LOVE ME BOLDLY

A DEER CREEK NOVEL BOOK TWO

STACEY LYNN

Love Me Boldly

A Deer Creek Novel

Book Two

Stacey Lynn

ONE
HOLLY

Then

FREEDOM.

The glittery blue word was the only bright thing in this run-down trailer. It didn't matter how often I scrubbed and cleaned, the lingering odors of beer, marijuana, and other scents I not only didn't recognize, but wouldn't think about, remained.

"Looks good," Tracey said. Her stance mirrored mine, with our hands on our hips. A ghost of a smile crinkled her eyes as she surveyed our boards.

Vision boards. Her suggestion. I'd rolled my eyes at her.

Hers boasted of ocean pictures and the University of Tennessee, where she wanted to go to grad school for a masters in software engineering. Hot guys with chiseled abs in swim trunks made a strong, third showing.

Success was her chosen word. In complete contrast—and not surprising because we were one hundred and eighty degrees different—mine was more realistic, less "get me a hunky guy" dreamy.

An apartment building. Graduation cap. Picture of an open highway.

I wanted to get out of this trailer, into my own place, and for the first time in my life, finally find some freedom from the life and family I was born into.

Tracey's board was hot pink and lavender. Mine was dark blue and silver, and only silver because black clashed with the blue.

Tracey insisted I go for something brighter. I caved because it wasn't worth arguing about, but now, with the canvas drying and propped on my television stand in front of the broken TV, the blue was harsh.

Happy. Bright. Shiny. Out of place in the dark cesspool of a home I'd lived in for far too long.

Not forever. I had a few memories that reminded me of a time when life was different. A life *before*.

Thankfully I had Tracey to pull me out of the muck and mire, and she'd done it again.

"Thanks again for coming," I whispered. I hated the vulnerability in my voice.

I didn't mind being alone. I was used to it. But being alone for your first holiday break because your drunk of a father was in prison was an entirely new level of loneliness.

When Tracey showed up at my door with a suitcase at her feet, arms laden with plastic bags and hugging two large art canvases to her chest, I'd burst into tears.

"You're my BFF. Where else would I be?" She took my hand and squeezed.

We were entirely different, practically from two different worlds. She came from happy parents with a happy marriage, was equally happy herself, and had three little brothers she treated like they were her children instead of siblings. Her family took two vacations a year—one to the beach and one somewhere else in the country—and an Instagram feed full of smiling people with affection and joy and all the normal things I could only envision.

I had a mom who took off. A father in prison. At some point, I'd had a chance of having Tracey's life, or something similar, but that was before Mom's surgery. Before the addiction. Before she took off to chase her high and Dad crumbled to his knees while hugging a case of Natural Light.

I had an aunt and uncle who did their best to fill in the gaps my parents created, and I had Tracey.

Some days it wasn't nearly enough.

Today, like others, it was more than I deserved.

"What now?" I asked, looking at the canvases. My dream of freedom. Get my degree, get out of this town. Get a job, a home of my own, and leave Deer Creek and all its horrific memories behind.

Tracey's wine-deep red fingernail tapped the fireworks on my vision board. They were meant to celebrate graduating college after this last upcoming semester. "We celebrate. You made it through a crummy year, the worst of the worst. Your best is on the horizon. Which means...we have some hotties to find."

I groaned. "You have hotties to find."

"Nah." She shrugged and reached for her purse. While she pulled out her ID, bank card, ChapStick, and car keys, she continued. "You need a hottie in your life, too. Remember what my grandma always said?"

"Marry a rich man. They're just as easy to love, only harder to find." I repeated the words in a robotic tone.

Tracey's grandma, Mary, repeated that so often I had dreams about it.

"Exactly." Tracey flashed me a manic grin, grabbed my hand, and tugged me toward the door of my trailer.

I didn't bother locking it as we tumbled down the rickety stairs to the BMW SUV her parents bought her for her twenty-first birthday. There was nothing inside worth stealing.

The most valuable thing I now owned was that ridiculous vision board. And that included the cost of supplies.

"SEE?" Tracey shouted in my ear with a glass of foamy beer held high above her head. "Fun, right!?"

I tipped my club soda in her direction. "Loads."

She rolled her eyes at me and grabbed my free hand. Dragging me along behind her, I had to hurry so I didn't end up face-planting onto the sticky, beer-stained floor.

When Tracey said we were heading out to the bars, I thought she was taking me back to Boone, thirty minutes away where we went to college, but nope. She meant staying close to home. Deer Creek wasn't any place special. A small mountain town in northern North Carolina, my paw-paw, Dad's dad, used to say that from the top of Crystal Mountain, we were close enough to the border to spit into Tennessee. Based on the way the man spit his chew, I figured maybe *he* could do it, but I'd never attempted it.

The Golden Eye was the same as it'd always been. Considering it hadn't been updated in my twenty-two years of life, it was surprisingly clean, minus the sticky floors. A long brass handle that rimmed the bar shone like it'd been recently polished. The brass coverings on the lights hanging from the ceiling were in equally good condition. Pretty sure the only thing that'd been added to Golden's was the number of bras tacked to the walls. Why women got drunk and flung their bras around only to have them stapled to a grungy wall was something I never understood, and my dad had been dragging me in there to do my homework since I was old enough to carry my own backpack into it.

Didn't women know how expensive those things were?

Or maybe tourists didn't care. Maybe those women had more money than my family.

Not a stretch, considering.

"This really isn't a good idea," I called out to Tracey as she weaved around tables. I tried to avoid eye contact with every familiar face, but it was difficult. Several who met my gaze before I could look away sneered.

Tracey didn't understand, and I was loath to ruin her good mood even at the risk of my own. One night. I could do this for one night. In a week, she'd be back in her apartment, and I'd be spending the weekend working and studying in my drafty trailer.

"It'll be fine. I swear it! Besides, I ran into some hotties while you were getting our drinks!"

She grinned at me over her shoulder, hazel eyes lit with the promise of a good time.

I'd walk through fire for Tracey, I trusted her beyond reason. She was truly the smartest person I knew, but in this she was wrong. Me? Have a good time at a bar in Deer Creek? Never gonna happen.

She'd have a good time though, especially if guys were involved. She had brains, an incredible body, and a fantastic sense of humor. A triple threat, my best friend was, and men flocked to her like bees to nectar after a starving winter.

She dragged me to the back. At least we were in the corner. Opposite the hall to the bathrooms and far from the thickest crowd near the bar, if I hid by the dartboard all night, I'd probably be okay.

"Holly, this is Tucker and Graham. Our new friends."

I fought the roll of my eyes. Tracey made new friends everywhere, and those friends usually stuck around until the tab was paid.

I held up my club soda and grenadine instead of a handshake. "Hi there."

Tracey sure knew how to pick them. Both dark-haired, both a full head taller than me at my five-five stature, they had to hover right around six feet. One had fuller lips and thick brows. The other was...well, *wow*.

A mop of thick dark hair had a curl to it on the top of his head, slightly falling to the sides that tapered to practically nothing at the base of his neck. His dark eyes were pools of mystery as his gaze lingered on me.

"Graham," the man said, barely moving his lips as he spoke his name.

I felt that name in hidden places. It was a caress against my skin, and I fought the urge to shake off prickles that were slipping down my spine.

Oh...yeah. He was a hottie all right. Based on the cut of his shirt, he worked out *often* to become such a hottie based on the build, but it was also the clothes. The fabric. He was wearing a fitted gray Henley and light denim jeans that fell loosely over scuffed and worn black Doc Martens.

He wasn't from here.

And he had money.

So...great. He wasn't for me. I wasn't like Tracey. Her grandma's advice was entertaining, but there was no point in hoping some guy would come in and sweep me off my feet straight out of my trailer.

Rich men would get one whiff of my life and take me for a gold digger. And if they didn't, their mothers certainly would.

I gave Tanner a quick scan and found him the same. No wonder Tracey latched on to them in my three-minute wait at the bar. They screamed rich tourists, down for a good time with a local.

Except Tracey wasn't a local, and this one knew better.

"You guys here for the weekend?" I asked and caught sight of Tracey sliding closer to Tanner.

He was attractive. That couldn't be argued, but he definitely looked like a guy ready for a good one-night stand than anything else.

"Just the night. Wanted to get out of Boone."

Boone. And they were our age. That meant... "You're students?"

Graham smirked, eyes widening. "You don't sound like you like that."

He couldn't be a finance major. I would have seen him in the business classes building. Rather, I should have. I tended to keep my eyes down and my business to myself when I was on campus.

I ignored his statement. "Major?"

He rocked back on his heels, grinning like a fool. "Science education."

"Seriously?" I scoffed. Couldn't help it. No way a man who looked like that was an *education* major.

"Yeah. Wanna coach someday, and I like science."

"Huh."

"Wanna tell me why my answer makes you look like

you just sucked on a lemon and remembered you despise them?"

There was curiosity there, and interest. It sounded genuine too, but I quickly shook it off.

"Didn't peg you for the type, I guess."

"Yeah? What's my type?"

His eyes scanned my body. Oh yeah...definitely interest there. Too bad for him. I was staying far away from all college guys. The last thing I was going to do was end up like my mom. Knocked up, unmarried, life ruined, and bitterness growing with every breath.

"I wasn't talking about girls," I said and rolled my eyes.

He set his drink on the narrow shelf next to him and crossed his arms over my chest. "You don't like me."

"Don't take it personally. I rarely like anyone."

More than that, I'd learned early not to trust anyone. Tracey wormed her way into my heart against my defenses, but the people who did that were few and far between.

To my utter surprise, the man threw his head back and laughed. "Fair enough, Spitfire."

I scowled. Nicknames weren't my thing.

"What'd I do now?"

As he asked, his eyes narrowed on something other than me, and then a sharp, stabby point pushed into my upper arm.

"Ow." I jerked my shoulder back and turned.

Any amusement I'd had being at Golden's, which was already slim, vanished.

"Whattareyou doin' in here?"

"I'm allowed to be here, Mick." He and my father had a feud. I figured they'd once battled to become the town's largest drunks. The meanest drunk award always went to

Mick. At least I could count one blessing in my life. My dad didn't smash my face into walls like Mick did to his kids.

"Hey, maybe you should back off."

How sweet of Graham to jump in to the rescue. I held out my hand and put my body between his and Mick's. There was a chance Mick wouldn't hit me, but a stranger taking up for me wouldn't have the same chance. Snowball's chance in hell, as it was.

Mick's face was red and puffy, which wasn't only from years of drinking and doing who knows what else, but he grew larger and meaner every year. His stomach extended far over his belt buckle, and according to his son Mike, who I hadn't talked to since high school, the man had a mean right hook.

I felt the pressure of the stranger at my back, trying to get me out of the way.

"Keep your hands off her," Graham said and tried to tug me backward.

"Stop it," I hissed at him and dug my heels into the floor.

"We'll go," I told Mick, because now that Graham had stood up for me, if I left, the guys would have trouble too. "All of us."

"Never should have let trash like you in here in the first place."

"Yeah, well, they can't keep me out."

"That's enough, Mick."

I almost breathed a sigh of relief at Chanelle's presence as she sauntered up to us. A quick glance behind Mick made me cringe. He was causing a scene, and it was directing the attention of almost everyone in the place.

No one was going to have my back.

Chanelle wasn't standing up for me, either. It was her

bar. She didn't want broken tables and shattered glass all over.

"You know I don't hate you like everyone here, but you should take off," she warned, sliding in front of Mick.

He huffed and puffed behind her, and spittle might have hit the back of her head.

She'd had worse though, and if she felt it, she didn't flinch.

"*We* weren't causing problems," Graham said. He tugged at the back of my shirt again, and this time, I stepped back.

It wasn't to let him protect me, it was to grab Tracey.

"We're leaving," I told her. "Now."

"I'm sorry. I didn't think…"

"Yeah. Well, we're gone."

"Thassss right," Mick slurred. "Go back to that dumpster with the rest of the trash." He shoved his pudgy finger at Tracey and the guys.

"That's enough," Graham snapped. I was tugged back, and then he was in front of me. "You're a grown man and know better than to talk to women like that. So far, the only trash I see in this place is you."

"Graham. Don't."

"You disrespectful little sh—"

"Enough!" Chanelle shouted. She turned and faced Mick. "Back off or you're banned for a week!"

He scowled at her and grumbled something low enough I couldn't hear.

I tugged harder on Tracey's hand. "Now. We're leaving now."

"Right," she muttered. Regret was stamped all over her face, but I wasn't mad. This was standard operating procedure these days.

The freezing air slammed into my face, making my eyes water as soon as we reached the sidewalk.

"What the hell was that about? That guy puts his hands on you and *we* get kicked out?"

I shook my head. It hadn't come from Graham, and Tracey knew better. I left her to figure out what to say, even though it didn't matter. After tonight, I never had to worry about them returning to Deer Creek.

Lucky guys.

"Bye!" I called out and kept hurrying. Maybe it wasn't cold air stinging my eyes. Maybe that was pure embarrassment.

By the time I reached the gravel parking lot, booted steps were slapping behind me.

"I'm sorry!" Tracey called out.

"It's fine!"

"I didn't think they'd really react like this." She reached me at the back of her SUV, huffing and puffing. "Southern hospitality and all."

I snorted. Southern hospitality was real all right...until your dad did what mine did and the entire town turned on you.

"I can't wait to get out of this damn town." I moved toward the passenger door.

Once we were buckled, the car was on and the heaters along with the heated seats were blasting at full power, I faced Tracey. "What happened to the guys?"

"Who cares? You're the only one that matters."

At least I mattered to someone, and she was right about the boys. Who cared?

After tonight, neither of them would cross a sidewalk to say hi to me ever again.

It wasn't like I wanted them to.

Freedom. One more semester, and then I'd have it.

TWO
HOLLY

Winter was brutal. Wind whipped through me as I shoved my gloved hands into my puffer coat pockets and headed across campus. My scarf was wrapped around my neck, and I buried my mouth into the knitted, scratchy fabric. My hat was tugged low over my ears, and my toes were still freezing even though I was wearing boots and had doubled up on socks. We were in the midst of a heavy storm, with several inches of snow expected, but we were also a mountain town.

Life didn't stop. Classes were only cancelled when blowing snow reached blizzard conditions, but today's snow wasn't severe enough despite the burn stinging my cheeks. I wasn't the only miserable one. Days like this meant there wasn't time to stop and chat in the quad or throw a frisbee around in the open spaces outside dorms. Not that I ever did much of that, but chatter and shouts were nonexistent as I buried my face further into my scarf. The campus felt more like a ghost town even though there were dozens of us out.

My feet sank into the couple of inches of snow as I

hurried up the steps to the business building, careful not to slip on packed snow that was already icing over. I stomped loose snow off the bottom of my feet as I reached the top step and covered area and tugged open the doors. Immediately, a blast of heat slammed into me, making me shiver in my coat, but it was enough relief to unwrap the scarf from my neck and face.

"Ugh," someone said behind me. "Is it March yet?"

I recognized Dallas Bronx's voice and glanced back as he tore off his stocking cap and shook off his mop of thick blond hair.

"Bad day?" I asked.

"When isn't it? You ready for the test?"

"I better be, or else there wasn't a point in driving in today."

His brows arched. "You drive in this stuff?"

Southern kids. Most towns outside our area came to a complete halt at the mere threat of snow or ice. Granted, I knew we weren't as tough as those who lived in the Rockies or farther north, at least from what I'd heard, but kids like Dallas who grew up on the coast thought every heavy snowfall was the end of civilization as we knew it. "You could always transfer back to Wilmington if you can't handle it," I teased.

"Please. I can handle just about anything. Doesn't mean I'm not waiting for the sun to start shining again, though."

Couldn't blame him there. "You ready for the test then?"

"I'm never ready to listen to that man. Is he even alive?"

I snorted. Dallas wasn't far off. Sometimes I swore Professor Morgan talked in his sleep and only stayed on his feet by his firm grip on the pedestal he used for his handwritten notes. The man had to have a laptop or computer somewhere, but everything he taught was hand-scribbled messily on a large whiteboard. I started taking pictures at the end of every class so I could decipher his writing on my own time.

We'd gotten stuck with the hardest professor and the professor with the worst personality. He was dry as campfire wood in a drought, which only made staying awake for Derivatives and Financial Risk Management more difficult.

Ironically, I hated math. Finance degrees were not only highly employable, but careers with the degree not only made decent money but also came with a high percentage of stability. They were the only two requirements I had for a career. I didn't care what I did, as long as I made enough to someday have my own home and not worry about fighting for government assistance or worse, going without.

We headed up the stairs together. Dallas and I weren't close, but we'd had dozens of classes together, and the older we got, the classes shrunk, which meant we'd been in small group assignments and projects multiple times over the years.

"Any plans this weekend?" he asked as reached the top floor.

I opened my mouth to answer and then froze. Dallas didn't realize I was still stuck on the top step until he was five steps away.

"Holly?" He glanced at me over his shoulder and then shifted his gaze to what—or rather, whom—had snagged my attention.

Graham.

"What are you doing here?" My feet remembered how to work at the same time my mouth did, and I took one step toward him.

Graham was leaning back against the wall, one booted

foot propped against it. His arms were crossed, but our school's NCWU logo was plainly stamped in bright yellow against the forest green sweatshirt.

"You didn't answer your phone." He shrugged and gave me a look like it was possible the very idea of not calling him back or answering any of his dozen texts had simply slipped my mind. In the last month, probably more, since I met him, Graham hadn't only somehow secured my phone number—something I was blaming Tracey for even though she swore she didn't give it out—and had taken to texting. Calling. After his first dozen texts asking me how I was went unanswered, he switched courses. Now, the unanswered text threads from him had dozens of memes and even more TikToks. Most were stupid animal videos.

Almost all of them made me laugh.

He'd clearly never heard of the term *ghosting*.

"I figured you'd get what that meant eventually." I grabbed the straps of my backpack and rocked back on my heels.

"You coming, Holly?"

I glanced at Dallas, who stayed standing where I left him, glancing between the two of us. Clearly, he'd heard. "I'm good. Save me a seat."

Dallas gave one last lingering look toward Graham and then left.

"Is he the reason you haven't called me back?" Graham's gaze was on Dallas's back and stayed there until he opened the door to our classroom.

A half dozen other students headed down the hall toward us and the stairs that I was blocking, so I was forced to step closer to him.

Or run.

I preferred not to show fear. I made the step toward Graham.

He smelled like spring mountaintops and warm sun. Clean and fresh and my favorite time of year.

"He's none of your business." It came out harsher than I intended, and I sighed. I was used to being alone, but I wasn't *rude*. "And no. Maybe I'm not interested. Have you considered that?"

"No, actually, that thought hadn't crossed my mind." There was that boyish grin again. It did funny things to my stomach and to my common sense.

I tightened my grip on my straps so I didn't reach out and flick a lock of his hair out of his eye.

"What do you want?"

The guy was relentless. He clearly wanted my attention. I was certain he'd been only looking for a fun time, but he hadn't given up. And now he was in front of me, looking all shameless and cute.

And somehow...he knew exactly where I'd be.

"Dinner." He shrugged and uncurled his arms from where they'd been across his chest, pushed off the wall, and took one step toward me.

My boots dug into the ground so I didn't step back. "Why?"

"Because we both need to eat, and you seem like you'd be stellar company."

I huffed out a laugh. He had to be joking, but the longer I watched and waited for him to laugh it off with me, the more serious he grew.

"You're serious."

"Very rarely, but about dinner, yeah. I eat a lot."

This guy. He was making my head hurt.

"When?"

"Tonight."

"And if I go for dinner with you, you'll leave me alone after?"

"Probably not."

"Really?" I arched my brows in surprise.

He leaned in. It was the tiniest amount, and yet I was suddenly surrounded by him. His looks. The size of his shoulders. His mere presence was overwhelming. "Spitfire, if you really wanted me to leave you alone, you would have blocked my number."

He reached out and booped my nose. He *booped* my nose. My jaw unhinged in shock, and by the time I thought to say something, he was gone, his hand gripping the railing and ready to head off down the stairs.

"One dinner," I called out. "Where do I meet you?"

"Don't worry about it. I'll find you."

He vanished down the stairs, boots thumping and echoing with his hurried movements.

I gawked at the stairwell, filling with more bodies coming up the stairs.

He *knew* where I'd be. And he had my phone number...

I was going to go to dinner with him for the sole reason of finding out *how*.

Then I was putting an end to this. I didn't have time for his games, and I didn't have time for him. Not with graduation looming and my last semester in full swing.

I headed toward my classroom and slid in with seconds to spare and refocused.

Derivatives. Financial risk management. They were the only things I needed to focus on in my life.

But a girl did need to eat...

"HAVE A GOOD WEEKEND." I handed the purchase to the customer and glanced at my phone.

I wasn't checking to see if Graham texted. I wasn't keeping an obsessive eye on it, hoping it'd light up. I wasn't at all getting nervous about having dinner with him.

I also hadn't canceled...nor had I blocked him...

A sharp poke hit my shoulder, and I spun, only to come face-to-face with Tracey, grinning from ear to ear. "I *told* you I didn't give him your phone number."

I texted her as soon as I finished my financial risk exam, before grabbing lunch at the student center. Fortunately, while the wind was still rough, the snow had slowed.

"Unless you also gave him my class schedule."

"Like I have that memorized."

"Then how'd he get it?" I grabbed a paper clip off the counter in the university's bookstore and started unbending it.

Tracey and I met on our dorm floor freshman year. Back when Dad was still able to occasionally hold down a job and help me with tuition so my loans weren't sky high. I'd lasted in the dorms for a year, then had to move back home by sophomore year, and by the end of my junior year, I was alone.

Back when we shared a wall in the dorm, we'd known everything about each other. Since then, that'd become more difficult but given that I worked two jobs and her propensity to spend the majority of her non-class hours either sleeping or partying, that was understandable.

"Have you talked to his friend at all?"

"Tucker?"

That was a no. "Wasn't it Tanner?"

She giggled. "Probably. So no, obviously."

I wasn't surprised. She tended to pick up strays but

discarded them just as quickly. Given how quickly and abruptly that night ended, I suppose I wasn't surprised they didn't exchange numbers or snaps or whatever. Which meant Graham couldn't have easily reached out to Tracey, anyway.

"It's so weird," I muttered.

"What's weird?"

We both jerked at the new arrival, and this time I *was* surprised. I hadn't seen Graham come down the stairs to the bookstore, and I was usually pretty alert.

"You," I said, but there was a tease to my tone. "You know my work schedule?"

He gave that same shameless shrug. "Maybe I'm here for school supplies."

"By coming to the bookstore"—I glanced at the clock at the top of my laptop—"exactly two minutes before I get off shift?"

"Coincidental."

Sure it was. The look I gave him said it, but his smirk turned into a grin.

"You can go," Tracey said, nudging me. "I'll clock you out."

I faced her. The traitor. She knew I'd been blowing him off.

"Go have fun," she whispered, but I had no doubt he could hear even as he turned toward a nearby shelf and flipped through packages of pens and pencils. "You've earned it. Take the free meal if that's all you want to do."

"Classy," I muttered, and from his profile, Graham's lips lifted a smidge.

Graham dropped the pretense of shopping and glanced at me. "Ready for your free meal?"

Tracey chuckled.

I rolled my eyes, and then I grabbed my coat and back-pack, because Tracey was right.

A free meal never hurt anyone.

"Fine. But I'm driving."

A girl needed to have some boundaries.

"Perfect. Because I don't have a car."

Wonderful.

THREE
HOLLY

"Here?" I turned my shocked eyes in Graham's direction where he sat smugly in my car.

Embarrassment at driving him in my GMC Jimmy, a car that was older than me, fled as soon as Graham flung his body into the passenger seat, belted in, and said, "Bet this works great in the snow."

There wasn't a hint of judgment in his eyes, no pity. He hadn't even hesitated to get into it, like it wasn't too old, too run-down, and *way* too rusty for him.

He started giving me directions that were so quick there was barely room to speak about anything else until I was pulling into the parking lot of the restaurant.

We weren't just going out for dinner at a diner or pizza joint or regular close-to-campus American grill—we were at a steakhouse.

An expensive steakhouse.

"You can't be serious." How could he even afford this? We were college students, for crying out loud.

"Sure I am. Why wouldn't I be?"

"Because the meals in this place cost more than my car is worth."

Graham was still grinning that cocksure grin, and for the first time, I truly wanted to slap it off his face. What in the world was he thinking? That'd we'd work enough hours washing dishes and then be able to afford to eat here?

"That's not true. Your car is definitely worth more than a dinner here." He slapped the dashboard, and I was surprised it didn't crack. "It's sturdy. Runs great. Practically a classic."

"Graham." It was meant to be scolding.

His answering smile said he didn't take it as such.

"I think that's the first time you've said my name, Holly. I like it. Come on, I'm starving, and stop worrying. Everything will be fine."

I glanced at him, his expression so confident it edged on arrogance, and back to the restaurant. Outside, it didn't look anything special. Dark wood and beams made it fit perfectly into the mountain-town vibe, but this was a place that hand-carved your steak at the table.

Just because I was poor didn't mean I hadn't heard of the place. Half of my high school's senior class had come here for prom night and then spent the rest of the following week raving about the food.

It should have excited me to finally step inside, but I'd also heard they only took reservations.

"When did you make the reservation?" I asked Graham as he wrapped his hand around the door handle.

"What do you mean?"

"You need reservations to eat here. When did you make them?"

"Does it matter?"

It didn't. And yet it did. For some reason, it really did. "Before or after you stalked me this morning?"

"Ah..." He wagged his finger at me. "Not stalking if I knew exactly where you'd be—"

"Speaking of—"

"And last night," he stated, not letting me speak.

"Last night?"

"Yeah. I was hopeful. You hungry yet?"

Starving. The small chicken salad I'd scarfed down at the student union had worn off hours ago, but I was used to the ache of an empty stomach.

"I'm already regretting agreeing to this."

Yet I opened the door and climbed out, and Graham reached me at the front of the Jimmy. He then led me to the door, opened it like a true gentleman, and when he gave his name to the hostess, her smile was soft and welcoming.

"Right this way. Your table is ready."

She guided us toward the left, away from the open bar area. On the far left side of the entire restaurant sat an enormous bouquet of pale pink roses and baby's breath, the bouquet so large it'd be impossible to see the person on the other side and entirely out of place with the worn wood tables, flickering faux candles as centerpieces, and tables already prepped with silverware wrapped with fabric napkins. A light jazzy instrumental music filtered through unseen speakers, and the dining area was lit by chandeliers hanging from the ceilings with warm, candle-looking light bulbs.

It was elegant. Woodsy. Romantic and warm.

And my heart dropped to the soles of my boots when the hostess stopped at that very table with the massive bouquet of flowers.

"Is this table acceptable for you, Mr. Marchese?"

Mr. Marchese? Who was this guy?

"Absolutely. And thank you so much for the help."

She left, and while I'd heard the conversation, it was muffled behind the rushing roar of *whatever the heck this was* going through my mind.

I found the strength to lift my head and meet Graham's gaze.

His hand rested on my lower back, and he gently guided me toward the booth's seat.

"What is this?"

Stunned didn't begin to describe my emotions. Or lack of them.

I woodenly collapsed into the booth and stared at the flowers. Graham must have been moved into the seat across from me because the flowers were pushed to the side, giving me a relatively decent view of him through the falling wisps of baby's breath.

"What *is* this?" I repeated.

Graham leaned forward, elbows on the table, and clasped his hands. "Happy Valentine's Day, Holly."

My mouth dropped open, and I sucked in a lungful of air. "What?" I managed to ask, but it came out on a wheeze, then a cough.

Humor fled Graham's face as concern replaced it. He stood, reaching across the table for me, but I threw myself back in my seat and shook him off with a hand.

"Don't." I coughed and then kept coughing while I forced my body to start working again. Forced my breaths to slow down. "I...what...?"

For once, Graham didn't look so sure of himself. He glanced at the flowers and pushed out his lips before looking at me again.

"It's Valentine's Day. I thought you'd like them."

I gaped at him and then truly looked at him, and my shoulders fell. I didn't have the heart to ask him what he was thinking or question him again.

He looked almost crushed that I hadn't fallen over myself to thank him. "They're beautiful," I admitted. "I'm not used to such nice things. And I didn't realize it was Valentine's Day."

With his head tilted to the side, that curly lock of hair flopped into his eye, and slowly, his lips spread into a grin. "Then I'm glad I could give that to you, and trust me, I was hoping you hadn't realized what today was. Figured that would have sent you running."

"If I did, would you have known where I was running to?"

He chuckled then and shook his head. "Probably not."

"So there are some things that you don't know about me."

He leaned back in his chair and flashed that cocksure grin. "Hopefully not for long."

DINNER WAS a strange mix of awkward silences, smooth conversation, and the most incredible food I'd ever tasted. My steak was so delicious I would have dreams about it, and Graham gave me another surprise by adding lobster tails to our entrées, something I'd never considered *ever* ordering. I'd never been in a restaurant where it was on the menu. My salad had almost forty topping options to choose from, and the entire dinner was an experience. If I were the kind of girl who journaled every major experience in her life, I'd record this one in detail.

It was Graham who kept the conversation flowing, and

while he shared bits and pieces of himself, I got the sense he was keeping it pretty surface level, which helped me do the same.

I told him why I was a finance major—because of the stability. He told me he'd played hockey his entire life, had loved his high school coach, and wanted to inspire others the way he'd been inspired. Science came easy for him, so that's why he majored in it. It was hard not to feel a twinge of something warm when he talked about coaching. Most of the guys I met either had no direction in their lives, had no desire to make a better life for themselves than where they came from, or had dreams of playing professional sports, and that was all they talked about.

The comfort I felt through it all slithered beneath my walls. Somehow, slowly, his easy manner and mildly flirtatious smiles and teasing disarmed me. I blamed him for why I found myself asking the one question I *never* asked simply because I never wanted to have to answer it.

"What about your parents? What's your family like?"

The words were out before I could suck them in faster than I'd eaten my ribeye.

"They're parents." He shrugged, but the softness in his eyes told the truth.

"Good ones?"

Why was I continuing this? At some point, these questions would come right back around to me, and then the ease of the night would drop like a weighted balloon.

"They're old, overprotective, and also, I guess, kind of great."

Kind of great. I got the sense he was minimizing how much he liked them in the same way Tracey tended to do when she was around me. Like because I had such crappy ones, she was loath to talk about how much she liked hers.

This was the same hesitancy, but the guy had seen me kicked out of a bar and berated by a grown man, so he had to know mine weren't the best.

I wasn't even quite sure I cared. I never had before. I'd spent my entire life being judged by my parents' actions, but that was Deer Creek, and the judgment typically stayed there.

I didn't need more gossip or news about me spreading. I was still putting last year's local headlines behind me, and thankfully I'd been able to go mostly unnoticed on campus.

"Can I ask you something?" Graham asked.

"You can ask anything you want."

"But you might not answer?"

"It's always a risk." I grabbed my water with lemon and took a sip. Ice cubes clinked against my teeth, making me shiver from the sudden cold sensation.

"You knew that guy at the bar that night."

Of course he'd bring up Mick. The chill from the ice spread further through my veins. I should have remembered this was coming, yet I'd been so focused on dodging questions about my family, I'd forgotten how we'd met.

"That's not a question," I teased and tried to keep it light, but inside, my heart was racing.

This was it. The last of my free meals.

Graham chuckled and shoved his floppy hair out of his face. "He didn't seem to like you very much. I'm just wondering how that's possible."

It still wasn't quite a question, but at least there was an easy answer to this. At least a rumor of it. And if he didn't *know* why I was hated, then he hadn't looked into me any further than my school and work schedule. "There's a rumor in town that way back when, Mick wanted my mom, and she chose my dad instead. He's carried a grudge ever since."

Considering Mom took off, and Dad became a drunk and refused to let me talk about her, I was never able to get his perspective on that rumor, but since Mick had seemingly hated me since the day I was born, it made sense.

"Wow. That seems like a long time to hold that kind of grudge."

The fact that Mom disappeared made it stranger, but my guess was that Mick was arrogant and delusional enough to believe that if Mom had chosen him, she would have stuck around.

"Mick's that kind of guy." I gave a halfhearted shrug. He'd seen the man.

"And you're from Deer Creek, then."

"Born and raised. Still live there."

"You commute?"

"Doesn't make much sense to pay to live closer when it's twenty minutes away." Tuition wasn't the largest cost of going to college, and my loans were going to be more manageable now that I wasn't. But man, the day I'd *had* to move back to Deer Creek had been depressing. Felt like such a step backward.

As long as I didn't stay stuck backward, then I was okay with it being temporary.

My phone rang, buzzing against my hip where it was next to me on the booth. I ignored it, but Graham glanced in that direction. "Do you need to get that?"

"The only calls I get are spam callers."

"And me." He smirked.

I rolled my eyes as my phone stopped. "And you, and see? Silent now."

It immediately started vibrating again, though, and this

time, knowledge of who it could be sent a rush of ice picks to my head, giving me an instant headache. "Crap," I muttered and rubbed my forehead.

"So people do call you."

"No one I want to talk to." I picked up my phone, checked the caller, and sighed. Of course it was him. My dad, calling from prison. Probably demanding more money as if I had piles of it lying around to spare.

Graham's brows rose. I was beginning to think the man had a sixth sense because it seemed like he knew I wouldn't talk about this. Like he could see my pulse racing, thumping in my ears and my inner wrists. "So then it's not just me you avoid."

A burst of laughter came through me, breaking my anger and fear and worry like a snap. "No." I shook my head. "I suppose it's not just you I avoid."

I was saved from further talking about it when the waitress came. I tucked my phone into my coat pocket so I wouldn't hear it vibrate again. Graham pulled out a credit card from his wallet, handing it to her without bothering to look at the check.

When she was gone, I asked, "Are your parents going to be okay with this? The meal, I mean?"

"Yeah. Of course. That's why my dad gave it to me."

"He gave you a credit card so you could take girls out to eat? Sounds like an interesting Dad."

"No." He laughed. "My dad gave it to me for emergencies."

"And I'm an emergency?"

"Getting to know you is, yeah."

Wow. He had all the right words, all the right jokes, and his flirtatious banter was top-notch. It was almost too easy to trust him and equally easy to believe he used all these lines on every other girl who threw herself in front of him. With his looks and personality, I assumed they were lined up.

"I'm not sure if I should trust you or run in the opposite direction," I admitted.

Graham leaned forward, resting his forearms on the table. "I don't ask for trust from a lot of people. I'm used to people abusing it, but if you gave me yours, I can promise you I wouldn't betray that or take it for granted."

His stern expression had me melting. Maybe he wasn't the player I thought he was. There was something so endearing about him, something that made me want to take the risk.

"Why me?" I asked.

An edge of his lips quirked up. "Why not you?"

FOUR

HOLLY

"No kisses? Not even one on the cheek? I'm so disappointed in you."

Tracey flung herself back on my worn, green sofa. I'd texted her as soon as I got back home, and she showed up ten minutes later. She was either waiting in town for my text or sped like a demon to get to me. I didn't bother asking. Both were equally plausible.

"We said goodbye outside, and he ordered an Uber to get him back home. No kisses."

Just laughter. His question *why not you* that I couldn't get out of my head. I'd even offered to take him home, which was *not* like me. He declined, saying he didn't want me to go out of my way.

"So how did you leave it then?"

"Are you going to block me after this?" he asked, the cold darkening his cheeks but not the shine of his dark eyes.

I opened my mouth to say yes. He was a risk I wasn't sure I could afford despite how easily his flattery came. "Not tonight" *came out instead.*

His grin was as large as the mountain range as I climbed into my Jimmy and shut the door.

"He said he'd call me," I told Tracey.

"Given the last few weeks, has he called yet?"

Chuckling, I checked my phone and found it blank of all notifications. "Nope."

"He will."

"What makes you so sure?"

"Because he likes you, which means he has good taste."

I rolled my eyes. She flung a pillow into my face. For a brief moment, I was assaulted with the scent of stale smoke and beer before it evaporated into the air with dust. "Ugh. Gross. And yeah, he obviously likes me. It's impossible not to."

Which wasn't true. Lots of people despised me, but they hated me because of who my parents were. On a good day, I had a pretty decent level of self-confidence, but it was nowhere close to Graham's. It didn't mean I thought he and I would ever work, and unlike Tracey, I wasn't the stray-collecting type. I'd been so busy proving myself over the last few years I wasn't sure I was any kind of type, but if I was, I wouldn't have imagined choosing the smirking, flirtatious boy.

And I still couldn't figure out if he was playing me or genuine. *I would never betray that trust...*

He'd seemed genuine then...

"I hate that I'm so worked up about this."

"Maybe that's because you like him, too." Tracey suggested it in a voice that was far too sweet, almost like she was afraid I'd throw the pillow back at her but load it with bricks first.

I couldn't argue with that. Maybe I was starting to like him, but liking Graham wasn't my only problem.

"My dad called at dinner," I admitted to her. "I didn't answer."

"Has he called back?"

"No, but I haven't heard from him in a few weeks, so he'll keep calling whenever he can get to the phones."

Her face scrunched up. "I'm sorry. Did Graham know?"

"No. But he definitely thought it was weird."

"You know." Tracey sat up, kicked her feet off the couch to the worn floor, and leaned toward me. "If he's as nice as he seems, I doubt he'll care."

"That my mom took off and my dad's in prison? Tell me who in the world wouldn't judge someone after hearing that?"

"I'm still your friend."

"That's because you have no common sense."

She laughed and couldn't deny it. We both knew it was true.

"It's getting late. I should head back."

"Drive safe."

I walked her to the door, the whole six steps it took to get there, and waited while she bundled up in her coat and scarf and then stood in the cold doorway until her car backed completely out of our snow-covered, dirty driveway and out onto the main road.

Once her taillights disappeared through the tree-lined, winding road, I stepped back inside and locked my door.

What a day.

What a really strange day.

My stomach was still full from dinner, so I forewent my snack, grabbed my backpack, and plopped down onto the couch to get started on homework.

Except the flowers kept grabbing my attention. The beautiful bouquet that had three dozen roses. I knew it was that many because Tracey had counted them, twice, as soon as she saw them. They were tucked onto the small counter space in my kitchen, and every few minutes I found myself staring at them. Like my vision board, they looked so out of place. So sweet and pretty. And fragrant. I swore they were making the entire trailer smell better.

Graham hadn't just taken me out to dinner. He'd made it special. On Valentine's Day. Those flowers had to have cost a *fortune* given the day. I wasn't sure I'd ever felt so special and seen.

I was certain no one had ever done something so nice for me.

I was equally certain I hadn't been nearly appreciative enough.

Which was probably why I set aside my homework and grabbed my phone.

Me: Thank you again for dinner. And the flowers. They're gorgeous.

Given how frequently he'd texted me before, I almost expected my phone to vibrate as soon as I set it down. Instead, it stayed silent. I got up, went to the kitchen, and poured a glass of water, rifled through the cupboards, and jotted down a quick grocery list. Between working my second job in town, studying, and running to the grocery store, my weekend was already booked. Which meant I shouldn't have been spending my time thinking about a boy.

My phone vibrated on my coffee table, and thank goodness Tracey was already gone. I moved way too quickly. She would have been in a laughing fit over my hurry to get to the phone. Water splashed over the rim of my glass in my rush to set it down.

Graham: Food was good. Flowers were pretty. How was the company?

Please. Like he had to hunt for compliments. I wasn't ready to put myself fully out there. That required a vulnerability I didn't possess.

Me: It didn't suck.

A laughing emoji appeared like he knew I would say something like that.

Graham: From you, I consider that a compliment. Plans this weekend?

Me: Yeah, hopping on my private jet to Bora Bora.

What did he think I did on the weekends?

I threw in an eye roll and then typed:

Me: **Grocery shopping and work. You?**

Graham: Asking me questions? I knew you were interested.

Please...well, maybe.

Graham: I'm headed out of town, actually. Nowhere as exciting as Bora Bora, though.

I sat there, fingers poised to see if he'd tell me where he was going. Debated if I should ask when he took the chance from me.

Graham: I need to get to bed early tonight. I'll see you when I get back.

For some reason, that made me smile. The audacity of this man.

Me: You're assuming I want to see you. Not even going to ask?

Graham: You haven't blocked me. You want to see me.

Ugh. I could practically see his smirk coming through his text. Based on the way my cheeks were burning, he wasn't wrong. Not like I was going to tell him that.

Me: We'll see what tomorrow brings.

I tossed my phone to the couch, grabbed my water and television remote, and pretended that hadn't just happened. That I hadn't flirted back.

That I wasn't interested in this guy. Not even a little bit.

———

I USED my key to unlock the back door of The Premiere Grille, what most locals simply called The Grille. One of the first two restaurants in Deer Creek, it was a staple in town, and my grandparents on my mother's side had proudly bought it and taken it over when my mom and her sister, Caroline, were young girls. They grew up in this restaurant that was more of a diner than fine dining, and on the days I wasn't with my father, I was in the office, working on school work. As soon as I was old enough, I started washing dishes. Every year older I grew, more age-appropriate responsibilities came my way.

By now, I could walk through this restaurant blindfolded and find my way to every cooking station and weave around every table and booth without so much as stubbing a toe.

Inside, I shook off the shivers from the frigid cold air outside and unwrapped my scarf. I took the first right into the back office. Caroline's scattered and messy office was piled with a mess of over-orders and folders. Every spare inch of space was covered in something, so I took one pile and set it on top of another. It was precariously close to tipping, but fortunately, the weight of my purse, coat, and gloves on the table didn't send it tumbling to the floor.

Although organizing papers might end up being more productive than working out front, it was Saturday, which meant all hands on deck.

I grabbed a server's apron, tied it around my lower back, and gave Caroline's office one last scan. Soon, I'd start working on her taxes, and while I was doing so, I'd get this place cleaned and organized.

My aunt fell in love with this restaurant from the very beginning. She not only owned and managed it now, but she spent time cooking, prepping, and serving. It was in her blood.

For my mother, it'd been a job. One she apparently hadn't liked enough in the end.

For me, it was a means to an end. There was peace in this restaurant, memories of my entire life, both good and bad. But in the end, the bad outweighed the good, and this wasn't where I wanted to stay forever.

I waved hello to the cooks and the dishwasher, checked the salad station to make sure it was stocked, and found everything cleaned, filled, and ready to go for the day.

Pushing open the swinging metal doors that separated the kitchen from the dining area, I gave the restaurant another scan on instinct. A plastic bin was overflowing with napkin-rolled silverware. Next to it, the water glasses were stacked, and the trays were ready to grab and go. Tables were cleaned. Everything was pristine and set up for the day.

Caroline was talking to one table of two retired teachers. The women came in every Saturday between the breakfast and lunch rushes and spent hours sipping coffee and talking about whatever books they had stacked off to the side. It was their own weekly book club, and there was something endearing about watching them and hearing their laughter.

The front door opened, and a tabletop of six greeted me, three men and three women. And so the weekend began...

"Hi, welcome to The Premier Grille. Six of you today?" I started piling menus into my arm.

"Eight actually," the gentleman said. "We're still waiting for two."

"Sounds good." I gave him a smile and led them to an area where I could quickly pull two four-top tables together. The men helped, and soon, they weren't the only ones entering the restaurant for lunch.

Luckily, we were busy, and I didn't have to spend all day thinking about last night's dinner. The flowers still sitting on my kitchen counter, the floral scent that filled my trailer, or the late-night flirtatious texts Graham and I had sent.

By the time we were midway through the dinner rush, I was finally able to catch my breath. Weekends at The Grille went either way. Sometimes it was full of locals, making my job difficult, or it was full of weekend vacationers who needed to come down from the mountain and get some food.

Tonight it was the latter, which meant my tip pocket in my apron was bulging. Things were good. I still had three tables, and then I'd be able to go grab my own meal.

I glanced at the door and immediately cringed as our weekend hostess, Emma, walked to the hostess stand.

Mia and Hannah, two girls from my high school, walked in, unzipping their coats as they reached her. "Two, please," Hannah said. "And *not* in her section."

She skewered me with a look that had long since stopped hurting. She didn't hate me because of my dad. She hated me because in seventh grade Corey Franklin asked me to the middle school dance, and she'd had a crush on him. Ironic that Mia was now engaged to that same boy, and they were still best friends.

Whatever. I rolled my eyes and walked away, going back to help a table that *always* requested my section, tipped well, and didn't hold a single thing against me.

"Still having trouble with that?" Eddie Ferentz asked and glanced at the women Emma sat in her section instead. He was one of Deer Creek's police officers, one of the men who'd showed up at my trailer after the accident to let me know about my dad. Across from him was his partner, Cole Paxton.

"It's nothing." I shook my head.

"We can help, you know."

I smirked at Cole and refilled his water. "What are you going to do? Arrest them for unkindness?"

"I can think of something. You shouldn't have to deal with that crap."

There were a lot of things in my life I shouldn't have to deal with.

"Can't save everyone, Officer," I teased.

"I can sure try." He glared at me, but it wasn't in anger at me. Protecting people was what he did, and he took his job seriously.

"Let it go, guys. I appreciate you, you know that, but you have to know by now that the town seeing you in here talking to me hasn't changed a thing and it won't." They started coming in after my dad's arrest to show their support for not only me, but Caroline and The Grille.

It'd been a sweet gesture, and considering *no one* wanted to be sat in my section at the time, something I was sure they'd gotten wind of through the gossip mill, their generous tips had helped.

But it'd been a full year, and while some people reluctantly let me serve them and take care of them, more than most refused.

"I don't know what you're talking about." Eddie leaned back in the chair and grinned. "We come for the pleasant company."

I snorted. "Sure you do."

Both men chuckled. "I'll be back with your checks."

They came, they ate, we chatted, but they didn't linger, considering they usually stopped in while they were on duty. And I knew they did that to show up in uniform, making it clear they wouldn't allow any harassment.

I returned with their checks and set them both in folders on the table. "Have a good night, guys. Thanks for stopping in."

Cole leaned in closer. "I hope you know that you *can* always come to us. If anyone harasses you, Holly, or does anything they shouldn't. You don't have to keep taking it and putting up with it."

"I know. I appreciate it."

We both knew I wouldn't. Not unless it was serious.

"Take care," I told them both and went back to work.

It was nice to know I had people at my back, but I'd learned a long time ago to let it go. Sometimes fighting for fairness only made life more difficult, and I'd had enough difficulty.

BY MONDAY, most of the snow from Friday had melted, leaving the streets and parking lots slushy with small piles of darkening snow scraped off to the edges of the campus sidewalks. The campus was drying by Tuesday, and even better, I found a spot in the covered parking garage. I grabbed my scarf and hat, tugged on my mittens, and then slipped my backpack over my shoulders. By the time I got outside the ramp, I flinched from the bright sun. It took my eyes a second to adjust, and when they did, I cursed at the vision in front of me.

I'd spent far too much time over the weekend consumed with thoughts of that certain smirk and lock of curly dark hair.

"How's it going?"

Oh. So it wasn't a mirage or a trick of the sun's blinding glare.

I stumbled over nothing and righted myself as Graham stepped closer.

"How in the *world* did you know where I parked?" My eyes narrowed on him. "Are you tracking me? Slip an AirTag into my coat or something?"

As I asked, I patted the sides of my coat. There was no way he knew my parking preference, and I hadn't been able to get a covered spot last Friday.

"Settle, Spitfire," he teased, laughing. "This was a best guess based on the business building."

Well, that made sense. "Oh," I mumbled.

"Thought I'd walk you to class."

"How gentlemanly of you."

"I can be." He shrugged and grabbed the straps of his backpack as he fell into step with me. "How was work this weekend?"

"Busy." I squinted from the bright sun. "I work at a diner in Deer Creek that my aunt owns. It's near the Crystal Mountain ski slopes, so it's always busy this time of year."

I felt, more than saw, the weight of Graham's gaze on me.

"What?" I asked, glancing at him.

"Nothing." He faced forward. "Just that's the first information you've given me without me having to ask."

Man, he made me sound super fun and nice. I stopped walking, and it took him a step to notice.

"What'd I say?" he asked. There was a line between his thick black brows.

"Why are you talking to me?"

"What?" He leaned back and scanned the area around us that was quickly filling with students. His chin dipped in someone's direction before coming back to mine. That same, confused expression on his face. "What do you mean?"

I shrugged. That was a stupid thing to say. "It's just...I have a lot going on, and I haven't had a great year, so if this is just a way to pass the time or have some fun..."

"You're not," he said, and it was said with such confidence, such depth, I sucked in a breath. "I saw you at Golden's and thought you were hot, yeah. But you dish out sass, and I don't have a lot of people willing to be honest with me, so yeah, I like that too. Is it a crime to get to know you?"

Getting to know me wasn't a crime, but would he be so flippant if I pulled up an article from last winter? Or the summer after my father's trial?

"Hey, Graham!"

"Marchese!"

People around us shouted his name as they passed. Some grinned and dipped their chins. More than one group of girls laughed as they said hi to him.

I glanced around. "You know a lot of people."

Graham chuckled. "We've been here four years, you probably know a lot."

I didn't. I'd always kept to myself even before, and while I didn't particularly like being alone, I did like not having gaggles of friends ghosting me and spending their time gossiping about me. In hindsight, I was pretty thankful. At least this way if people gossiped, it wasn't personal...just ignorant.

We stopped walking once we reached the business building. "Thanks for letting me walk you to class, Holly."

I shook my head. As if I'd had a choice. "Thanks for stalking me."

He chuckled. "See you around?"

"Do I have a choice?"

"You *could* have told me to go away, you know."

Odd. I hadn't even considered it.

"Maybe tomorrow I will," I said, but I was laughing, and somehow I think we both knew I wasn't serious.

Graham stopped laughing first and took a step closer to me. "Can I tell you something that might scare you?"

"Maybe?"

His smile vanished, and something dark flared in his eyes. "You made me laugh that first night, and I liked it. You're not the only one who's had a hard year."

With that, he turned on his heels and sauntered away, leaving me gaping after him.

I was bumped on the sidewalk and shook my head. Whatever that meant, I doubted he'd tell me if asked. Somehow it seemed he knew how to avoid questions as easily as I did.

And I hadn't even asked him about his weekend.

"How'd you do it?" A blond stepped in front of me. Several inches shorter than me, I jerked back when I realized she was talking to me.

"How'd I do what?"

"Graham Marchese. He never talks to girls. So what's so special about you?"

She seemed pissed. All dolled up with a face full of

makeup and in jeans and a lacy shirt beneath an opened fuzzy coat. She was dressed inappropriately for winter, and most likely whatever class she was going to... unless it was fashion.

"I have no idea what you're talking about."

I went to move around her, but she slid in front of me. "Seriously. What makes you think you're special enough to be talking to Graham?"

"Nothing," I told her and absolutely meant it.

I slid past her and dipped into the building.

Who *was* this guy? And how did half of this morning's campus seem to know him?

FIVE
HOLLY

"Lambda Nu Chi." Tracey pointed to the girl who'd stepped in front of me earlier in line outside Starbuck's in our school student union building. She was flanked by two other busty blonds, all of them looking like they were on their way to a shopping spree at Nordstrom and not their next class.

"That explains it," I muttered. The sorority was known for welcoming only the richest girls and called themselves the *Ladies of North Carolina*, regardless that it was an international sorority and originated at a California school. Usually I paid no attention to the Greek system on campus, social or otherwise, but I'd spilled what happened with Tracey as soon as I saw her.

"Did you ask him?"

"Pfft. No. Why would I do that?"

"Um, because you like him, and that girl was rude?"

"So?" I scoffed and stabbed my homemade Caesar salad with my fork. "Haven't you learned yet how normal that is for me?"

I took a bite, and when I glanced at Tracey, she was scowling at me.

For as wild as she was, her middle name should have been Sweet. I hated that the reminder of how I was treated bothered her. Possibly more than it bothered me. "I'm sure I'll figure it out."

"What else is going on? Any more phone calls?"

"No, thank goodness. But that can mean anything."

Dad was given a certain number of minutes every month for calling, and those could be decreased by his behavior or restricted altogether. He could also call me without calling collect, but then that cost would be taken out of the money I sent him. So really, he screwed me over every time he made a collect call, and I was dumb enough to answer.

I'd written to him frequently and asked him to stop and to use the money I gave him to call and ask for more or write a letter and ask instead. The fact he continued to ignore my wishes showed how little my father respected and cared about me.

The man stopped caring about anything and anyone but himself the day Mom left. Some days I wondered if all of my "happy" family memories before the age of seven were a lie in the first place. A fantasy I'd made up for my own survival.

"Tell me something good and fun," I told Tracey. "It was kind of a crummy weekend, and I need to hear something good."

"I met a guy at the SigEp party on Saturday night."

"Of course you did," I teased. "Remember this one's name?"

"Asher and be nice. He's cute."

"Cute?" My brows rose, and my next bite of salad on my fork froze halfway to my mouth. "How cute?"

"I dunno, cute-cute. And he was cool. We talked for quite a while."

"Huh." I shoved my fork into my mouth and chewed my salad. It was drenched in dressing, the only way I could eat a salad, but I kept forcing my body to believe salads and vegetables were good for me.

So far, I was sure my body only believed me when I used enough dip or dressing to counteract the health effects.

"You're making a face," Tracey said and pointed at me before taking a bite of her meat-covered, grease factory pizza.

"What face?"

"The face you make when you think I'm weird, but you're too nice to say anything."

"I don't think you're weird." I was definitely making that face. "I think it's weird you said you spent the night talking to a boy."

She rolled her eyes, but a pale pink crept up her neck. "Maybe I finally found someone worth talking to."

"Hearing this feels like I should go buy a lottery ticket," I teased.

Tracey laughed, and then a voice next to us said, "Why? Feeling lucky you get to see me twice in one day?"

We both jumped and spun, taken off guard by Graham's arrival. My hand flew to my chest as I huffed out a laugh. "You scared me."

He slid into the chair next to me like he'd been invited and dropped his backpack on the floor. "What's this about a lottery ticket?"

I glanced at Tracey. "Nothing," we both said, staring at each other.

She gave me wide eyes. I rolled mine before turning back to Graham. "What are you doing here?"

"Stalking the most gorgeous girl at NC Western in hopes of getting another date."

He plopped his forearms onto the table and clasped his hands together, looking so disarmingly sweet. But there was nothing sweet about the look in his eyes. Or the strength in his body.

"Oh, look at that," Tracey sang. "I'm late for class."

"You don't have another class," I drawled.

"Right. Vet appointment. For my cat." She glanced at Graham. "Not me. My cat."

She grabbed her tray and backpack and hurried out of there like I'd told her it was going to blow up in less than ten seconds.

When we were alone, Graham tapped his fingers on the tabletop. "I don't really believe she has a vet appointment."

"You shouldn't. She doesn't have a cat." I stabbed the last crouton in my salad, frowning when I learned it was more soggy than crunchy. I chomped on it anyway.

He chuckled and leaned back in his chair, draping one of his arms over the back of it. The move stretched out his chest, and as he tilted his head, that same lock of hair fell over his forehead. Did he style it like that? Or was he just inept at doing his hair?

"So, I guess I'm not going to hear about your lucky day, huh?"

"She spent the night talking to a guy."

"And that's worthy of a lottery ticket because...?"

"Because she doesn't usually do a lot of talking."

"Ah." Graham laughed, shaking his head. "I get it. And you? Do you like...talking?"

"No, actually. I prefer being alone."

"No, you don't."

"I don't?"

"Nope." He shook his head. "Wanna know how I know?"

This should be good. Let the gorgeous man who knew half of campus read me like a tarot card. I leaned back and crossed my arms over my chest. "Sure. Go for it."

One edge of his lips curled up. "You *think* you like being alone because you spent a lot of time that way. But you don't like it because if you did, you wouldn't have texted me so late on a Friday. You wouldn't have even still been thinking of our date."

He let that linger, and I couldn't argue. I *had* still been thinking of our date hours after it was over, and I didn't even realize I'd showed my hand then.

Not that I'd let him know that.

"It was impossible not to think about it when the roses took up my entire kitchen."

"Besides," he continued, like I hadn't made a half-hearted attempt to prove him wrong. "I'm still not blocked, which tells me you hope to hear from me again. *And* you could have thrown away the flowers."

Man, this guy was *smooth*.

"Maybe I'm saving the texts for the police when I decide to get a restraining order."

His laugh boomed throughout the café, causing dozens of students to glance in our direction.

"You're something else, Spitfire. Are you going to tell me how close I was to the truth?"

"Not particularly." But he was close. Walking the edge of it, anyway.

He slid off the chair and reached for his backpack. "Want to know how I know and can read you so well?"

As he asked, he leaned down, setting his hand at the back of my chair. His thumb brushed against my sweater, and as I glanced up at him, our gazes met.

Mine froze on him. Gone was the teasing and the flirting in his eyes. Something else had replaced it. Something that looked familiar. "I'm not sure," I admitted.

"You're not the only one with a closet full of secrets you'd prefer to keep locked up." He blinked, and all the brightness returned to his eyes, and I was still frozen, stuck on what I swore I'd seen.

The haunted look of someone who had a past that could only be similar to mine. But that couldn't be...

"Come on," he said. "You have class."

I shook the surprise off me and woodenly stacked my containers back into my lunch bag. When I reached for my backpack, it wasn't on the floor next to me.

"Here." Graham handed it out to me, holding it in his hand, the top unzipped so I could easily drop my lunch bag into it.

I did it without thought and then got to my feet.

"Wait a second." I reached for my backpack and took it from him. "Are you ever going to tell me how you know my schedule?"

He tipped his head toward the door, giving me that smirk I knew so well I could probably draw it in my sleep.

"Are you going to block me today?"

"Haven't decided." I slipped my coat on, dragged my bag's straps over my shoulders, and followed him out of the union.

"Well, when you make a decision on that one, then I'll clue you in."

And yet somehow, I still ended up following him, walking out of the student union where his name was called a dozen times. Where even more people seemed to know him.

He waved or smiled or said hello to most, but through it all, kept pace with me, asking about my class. If I had to work later.

He rarely took his eyes off me when someone called his name.

And for the first time in my life, I felt seen. I wasn't an afterthought, or someone to pity, or someone to ignore. I actually felt wanted.

What in the world was I supposed to do with *that*?

SIX
HOLLY

February slowly turned to March and with it, the hope of spring. Most days, I left my winter coat in the car and was able to survive with a heavy sweatshirt. Occasionally, I was carrying the sweatshirt by the afternoon and soaking in the warmth of the sun in just a T-shirt.

It had been over three weeks since that first date with Graham, and I was no longer surprised when he popped up at random times and random places, always knowing exactly where to find me.

Odd, because whenever I looked around the campus, I never saw him. He was a ghost who appeared and vanished at will, while also becoming so real to me sometimes my chest squeezed with a pain so severe I feared a heart attack.

Tracey assured me this was what happened when you started liking someone for the first time. Your brain went a little haywire, your hormones ran amok, and all the sensible and safe choices you spent your entire life making somehow started to seem too constricting.

If I could have, I would have stopped this falling for Graham train weeks ago, turned down that first date, and never stepped foot on campus again. Liking him left me feeling more self-conscious and more suspicious than I ever had in my life. Which said quite enough.

But there were flags, as I called them, popping up. He was almost always out of town on the weekends. We saw each other off campus, but aside from him randomly walking me to a class every couple of days, I never saw him. I spent one night at his apartment, one he lived in *alone* of all things, and after we ordered pizza and watched a movie, he walked me to my car and gave me a kiss on the cheek. "Drive safe," he'd whispered, like he wasn't basically kicking me out of his apartment by nine o'clock on a Thursday—prime college getting ready to go out time.

There was the fact he still hadn't told me how he got my schedule, but he somehow always had an answer when I asked and smoothly changed the subject.

And yet he texted. All the time. Morning, afternoon, night. Weekends he was out of town, where he didn't tell me where he was except that he had *things to do*. One was a trip with some friends. One weekend he had to go to Raleigh, and I assumed that meant home, but then he never said anything about it except that it was good. Or exhausting.

Closet full of secrets. That's what he called them.

Like called to like, I supposed, because I hadn't exactly opened up to him and let him read my entire life story. Our time was spent laughing and teasing. Walking to class. All very middle-school, G-rated behavior.

And wasn't that alone a strange thing?

Was he...just becoming my friend?

All of it left me antsy and anxious, and at the diner yesterday, I'd gotten three orders wrong. I started letting some boy into my head, and all of a sudden my critical-thinking skills were misfiring.

Which meant it was probably time to bring this ridiculousness to an end. He had to be having fun with me, playing some game.

He seemed genuine when we were together—and even through the texts—but that wasn't enough.

It'd be simpler, easier for me for sure, and for Tracey because she wouldn't have to hear me whine about it anymore if I just ended it.

I could block him. Clean break. That alone would tell him all he needed to know.

I was done.

Surely we hadn't spent nearly enough time together to owe each other more explanations....

"Hey! Holly!"

I looked around, but I didn't recognize anyone, so I turned back and kept walking.

Footsteps thundered behind me on the cement, and I straightened my back. We were on campus, and it was midday, but I still gripped the straps of my backpack in case I needed to fling it at someone.

"Hey. Holly, right? You're Holly?"

I stopped then as a guy with labored breath slowed down as he neared me.

"Who are you?" I stopped and turned to face him.

He glanced back and forth up and down the sidewalk and shoved a hand through his chocolate brown hair. "I'm Eli. A friend of Graham's."

"If you're looking for him, I don't know where he is."

"No, that's not it. I just...he talks about you, you know? When we're out of town and stuff."

"Oh...you're one of the guys he went on a trip with last week?"

Eli's brows tugged low. "Trip? I mean. Yeah. We were together, but I saw you. He showed us a picture, and I guess I wanted to...shit...I don't know. Not warn you or anything. That sounds bad, but ask for a favor, I guess?" He kicked at the cement, his unease growing.

It didn't rival mine.

"You want me to do *you* a favor? A guy I don't know? About a guy I barely know?"

"Barely know? Graham says you talk all the time." His confusion increased. It was still nowhere near mine. He shook it off quicker than I did. "Listen, then yeah...I mean, if he's just some guy to you, I'm going to ask you to cut him loose."

"Excuse me?"

"He's had a crap year. Worse than most. I guess my favor was going to be if you don't like him, really like him, then bow out now before he gets hurt. I'm not sure he can handle any more and the guys...well, me...*us*...well, we need him healthy."

My head spun as the guy babbled, and all those flags that had been popping lit on fire until my blood was boiling. *He* had a hard year? His *guys* needed him?

"I'm not talking about him with someone I don't know." I turned to head off toward class, where I should have kept going before someone started shouting at me, and *how* did he recognize me anyway? Questions kept coming, but the one who had the answers was *busy* tonight.

Like he usually was.

Unfortunately for me, Eli kept following.

"Crap, he's going to kick my butt for this. Probably put me through hell later. I didn't mean to make you mad. I'm just having my boy's back, you know? Someone had to say something."

I kept walking. Anger made my shoes slap against the pavement as I tried to put distance between Eli and me, but he was tall. Taller than Graham, and man, he had long legs. He didn't have to hurry to catch up to me at all.

"You're going to tell him I said this, aren't you?"

There was something—a terror or sadness or maybe the guy was just realizing how badly he'd messed up that I paused. Looked at him. Arched my brows. Did he think I was an *idiot*?

"Yeah, Eli. I'm going to tell him about some guy chasing me down on campus to tell me to stay away from him. Stop following me."

Once I told him about this lovely, interesting conversation, I'd be getting answers.

Or my contact list would have one less number in it.

———

IT WAS WELL AFTER DINNER. I'd worked the shift at the University bookstore before stopping by The Grille to grab dinner to go. One of the servers was sick, so I ended up staying through the dinner shift. At all points, the bookstore and then the diner, I was half-expecting Graham to appear out of nowhere, somehow knowing what his friend had said to me and wanting to make things right.

I found myself disappointed he didn't, and then jumping and feeling my cheeks heat when my phone finally rang. Only for it to be a blocked number.

Dread settled as I debated answering and then hit the End button without bothering. My dad had once been the kind of man who picked me up from preschool and took me to get ice cream instead of real food for lunch. He sang and danced in our living room. He shouted at football games on television without them ruining his mood. He did all those things without requiring a twelve-pack at his side.

I didn't lose my mom the day her addiction swallowed her whole and she took off in search of her next high, completely forgetting she had a husband and daughter who adored her. My dad died that day. My mom was *gone*, but Dad turned into a walking, drunken zombie, shriveling a little bit more right in front of me.

I was eight the first time I cleaned up his vomit. Ten when he lost his job at the city and found a part-time job doing maintenance for one of the hotels in town, one job that would lead to dozens off and on over the years. Fourteen the first time he handed me the keys and told me to drive him home from the bar. I hadn't even taken driver's education yet. Not like he knew or cared.

I turned twenty-one the day before he got drunk, got pissed, and then drove a small SUV off the road on the way down Crystal Mountain Highway, killing the driver, a college student at Duke. A girl my age.

He'd never apologized. Never showed remorse. He lost our home years before, and he never apologized for that, either. In all my years of living, I had a mom who abandoned me and a father who quit knowing I was alive while staring at my face daily.

That was why I despised him. It wasn't his mistakes. It wasn't his own grief. It was the fact that as soon as Mom left, he never saw me. When he was being taken to prison, right after his sentencing, he didn't share fatherly advice or a hug or an apology. He glared at me and grumbled, "This is such a bunch of bullshit."

Those were the last words my father said to me before I

started getting calls demanding more money on his federal account. He left me with nothing but a run-down trailer and my plans to leave this town shriveling down to almost nothing considering the statewide news his horrible decisions made...and then decided *I* owed *him*.

And I was still the little girl who remembered her father's booming laughter and his comforting embrace. In my weak moments, I hoped that if I gave him more than he asked for, he'd see me again. That he'd become the dad I needed for the last decade even if it was from a distance.

My phone rang again, and I went to hit End, but it wasn't a blocked call.

It was Graham.

I debated. Thumb poised over the red circle.

And then... I answered instead. "Hey."

"I'm gonna kill him," Graham said in lieu of the appropriate greeting. Like hello or hey, back. "You've gotta be pissed, and I wish you would have texted me when it happened."

I had to give him credit for not hesitating to jump right in. "I didn't think your friend would tell you, and I didn't want to cause problems."

"You wouldn't cause a problem. *Eli* caused a problem, and it was ridiculous because he doesn't know what he's talking about."

"No? Because he seemed pretty certain he did."

You're not the only one with a closet full of secrets...

I've had a bad year...

"Yeah, well, you're not exactly an open book either. Did you consider I needed time to warm up to tell you stuff, too?"

"So this is *my* fault?" Oh, that was definite sass in my tone and not the fun kind. But if he thought for a second that I could be approached by a strange guy on campus warning me away from his friend and then blame me for it...

"No. Sorry. That's not what I meant. I'm ticked at Eli and had a crap night because of it. So I'm sorry. Really. I just...I don't talk about it, but I know I haven't been honest with you about things."

"Like how you got my schedule?"

It seemed easier to tease him about something trivial. If he started being honest, he might demand the same from me, and all of a sudden, with thoughts of my dad and his phone call on my mind, I was staring at a door I was asking him to open, but I wasn't ready to give the same back.

"My aunt Denise works in the campus career center. I told her if she gave me your schedule, I'd commit to having six Sunday dinners with her."

The truth spilled from him so easily, I wished we were on a FaceTime call so I could see his face. Sure, he could be lying, but...why?

"Denise?" I asked.

"Denise Campbell. My mom's sister. It's only one of the reasons I chose NCWU, because I like being close to family. You can go say hi to her if you want. I'm sure she's curious to know why I asked her for it."

"Well, aren't you just turning into being super honest tonight, but I think I'll pass." I tried to laugh it off, but a heavy sigh came from his side of the phone.

All the secrets of my own I was hiding came back to me, and now that we were talking, I wasn't sure I wanted to know his.

My phone buzzed, and before I could look, Graham asked, "Need to take that?"

He'd clearly heard the pause through the phone.

"No."

I didn't bother peeking. Dad's habit was to call at least three times before giving up on me. If he paid for the call himself with *my* money instead of expecting me to pay more than double for it to call collect, he'd be able to leave a voicemail.

"I *am* sorry about Eli, Holly. He spoke when he shouldn't have."

"He sounded like a friend concerned, that's not a bad thing to have."

There was the heavy beat of silence before he cleared his throat. "I went through a hard year. Last spring was especially tough."

We actually had that in common. We also both had aunts we liked. And we both had secrets.

Maybe we had more in common than I originally thought.

"You don't have to tell me," I said. "Because it's none of my business, but I do have to admit that you worry me."

He chuckled, almost in surprise. "I worry *you*?"

"Yeah...you're gone on the weekends, you show up at random times when you know where I'll be, but I never see you, and when we're together, you don't..."

That *cheek* kiss outside his apartment came back to me, but I couldn't finish it.

"I don't what? Show you how much I want you? How much I think about you and like being around you?"

When he put it like that...

"Yeah, kind of."

"I do," he whispered. My heart leaped straight into my throat, making it difficult to breathe and to think clearly. "I do like you, but I didn't want to scare you off. Figured if I did, that'd definitely send you running."

Once again, silence stole my thoughts. I wasn't prepared

for this. I wasn't prepared to meet someone who did these things to me. Made me feel something.

Made me hope.

Graham was becoming more dangerous by the minute.

"How about this?" he asked, and that teasing tone was back in his voice.

"What?" I couldn't help it. He teased me, and I fell for it. He was pulling me in when I should have been showing him my back.

"Friday, you'll have to come find me."

"And how do I do that?"

"I'll give you a clue. Later."

"That's it?" I laughed. "A clue?"

"You're a smart girl, you'll figure it out. Are we okay?"

He'd managed to be honest without telling me everything, or much at all. Which was okay because I wasn't ready to give him everything of me. But he was trying.

Maybe it was time I started thinking about doing the same.

"We'll see."

SEVEN
HOLLY

"Hockey," Tracey stated. "We should have known he was an athlete."

Before I left for campus, I'd received a text from Graham.

Bring a blanket.

Choosing to trust him, said blanket was now draped over my arm as Tracey and I walked into the campus's ice arena. And I figured *that* out because my second text came from Graham two hours later. I was sitting in my finance class next to Dallas when a picture popped up.

It was a picture of clear glass walls with metal bleachers behind it. The half wall beneath the glass had NCWU's painted Wolf mascot on it.

For assuming I was such a smart girl, I had to show the picture to Dallas.

"What is this?"

His eyes narrowed on the picture. "Ice arena. You've never been? They do open skate every week. It's a blast."

No, I'd never been to the arena for a fun night of ice

skating. I didn't tell Dallas that. I thanked him, took my phone back, and then it clicked.

A quick search of NCWU's hockey roster proved me right. Graham Marchese, forward, whatever that meant. His face was a bit blurry due to the thumbnail picture provided, but as I scrolled through the rest of the roster, other names jumped out at me. Eli. Tanner.

Well, surprise, surprise.

Another search of their schedule had most of my other doubts about Graham clicking into place. Every night he was out of town? He was at an away game. On nights when he was "busy?" He had a home game. Nights when he went to bed early? He'd had to leave the next morning for a trip.

I should have been able to figure it out sooner given his propensity for wearing sweatshirts and hats with our school's logo all over it. I'd assumed he was big into school spirit.

"You owe me for this," Tracey muttered, and her body shivered as we set our phones beneath the school's ticket scanner. "It's freezing in here."

It was cold, and the air was different from outside. Staler and not as crisp as the freezing temps outside.

"It's not like they can heat the place," I muttered.

We headed to the concession stand and bought hot chocolates and then scanned the arena. A small cheering section was decked out in green and gold hats and scarves on the opposite side of the rink beneath the massive HOME SEATING green banner.

And on the ice?

The team was warming up. Charleston University was their opponent, and they were closest to us in their red and white jerseys.

"Looks like we go this way."

I followed her around the edge of the arena, keeping one eye on the hockey teams, and trying to figure out which one was Graham. They all had on helmets and pads, and there weren't names on the back of the jerseys to help me out.

We reached the bleacher section, and as Tracey started walking toward the small crowd that looked to be students, most of them blonds, I grabbed the back of her coat.

"Don't."

"What?"

"That girl." I gestured to the blond closest to the glass wall. She was decked out in green and gold. It also looked like she'd added strands of green tinsel to her hair.

The rest of the girls around her looked similar. Apparently the Lambda Nu Chi girls were fans...maybe not of hockey, but definitely of the players.

Tracey made a face as she looked at me over her shoulder. "We should probably figure out who she is."

"Explains why she approached me about Graham."

We avoided the students and climbed the steps to the back row, passing a dozen or more adults gathered close together in the bleachers at the center of the rink. We grabbed our seats, separated from both adults and students, and off to the side, giving me a clear view of the ice rink.

"Graham's number eight," she said, and then flashed me a picture on her phone.

I leaned in closer. "What about Eli and Tanner?"

She scrolled through the roster pics, moving slow enough I could pick out their faces. "Tanner is twenty-two, and Eli...six," she said once she found them.

"Wonderful." I focused on the team.

They were set up in three lines, and the guys skated so fast, slapped the puck back and forth so quickly, I kept losing sight of it. It looked like a drills practice, and after every shot at the small goal, they skated leisurely back to the lines. It was impressive any of the pucks went in considering the goalie was about twice the size of the small goal he skated in front of.

Everything moved so fast, and the constant *swish* of skates on ice and the *smack* of the puck soon became nothing but background noise.

Tracey sat and bumped my shoulder as we huddled close to each other and wrapped my blanket around us. "I can't believe you're dating a hockey player."

"I'm not dating anyone."

She chortled. "Right. Sure you're not."

"We went on *one* date. That's not dating."

"I think the fact he said he likes you and thinks about you and invited you to his place says you are."

"Whatever." I shivered and grabbed my hat from my pocket and tugged it onto my head.

"Do we know anything about hockey?"

"I used to watch with my dad. Pretty sure he put it on when it was my nap time, so unless I learned through sleep, probably not."

"My brother played. I just read books and colored and ignored everything about the game."

"So we're mostly screwed," I said.

She held up her phone and wiggled it. "They hit the puck into the goal and try to win. How much more do we need to know?"

I wanted to know why Graham kept this from me. That wasn't normal, was it? Didn't athletes like to tell everyone how awesome they were?

A horn blared, and Tracy and I both jumped.

"Wowzers," she whispered, pressing her heart to her chest. "That was loud."

That horn meant something because the teams skated to the benches and cleared the ice.

A loud voice squawked through the speakers. "Ladies and gentlemen. Please rise for the singing of our national anthem, performed today by North Carolina Western University's very own Megan Schleppe."

As the announcer spoke, guys from both benches came back out onto the ice, this time without their sticks, and lined up, each team on a blue line, and faced the flag hanging next to a scoreboard.

The singer's voice filled the arena, and I scanned the rink and then found her at the edge of the ice on the far end, standing right at the edge in front of a door to the rink that had opened. Her voice was rich and pure, and she sang it a cappella, which was probably more impressive than anything I'd ever seen.

When she was done, the small crowd cheered, the Lambda Nu Chi's loudest of all. Both teams skated back to their benches, grabbed their sticks, and then stood in the doorway.

And then the announcer came back on. "Charleston University's starting lineup..." he droned on, rattling off a bunch of names as the visiting team skated out, one by one, to the ice.

The lights turned dark, and eerie, low music came on building and growing louder. My heart rate matched the beat, thumping harder and faster as it crescendoed. Spotlights appeared and flashes of green and gold filled the area.

"Whoa," I muttered. They were putting on a show, and it was pretty cool to see.

"And now...for your North Western Carolina University starting lineup!"

The small crowd cheered and got to their feet. Every time a name was called, a player skated onto the ice and did a lap around the rink until they landed at a specific spot on the ice.

I wished I would have gotten earlier clues so I had time to do basic research on the game. I was totally lost.

Finally, Graham's name was called. A woman six rows away from us jumped to her feet, grabbing my attention. She was older, dressed in a thick sweater, a winter coat, and had a striped scarf wrapped at least three times around her neck. "Go Graham!"

"That must be his aunt," I muttered to Tracey.

"And he has his own fan club." She elbowed me in my side, but I didn't need her nudge to know who she was talking about. The blond who had stopped me in my tracks was jumping up and down, cheering for him, louder than anyone else.

To Graham's credit, if he heard the noise, he ignored it and skated to his spot in the center of the ice, inside a blue circle, and across from the team's other player.

He tapped his stick to the ice, stood, and turned his head, stopping when he found me like he knew exactly where I'd be sitting. He reached up and tugged at his helmet before dipping his chin and then turned back to the opponent across from him.

But I swore, in that brief moment when our eyes met, there was a smile curling the edges of his lips.

"Yeah. If you're not dating, fine, I'll give you that. But after that, I'm pretty sure you're about to be. And someone isn't happy about it."

I didn't need to look toward the other students to know who she was talking about.

I could feel her heated glare from across the space between us.

HOCKEY WAS WILDLY CRAZY. There were fights and shouts. The puck flew across the ice so quickly I kept losing it and then finding it when the players were suddenly fighting behind the net at the opposite end of the ice. Every time our team scored, a horn blared, and lights went off through the arena. The music was loud, the announcer explained everything that was happening, and while Tracey and I tried to watch every minute, I had absolutely *no clue* what was going on.

The most terrifying moment came when Eli got in a fight across the ice from us. Helmets and gloves went flying. Fists started slamming into each other's faces. More players from both teams joined in, and soon, Graham's fists were flying as fast as everyone else's.

No one was bothered by this. In fact, the arena turned electric. Parents and students and even the away team across the rink jumped to their feet, clapped, and cheered.

By the time uninvolved teammates and the referees separated the players, blood was dripping from more than one player's nose or from a cut by their eye, and players from both sides were shoved into a small, enclosed bench area off to the sides of their teams.

"Sin bin," Tracey had muttered, clearly trying to learn about the game by Googling it on her phone. "It's actually called a penalty box, but it's most commonly referred to as the sin bin."

"Thank you, Mrs. Google."

"Shut up." She chuckled and bounced her shoulder against mine. "I'm learning. Consider me your new hockey tutor."

"Thanks."

Whatever had happened, and whatever the reason for the fight, everyone quickly settled down, and the game resumed like it hadn't happened at all.

The entire experience was confusing, but there was no hiding the fact that Graham Marchese was by far, the leader of the team. He moved faster, and out of all the shots on goal, he had landed two, putting the Wolves ahead by four to zero.

The buzzer went off, signaling the end of the second period.

"I'm freezing," Tracey muttered. "I need more hot chocolate. Want some?"

"No thanks." She tossed her half of the blanket onto my lap and headed down the stairs. Thanks to my hockey tutor, I now knew there was a fifteen-minute break and then one final twenty-minute period.

While Tracey was gone, I did my own research about hockey and pulled up the site Tracey had been using. Apparently hockey teams fought for all sorts of reasons. They weren't only an expected part of the game, but one of the most exciting.

"Who knew?" I mumbled and kept reading.

Tracey came back before long, hot chocolates in both hands and handed one to me. "I know you said you didn't want it, but I bought you one anyway."

"Thanks." As soon as the warm cup was in my hand, I definitely wanted it. The heat alone helped.

"Anything exciting happen while I was gone?"

"It's intermission. What could happen?"

"With you around? Who knows." She shrugged like *I* was the wild and crazy one out of the two of us.

I laughed her off, sipped on my hot chocolate, and then pulled up NCWU's hockey Instagram page. "Apparently they're pretty good," I told Tracey as I saw a graphic with their conference standing. "Number two in the conference right now."

"I don't know what that means," she said.

"You know?" I closed my phone and slipped it into my coat pocket. "I don't really either."

We dissolved into laughter, drank our hot chocolate, and by the time the third period started, I was ready for my backside to stop feeling like a block of ice, but I was actually looking forward to the end of the game.

"Man," Tracey muttered, as the team took their spots back on the ice. "Is it weird that I think all that gear makes the guys look kinda sexy?"

"Considering you can't see their faces or what's hiding under all of it? Yes."

"Maybe I like the appeal of mystery."

She was a nut. An absolute nut.

The third period started with Graham once again at the center. He got the puck and passed it to another player. The game flew by, neither team scoring, but it didn't matter. Halfway through the period, I was sitting on the front edge of the bleacher, my hands fisted and pulled tight to my chest. The other team hadn't scored, and our team hadn't scored another.

They were fighting for the puck behind the net with our goalie in it, four players slamming each other into boards and kicking at the puck with their skates. Somehow, it got kicked or smacked to the side, and there was Graham, flying out of the tangle at the boards and racing down to get the puck.

"Oh my gosh!" Tracey's hand landed on my thigh and squeezed.

He was skating, moving the puck back and forth with his stick.

Their announcer called out, "Marchese with a break-away! He shoots...he...."

The horn blared, and the lights went out. "SCORES!"

Every single person on this side of the arena jumped to their feet and started screaming.

Tracey and I followed, slower. I glanced at her, and she shrugged. The claps in the building were louder than normal, and every student was jumping up and down on their feet.

"Hat trick! Marchese with the hat trick!"

A few seconds later, Tracey had her phone in her hand. "A hat trick is when a player scores three goals in a game. It's a huge thing. In pro sports, people actually toss hats onto the ice."

As she said it, two hats from the student section landed on the ice where Graham was getting bear-hugged by his teammates on the ice.

Whistles were being blown by the refs, but the chaos was too loud to get control. He skated over to his team, high-fived them all while they slammed their sticks against the boards and screamed and cheered along with everyone else.

"It's a really hard thing to get," Tracey continued.

I'd already figured that out.

"And rare."

I covered her phone's screen with my gloved hand and smiled at my friend. "I think I get it."

MY HEART WAS RACING. The game was over. We won five to nothing, but after the excitement of Graham's last goal, I couldn't calm down. Even as the final seconds ticked down, and it was obvious we would win, I was still leaning forward, moving left and right in the direction the playing happening in front of me.

Even now, as the players had shaken hands and were starting to skate off the ice and disappear under a walkway I assumed led to the locker rooms, I couldn't pull my focus off Graham. He skated like he was floating, and despite his size, he was graceful. Fast. So fast. He slapped the goalie's helmet as the guy stepped off the ice and disappeared.

I expected Graham to follow him, but he stopped at an area that didn't have glass and tugged off his helmet.

Immediately, his eyes met mine. "Get down here!"

"Go on," Tracey said, shoving my back. "Go see your man."

"Please." I huffed and felt the force of a thousand glares on me as the girls heading in the same direction where he was standing shouted his name.

"Good game," I told Graham, grinning down at him when I reached him.

"It was good. One of my best ever." He was smiling wide, sweating even though the weather was freezing.

"Really?"

"I haven't had a hat trick in two years. You must be my lucky charm."

My chest swelled, and my smile brightened. What a nice thought for someone to have of me.

"You have plans later?" he asked.

"Warming up as quickly as possible is the only thing on my agenda."

Graham laughed, bold and loudly, and it garnered attention because somebody stepped next to me, and the next thing I knew, I was shoved to the side and down a step.

"Hey!" Graham called and reached for me, but since I was above him, he couldn't do much. I grabbed the railing and steadied myself.

"Awesome game, G," the new person said.

I didn't have to look to know it was the blond.

"Thanks, Piper," he said, but he hadn't looked at her. Instead, he scooted to his left so he was in front of me again.

"Doing anything later?" she asked. "We hear the team is having a party."

Without taking his eyes off me, he replied, "Hoping to have a quiet night in. You in, Holly?"

Next to me, the girl—Piper—at least I now knew her name, scoffed. "Come on, Graham. You haven't had a hat trick in years. Come out with us. We'll make sure you have a good time."

He glanced at her, a slight frown tugging down his lips. "Not interested, but thanks."

He couldn't have sounded any less thankful.

When he turned to me, he was no longer looking amused at all. "What do you say? Dinner and a movie in? I need to shower and clean up, but I can meet you at my place in an hour?"

"Um. Sure?"

"Great." He grinned and skated off, leaving me alone with Piper and a gaggle of blonds behind her.

"He'll get bored of you. I've known him practically my whole life, and you're not what he'll want for anything long-term."

She wasn't saying anything I didn't already know, but the words, said with such nastiness, hurt more than they should have. "I'll keep that in mind."

I turned and hurried to where Tracey was standing near the bottom of the bleachers.

"Sorry, so sorry," she said. "I didn't think the girls would approach him with you there or I would have come with you."

"No worries."

"What'd she say to you?"

I rubbed my gloved hands together and then buried them into my coat pockets. "Nothing I didn't already know."

EIGHT

HOLLY

"So, you're some hotshot hockey player."

I was standing in the doorway to Graham's apartment. He had the door open wide, his arm straight out. His hair was wet and curly, and he was dressed in a pair of flannel pants and a long-sleeve NCWU hockey shirt. No socks, which somehow made me feel overdressed in my coat and gloves and everything else I'd layered on for the game.

"Not sure about hotshot, but yeah, I'm on the hockey team."

"You didn't mention that before."

"I didn't think you'd stick around if I did."

Would I have? I wasn't anti-athlete. Sure, there were stereotypical athletes that were all about being *jocks* and using that to get girls, but logically I was aware not all were like that. A few football players were in my finance classes, and they carried small Bibles with them and had started an on-campus Bible study for athletes. So yeah, not all were bad. On the flip side, attention seemed to follow athletes wherever they went, and I tried to stay out of the limelight. Case in point, *Piper*.

"If you've noticed, I haven't stepped foot inside yet."

Graham chuckled and stepped back, taking the door with him and swinging it wide open for me. "What are you waiting for?"

Nothing. If his being a hockey player bothered me, I wouldn't have come. I hadn't debated if I would or not. In fact, I was pretty sure I'd beaten him to the apartment building because I stayed in my car for twenty minutes waiting for the hour he requested to be up. And then I waited ten more minutes so I didn't come across as too eager.

I crossed the threshold, and a look of satisfaction flashed on Graham's face. I had the sudden rush that I'd pleased him, and that only increased when I removed my coat and hung it up on a set of empty hooks he had by his door.

"It certainly does explain a lot."

His "early" nights. The weekends. I was so used to people letting me down or flat-out lying to me that I'd built too many walls. It was too far ingrained in my nature to suspect wrongdoing everywhere I turned. Looking back, Graham had been honest with me. Sure, he'd kept things to himself, but I bet if I had tried to get to know him more, really dive in, he would have told me.

"If it helps, I didn't like not being fully honest with you."

"Like you said, we all have closets full of secrets. Was that yours?"

He rocked back on his heels, and for the first time since we'd met, he seemed uncomfortable. Like the question was diving in too deep. "One of them?"

He chewed his bottom lip. Did he want me to ask? Avoid it?

My curiosity was rising, but there were things I'd have

to tell him if I wanted to keep seeing him, and I wasn't ready for all of that. So avoidance it was.

Maybe I'd wait and see how the night went. I could always block him tomorrow.

"You mentioned dinner," I said, and relief washed through him, loosening the muscles around his eyes I hadn't realized had tightened and fell from his shoulders. "Are you going to feed me, or are we going to keep standing here?"

He chuckled and grabbed his phone. "Chinese? Pizza? Something else?" He waved his phone. "The world is our oyster...or whatever restaurants are available for delivery."

"Chipotle." As soon as I said it, my stomach rumbled.

"Guess I don't have to ask if you're sure," Graham said, laughing at me as I covered my stomach.

"Sorry. But chips and salsa and a massive burrito sound incredible right now."

He tapped on his screen, opened the app, and then handed me his phone. "Here. You order first."

"You're just handing me your phone?" I had my palm up, waiting for it, but...really?

Graham shook his head, and his dark hair swayed and swooshed with the movement. His eyes glimmered with amusement. "I don't have secrets, Holly. I have things I haven't told you yet, but the main word is yet."

"You're not asking about mine."

"Just because you have things you haven't told me *yet*, doesn't mean you won't. I figure I have to earn the honor of your trust first, so yeah...maybe that starts with you having access to my phone. But don't snoop for too long. I'm starving."

"Right." Of course. Because this was a Chipotle order, not unfettered access. Still, the urge to snoop slithered to my fingertips. Who did he Snap the most? How often did he and his mom talk? Or his dad? Did he have siblings?

They were probably all off doing equally amazing things like playing college or professional sports and being doctors or something. Maybe lawyers or engineers.

Was Piper at the top of any of those lists?

All the questions chased each other, giving me no break from my insanity and paranoia—at least I realized it—while I put in my order. I forewent a soda, figuring he had water and that was good enough for me, but threw in a large order of both queso cheese and guac.

I let him know as I handed the phone back to him.

"Extra food but no snooping?"

"You're right here," I drawled. "If I'm going to snoop, I'm not going to do it while you can watch."

"Shame...I'd like to see your reaction to my internet history."

A blush hit at the insinuation, and Graham's face went serious for a moment. Then two before he wiggled his brows.

"I...um...I don't need to see that..." I stuttered out.

Graham laughed as he finalized his order. "Don't know where your mind went, but I was talking about my search history of articles that start with '*How to get the girl you like but aren't sure if she likes you back.*'" He gave me that ridiculous eyebrow wiggle again with his standard shameless smirk.

An incredulous laugh fell from my lips. The audacity of this guy.

"I'm sure that's what's on there."

He held out his phone. "Wanna check?"

Tempting. So very tempting. Who wouldn't want to know if he really spent time searching for things like that?

Were they *Cosmo* articles? *Men's Health?* I highly doubted such things for guys existed. They were too confident. Too egotistical. *He* was too confident.

"I'll pass." I waved him off. "But I would like some water. Or hot tea if you have it."

"Sorry. Fresh out of tea," he teased. I doubted tea had ever made it on his grocery shopping list.

He went to the small kitchen, and I hung out on the other side through a pass-through hole in the wall where I could see him moving around, grabbing two bottled waters from the fridge. Which was basically all his fridge was stocked with.

"Don't do a lot of cooking?" I asked, but I wasn't surprised. Most college kids didn't, and if he was an athlete, they had their own dining and meal plans, and a lot of those were eaten in the athletic building.

"What gave it away?" He gestured to his fridge door like a classy Vanna White. "My vast selection of condiments?"

"Pretty much."

"I'll have you know, I *can* cook. I just don't like to. My dad did a lot of cooking in our house when I was growing up, and he made me help him. Said it was good for men to know so they didn't someday get married and expect the women in their lives to do it all."

"Well, isn't that progressive of him."

"My dad's a progressive guy." He shrugged it off like it was nothing, but it wasn't.

If my dad adopted that kind of mindset, he might not have fallen apart so spectacularly after Mom took off.

"Come on. The app said it'll be about forty minutes until our food gets here. Any movies you like to watch?"

"Was that a suggestion in all those articles you read?"

He barked out a laugh and plopped down on the couch. "No, Spitfire. That's because I'm a thoughtful guy."

He handed me my water, and I sat down close to him on the couch. "Can I ask a question?"

"You can ask anything." He untwisted his water and took a healthy swig.

"Who's Piper?"

He coughed, spewing water out of his mouth and then cussed as he jumped to his feet.

I laughed, more out of surprise than humor.

"Hold on. Crap." He brushed water off his shirt and then hurried to the kitchen, where he grabbed a roll of paper towels. Tearing off more than necessary for the few splatters on his table and couch, he came back and mopped it all up.

"How many cool guy points did that just make me lose?"

His cheeks were a dark pink. Was he really embarrassed?

"Zero, unless you're going to tell me there's something going on with you two."

"Piper? Me? No way." He shook his head, frowning, and then fell back onto the couch. "Why? Did she say something to you?"

"She told me she's known you almost her entire life."

"Yeah. I mean..." He paused, swiped at his hair, and then blew out a breath. "We've been friends a long time. She's...well...snotty is the best word, but she's got a heart of gold beneath all of that. We're just friends, though. That's all we've ever been."

His tone became more strained as he tried to explain.

"She made it sound like more."

His expression turned pained, and I was about to let it

go because this was another one of those things he seemed like he didn't want to talk about, but then he grumbled something I couldn't hear.

He closed his eyes. When he opened them, I expected to see the same playfulness he usually showed me, but there was something dark in them. Something cold. Like he was in the room physically, but he'd gone somewhere entirely else in the span of time it took him to blink.

"We lost someone last year. Someone important to both of us. Since then...I don't know. I think my family had always thought I'd end up with our friend, but she and I hadn't wanted that. Now that she's gone, Piper's been... territorial of me? I don't know if that's the right word. But yeah...I'm sorry if she said anything. I can talk to her."

"No." I shook my head. She'd questioned me, she'd made implications, but she also hadn't been wrong. I wasn't anything special, and whatever this was wouldn't be long-term.

"I'm sorry," I whispered. Because the pain of losing someone was difficult, and the way he said it made it seem like that loss was final. "Did you love her?"

It was absolutely none of my business, but Eli's words came back to me loud and clear. This explained his hard year. This explained why Piper said he never talked to girls. Was he...mourning?

"Yes? No? I mean, yeah. In a way, but not that way. We were just really good friends. Her dad and mine were super close. They hung out together all the time, so we were always together. And then Piper's family moved into our neighborhood when she was seven or something, and then it was the three of us. We were G, P, and Fee because parts of all of our names rhymed. I got older and obviously got guy friends and teammates and stuff, but for Piper, it was always

Fee. She's taken the loss harder and changed. I don't blame her for it. For me, it kind of opened my eyes to what I wanted out of life. Piper, well, she's struggling."

Now that I understood, I could sympathize with her. I didn't exactly want to feel bad about a girl who'd been rude to me, but we all struggled with something, and her current pains seemed to be pretty major.

"I'm sorry," I said again. I knew the pain of losing people, even if mine were still alive. It didn't make the loss easier knowing they chose to go away.

Graham shrugged and then took another pull of his water. I let him take the time he needed, drinking my own water, until he came back to me with that friendly grin.

"Did I scare you off yet?"

Bending my legs, I brought my heels to the couch and rested my cheek on my knees while facing him. If I was looking to leave, which I should have been, it would have been the perfect excuse. And yet, that's all it would have been—an excuse.

The more Graham opened up, the more I realized I was starting to fall for this guy, and not only was I doing it without a safety net...I couldn't bring myself to pull the cord, release my parachute, and get myself off this crazy trip.

"No. Not yet."

Had I been standing, his answering smile would have sent my knees wobbling.

NINE
HOLLY

Chipotle came. I was only mildly embarrassed by how quickly I devoured it along with the mess I made. Considering Graham ate his burrito bowl in half the time and we both annihilated the chips, queso, and guacamole, I wasn't *overly* embarrassed by my lack of manners or clean eating.

He put on a reality show where people lived on cruise ships, but most of the time, we talked. I moved us away from the loss of his friend after telling him I wasn't leaving, and somehow, that seemed to help him relax. I asked him if he wanted to go to that hockey party, and he asked if I drank.

When I said no, he shrugged. "That answers that then."

"I do go to parties. And we met at a bar."

"Yeah, well, I don't feel like going somewhere where people are already half drunk and stupid if we're both sober, so it's more for me."

"But you drink," I pointed out.

"Maybe one. Usually I sip a beer until it gets warm and then set it aside. I used to, but I think losing someone the way I have puts things in perspective. My friends know they can call me if they need rides, though."

He was more of an open book than I would have antici-
pated, and he kept surprising me. It wasn't only the kind of
guy he was or how much I was learning we had in common.

To some, maybe the heavy would have been too much,
but I'd lived with heavy my whole life.

Perhaps that was why my mouth opened, and I found
myself saying, "My mom took off when I was seven."

His body tensed. Out of the corner of my eye, I saw him
slowly readjust himself, curling toward me. His arm draped
over the back of the couch. I was close enough he could run
his fingers through my hair, and that was exactly what
he did.

"Yeah?"

I shrugged. I might as well have sliced my body open
right then and bled out in front of him for as vulnerable as I
was feeling. Admitting *that* was hard enough. The why was
harder.

"That must have been hard," Graham said, fingers still
running through my hair. His touch was gentle. Soothing.

I leaned back into the couch and faced him.

His eyes were on his hand in my hair. His curls were
now dry and slightly frizzy and wild. He was stretched out,
legs on the coffee table, one foot over the other. But for the
intense way he kept his eyes on my hair and not me, like he
didn't want me to know he was listening, I would have
thought he was uncaring.

Instead, he was giving me space. Time.

"She and I were at my gymnastics class. She put me in it
when I was really young, like three or something. But she'd
been a gymnast through high school and loved it. It was
before class, and I was warming up and begged her to show
me how she did her flips."

It was the last really good, true, and pure memory I had

of my mom. When she put me in gymnastics, she'd told me someday I could be better than her, maybe go to college on a scholarship or be in the Olympics. I'd been too young to understand then what that meant, but I remembered the way her face lit up when she talked about gymnastics and how much she loved it.

"What happened?" Graham asked. He glanced at me and waited.

I readjusted on the couch, the need to protect myself was strong, so I curled my legs up. "She tumbled. She fell. Landed wrong and broke her leg. Her body went one way, her leg went the other."

He cringed but stayed silent.

"We had to call an ambulance and everything. Her bone just *snapped*. I'll never forget that sound. Or her scream." I'd also never forget the smile she had on her face right before she agreed to try it. The way she crouched down low and kissed the tip of my nose. "Okay Holly, just for you..."

She'd taken off. Jumped. Fell. Screamed. And my life was shattered, right along with her leg.

"She had surgery," I told him, "and apparently had some really good drugs for pain after. She couldn't work for a while... and I don't really know what happened next. I was so young, but eventually I realized she got hooked on those pills and then other kinds of drugs. She decided she needed to chase the high more than she needed to get clean and be a mom."

The admission made my chest squeeze painfully tight, and all that pain rushed to my nose. My eyes. My sinuses.

"You know that's not what she chose, right?" Graham reached out and cupped my cheek and my jaw.

One thumb swiped across my cheek to gather tears, and

I leaned in closer, wanting that warm touch on my skin that felt rubbed and scraped until I bled. "People don't choose addiction, Holly. You know that."

Maybe. Maybe she didn't.

"I used to hear them fight—my parents. Dad begged her to get help, and she refused. Said he wasn't fun anymore. Said everything in her life was boring and tired and ugly and draining."

She hadn't specifically said *me*, but how could I not take it that way? She'd worked at The Grille but was always home with me. I *was* her life.

And I drained her.

"I'm really sorry," Graham said. "I'm so sorry you had to hear those things. It was the drugs talking, you know that, though. Right?"

"Well, she took off one day. Just *poof*, gone. And none of it would have happened if I wouldn't have been a spoiled brat and begged her to jump."

I couldn't stop the tears, and I closed my eyes, burrowing into a tighter ball until the weight of the couch shifted, and then Graham was tugging me closer to him. He set his hand at the back of my head, his other at my lower back, and wrapped me in arms so strong and tight I couldn't remember the last time I'd been held like this.

"It wasn't your fault," he whispered as I cried. "Maybe she wouldn't have gotten hooked on meds without that jump, but she was still your mom. She wanted you to be impressed by her. She wanted you to think she was amazing. And she loved you, I'm sure of it."

"I'm not."

"I am," he stated, and I swore his lips pressed to the top of my head. I cried, embarrassed at how I'd so easily folded into him, let him hold me for so long that even after the tears dried, it was hard to face him again.

"How'd your dad handle it?" he asked. It was said quietly, almost like he was scared.

"He fell apart. Needless to say, my dad didn't have the mindset about being partners in a marriage that yours did." I tried to joke, but it fell flat. Cringing, I pushed off Graham and wiped my eyes with the hem of my sweater.

"I got tears all over your shirt," I muttered.

"They'll dry. Stay here."

He got up, went to the bathroom, and when he returned, he had a box of tissues and some makeup remover wipes. Then he went to the kitchen and brought back another bottle of water.

"In the business of ruining women's makeup?" I asked, holding up the pale blue plastic packet.

"No, smart aleck. I use them. They're not so bad for a quick wash when I don't have time."

A guy who paid attention to his skin care?

Oddly attractive. Definitely impressive.

He gave me a few minutes to clean up, blow my nose, and was lounging on the couch like nothing happened. Like I hadn't fallen apart in his arms.

"So, I take it your dad wasn't so great after?"

"No." I shook my head. "Weirdly enough, for as much as he hated my mom doing drugs and her addiction, he didn't care or notice his own. His drug was alcohol, though...but it was what it was. He couldn't live without her, and he collapsed."

"You've been on your own a long time then, huh?"

As he asked, he reached out and covered his hand with mine. Pushing his fingers against mine, his filled the spaces between mine and then closed both of our hands into an entwined fist.

"I guess," I whispered. The warmth from his hand holding mine spread up my arm, sent warmth to my neck, my cheeks, and down to my lower stomach. I tried to pull away, and he held on tighter.

"My mom died when I was sixteen," he said, and it was so low I almost missed it.

"What?"

"Yeah. Cancer. She was diagnosed and then gone in six months, and it wasn't a pretty six months, either. But that's one of the reasons I came here for school. Her sister is the one who works on campus. She practically became my second mom after she died."

"And yet, you're not falling apart talking about it like I did."

He reached up and brushed hair off my cheeks and curled his around the back of my neck. My lips parted with surprise as he tugged me closer to him, not nearly close enough to kiss, but if I scooted toward him. If I leaned to the right a bit...

"I got help and had healthy outlets to deal with it, Holly. I have a feeling you didn't have that."

"No," I whispered. "I didn't have that."

His smile was soft, understanding. "I was also given the benefit of being able to say goodbye. To say all the things I needed to. To hear all the things she wanted to teach me. I'm sorry you haven't gotten that, either."

"Thank you." More tears burned. How did he *get* me? How was it possible this boy I met right before I got evicted from a bar I practically lived in while my dad drank his beers and I did my schoolwork could *see* me so much better than anyone?

He was right about everything. I hadn't had any of it. Caroline tried, but she and Paul had never been able to have kids, and the restaurant was her whole life. Mothering wasn't her instinct. Cooking was.

But I had this. This moment in time where there wasn't judgment in his eyes. Where I didn't see pity, only the deep well of understanding that could only come from a similar pain.

And it was for that reason I opened my mouth and told him, "You should know that that girl you like really likes you back."

"Yeah?" A corner of his mouth kicked up before he licked his bottom lip. "Then that girl should know I'm probably going to kiss her."

I chuckled, and then I was silenced. He leaned down and pressed his mouth to mine. His lips teased mine slowly and were as warm as the rest of him. His grip on me was strong. He unlinked our hands together and cupped both of my cheeks as he kept kissing. Kept teasing.

But he didn't push it farther. Didn't even slip his tongue inside. Didn't do anything more than kiss my lips and press his hands to my cheeks, and it was beautiful.

It was sincere and gentle. It was slow, and I had no doubt that while he kissed me, he wanted to do so much more but held himself back to gain my trust.

Which was probably what had me handing it to him without him even knowing.

TEN

HOLLY

"You doin' all right?"

Piles of paper and multiple spreadsheets in front of me almost hid the intruder from my view. I was working on Caroline's taxes, both The Premier Grille's and her personal ones.

Caroline was an incredible cook. Excellent at managing people and always had the front restaurant immaculate and was incredible with customers. Organization was her major fault, and I'd been staring at piles of receipts and unorganized spreadsheets. I'd been trying to reorganize her for so long that a dull throb had started behind my right eye.

She was leaning against the doorframe to her office, and I had no doubt she had one eye on me, one eye on everything else out front, even if she couldn't see it.

"You're a hot mess, Care. Have I ever told you that?"

"Just about every spring since you started doing this, so yeah."

I was thirteen the first time she asked me to help her get organized for her accountant. Fifteen when she decided she didn't need him for everything, and I started handling her personal taxes. Eighteen when I started figuring out the business end. There were plenty of accountants in town, but none she trusted for some reason only Caroline could understand.

"I swear I keep trying to do better. I start off the year well."

I laughed and held up one neatly piled set of receipts and printed bank statements from January and February of last year. "Two months. You did great. Do you need me out there?"

"The rush is slowing down, but there's a table that requested you."

"Me?" That hadn't happened since high school. "You sure?"

I was already pushing back from her desk and headed her way. "Who?"

"Some boys." She leaned in and whispered, "Cute ones."

Cute boys. That could only be one person...or, rather, three.

"Great," I muttered, and my hands went to my hair, smoothing back flyaways so I didn't *look* like I'd spent the last few hours wanting to tear my hair out by my roots.

"Is one of them the reason you've been different lately?"

"Different?" I glanced back at her over my shoulder.

"Yeah, your face has been different."

"Wow, Care. That's sweet of you. Thanks for the compliment."

She kicked the back of my shoe with hers, making me stumble. "Shut up. You've been smiling. It's weird."

"You're weird," I muttered and pushed through the metal doors.

I didn't have to look far to find them. Even among the

skiers and tubers and mountain hikers, there was something special about Graham. Perhaps it was the easy smile he wore as well as he wore his clothes and backward hat, curly hair concealed beneath the brim.

Maybe it was just him and the reminders of those kisses last night. The kisses we kept giving each other, the kisses I fell asleep thinking about and dreamed of. I woke up with my fingers pressed to my bottom lip like I'd spent the entire night trying to seal the taste of him into the deepest recesses of my memories.

"Which one is yours?" Caroline whispered, and I swear she was giddier than a kindergartener on their first day of school.

Yesterday, I would have said none of them.

But that was before he told me about his friend. Before I opened up about my mom. Before those kisses...

"Graham," I muttered, taking the minute while he talked with two guys opposite him and hadn't yet noticed me. "The one sitting by himself."

"Wowzers. He's *cute*. Could do worse, but not sure you could do better."

How odd. I was starting to think that too, but it had nothing to do with his looks. Well, not fully. He was gorgeous.

I nudged Caroline away with my shoulder. "Don't you have work to do? Tables to clean? People to help?"

"A niece to take care of," she added with her dry tone. "And that niece who I adore so much is finally smiling, and if it's because of that boy, I'm thrilled, but you deserve to smile even without a boy around."

"Thanks for the life lesson." I turned to the water station, grabbed a tray, and set three glasses on it. "You can go now."

"Get their drinks and their orders and then sit and enjoy yourself. I'll bring the food out when it's ready."

It was almost eight, and she'd been on her feet since six in the morning. How Caroline and Paul could have a happy marriage when she was on her feet for up to sixteen hours a day was beyond me, but except for the occasional stress that came with running a restaurant in a small town that relied heavily on tourism, I never heard Caroline complain.

And life hadn't been that much better to her than it had been to me, although she had someone to share it with.

I thought of this while I grabbed the water pitcher and headed toward Graham and his friends. Eli and Tanner sat across from him. I hadn't seen Tanner since the last time they were in Deer Creek, and Eli shot me a chagrined smile as I reached them.

"Hey," I said, glancing at all three of them. "Nothing going on in Boone that you had to head out this way?"

"Someone." Eli coughed as he said it. "Begged us."

"I didn't *beg*," Graham corrected. "I simply kept asking someone to come with me until I convinced them. I can be very convincing."

"Vomit," Tanner grumbled. "Seriously, it's right here in my throat." He pointed to the divot at the base of his throat and cleared it. "Please don't do that while I'm trying to think of food."

Graham rolled his eyes. "How's work going? Looks like you were plenty busy tonight."

I scanned the side of the restaurant they were in. Years ago, before smoking sections were outlawed, this had been that area, so it was tucked away and separated with a glass partition and two open walkways. Most of the tables were dirty. Some still had plates on them that hadn't been cleaned.

I cringed as I glanced around at the old restaurant. Back in the fifties, it'd been a diner, complete with poodle skirts and all. My grandparents had bought it after, taken out the jukebox and soda fountains, and remodeled it to have a rustic charm. I couldn't quite see the charm anymore. It'd faded after years of use, declining profits, and while Caroline was awesome and I loved Paul, neither were nearly as handy as my grandfather, or my dad had been when he'd helped out.

Caroline shouldn't have had me doing her taxes. I should have been out with customers and cleaning tables, but I couldn't fault her for tucking me away on a Saturday night. She needed as much business as she could get, and my presence tended to turn them away. We were at the end of ski season. It was probably one of the last few weekends that tourists would flock to our mountains and our town. Soon, we'd be spending our hours keeping the restaurant immaculately clean all for something to do with our time. The Grille needed every penny they could find to get them through the summer.

Right now, there was nothing special about the restaurant, and seeing it through the eyes of college students who had credit cards to pay for hundreds of dollars of flowers and dinners, I wasn't embarrassed necessarily...but it was humbling.

"Yeah." I poured their waters, set down the pitcher, and grabbed our old-school order pad. "It was pretty busy. You guys need something to drink?" I rattled off the beers on tap, but they all shook their heads.

"Hockey playoffs are soon," Eli said. "Need to watch that. I'm good with water."

"Same," Tanner and Graham said.

"Any chance you can take a break while we're here? Come and chill for a minute?"

"I'll try. I'll be back with your drinks in a minute. Take your time looking over the menu."

Not like it would take long to find something to order. The menu was only one page. Sandwiches, burgers, a couple of salads, and a half dozen actual entrées, Caroline always kept the menu simple. She switched things out every few months, though, to keep things new and interesting, keeping the best sellers always available.

I dropped my tray on the stand before pushing through the metal doors and found Caroline leaning up against the metal counter, arms crossed over her chest, like she'd been waiting for me.

"So...? Who's the guy? And why haven't I heard about him before?"

"I'm surprised you *hadn't* heard about him." It wasn't like gossip didn't travel. I'd been kicked out of Golden Eye on New Year's Eve. She *had* to have heard about that night.

"Chanelle didn't kick you out, she kept Mick from being a bigger asshole. You know that."

"Yeah, well, that was the night I met Graham and his friend Tanner, who's one of the guys with him, so it wasn't my finest moment."

"Doesn't seem to bother him." She shrugged. "He go to school?"

"Plays hockey at NCWU, majoring in chemistry, wants to be a science teacher and hockey coach. Any more questions, Your Honor?"

She chuckled and shook her head. "Don't get mad because I look after you, sweetheart. Life's handed you enough to deal with. You like him, though. I can see it."

I gave her the driest expression I could muster. "He's all right."

His kisses were far better than all right. His sense of humor was superior, and he never seemed bothered by the fact I didn't seem impressed with him. Which meant I was becoming a better liar, frankly, because so far I hadn't seen or learned anything about him that wasn't impressive.

She rolled her eyes and closed them. I was pretty sure she was praying for my soul, or for hers, so she didn't respond to my sass. "I'm forty-two, not ninety, and even then I'm pretty sure I'd still have eyes to see how good-looking he is. It's okay to live a little and have some fun. You know that, right?"

As she asked, she tucked wisps of my hair behind my ear.

In theory, I knew what she was saying. In reality, well, life hadn't given me a whole lot of chances to do whatever I wanted.

"I hear you, Caroline."

"Good. Get their orders and then get yourself a break. You're off the clock for an hour."

I gave her a look I'd learned from her. Probably why she didn't seem fazed by it. "When am I ever actually *on* the clock?"

"Perks from being part-owner. Now git."

"I'm gittin', I'm gittin'," I teased her, accentuating our southern mountain drawl, but that was only to avoid the whole part-owner comment.

It was in my mom's will that I took her half of the restaurant. Considering we had no idea if Mom was dead or alive, it wasn't *exactly* mine, but Caroline considered the fact that Mom had abandoned all of us as worthy enough for me to have it.

The problem was I didn't want it. I didn't want Caroline's life, and there was no way I could stay in Deer Creek. If the locals knew Caroline wanted to give me ownership, we'd go out of business faster than a summer flood could take out a bridge. The only bonus it offered was a safety net if I couldn't find a job right away. Or if something horrific happened. There was always The Grille to fall back on, even if relying on it would destroy me.

I headed toward Graham and his friends, took notice of a new table that'd been seated near them, and inwardly sighed.

Great. I had no doubt the girls at the new table had seen Graham and his friends and requested to be sitting within viewing distance. Hannah, Mia, and Kacey didn't hate me because my dad killed someone. They hated me because they were the quintessential small-town mean girls...

I ignored them as much as I possibly could while their snickers grew louder, no doubt directed at me in some way and smiled at the guys. Tanner glanced at the girls, then back to me. He was most likely replaying the last time he'd seen me in Deer Creek, being humiliated and then kicked out, because his brows tugged downward.

"Are you guys ready to order?"

"Yeah." Tanner looked to the table again and then back to me. "You good?"

"Always." I plastered on a fake smile that Graham read like a book.

"What's wrong?"

"Nothing. You guys need food, or did you come for the water?"

I went for sass. My backup.

Graham gritted his teeth together.

"Double cheeseburger, extra cheese and bacon," Eli ordered, "with fries."

"Okay." I reached for his menu, but he held it away from me.

"And I'd like to know why those girls are glaring at you and have been since you stepped foot out here."

"Because they're bored," I told him, "and I'd prefer it if you drop it."

That earned me scowls from all three guys, Graham mostly, but they at least complied quickly enough.

By the time their order was done, Caroline had come out and helped the girls, allowing me to breathe a sigh of relief as I headed to the back. Order entered, I took off my apron and went back to Caroline's office.

There, I rested against the wall, eyes closed, apron balled into a fist.

If I went back out there now, there'd be a scene. Caroline would be embarrassed. I'd end up in tears or a fight.

Graham was about to see the worst of me, all because I opened my mouth and told him where I worked and when. It wasn't like I expected him to show up or bring friends. It was just my luck those girls would be there tonight of all nights.

A knock hit the door, and before I could open it, the decision was taken from me. Graham stepped in, leaving me wide-eyed and slack-jawed as he closed it behind him.

"What are you doing here? You can't be here."

"Caroline said I could. Nice aunt, by the way. Seems feisty. That where you get it from?"

He crossed his arms over his chest, firmly fixing that smug grin of his into place. One simple smile from him and I was already wondering what I was so afraid of.

Against my better judgment and totally out of my

control, a smile broke out on my face. How was it possible he could disarm me with a grin and sarcasm?

"Why are you here?" I asked, but this time without panic lacing my words.

"Wanted to see if you're okay and wondering if you'd tell me why you knew what was going to happen as soon as you saw those girls?"

"You didn't hear them say anything about me before I came out?"

With the way Tanner had glared at them, I already knew the answer.

A muscle on the side of his nose jumped. "They did."

He wasn't going to tell me. Cool, cool. Back to secret keeping we went.

"Why'd you come here tonight?"

"Because I missed you and wanted to see you." He stepped toward me. "I don't care what those girls said, Holly. And I don't care about Piper's opinion either, although we already went over that last night. The only person I care about right now is you and making sure you're okay."

"I'm never okay," I admitted, and my stupid chin wobbled. I breathed in sharply and fought the surge of emotions. I'd been looked down on and pitied for years, and it'd been a full year since I became a pariah. None of it was any fault of my own.

I should have thicker armor by now, but whenever it happened around Graham, the walls I built crumbled and failed when I needed it the most.

He reached out and cupped my cheek. Thumb brushing along my cheekbone, he tipped his head until I met his eyes. So dark, they swirled with tiny flecks of yellow at the irises. "How can I help?"

The urge to suggest he get his food to go and leave came first but stalled before I could give voice to it. Instead, I suggested, "I know it's not really the ambiance you guys were going for, but what if you and the guys came back and ate in here?"

There was a round table with chairs in the corner. It'd work in a pinch, if he gave me a few minutes to clean off the stacks of boxes of extra napkins.

"We didn't come for ambiance or the food, Spitfire. We came for you, so where you want to be is where we'll be. Where I'll be."

Darn him. He was so sure. So confident. So *caring*. It was the last that shook me most. Outside of Caroline and Tracey, I couldn't remember the last time someone so easily cared about me. Certainly not a man.

"Thank you," I whispered.

"No thanks required. Being back here with you means I get to do this." He kissed me, brought my lips to his, and at the first heady inhale of his cologne and the taste of him, I lost track of where I was, what had bothered me only moments before, and a whole new fear raced across my mind.

If he truly cared about me...what would happen when he found out the truth?

And why in the world did I keep forgetting that this thing with him wasn't a good idea?

ELEVEN
HOLLY

The office door slammed open, banged against the wall behind it, and made us all jump.

"You're having a party and didn't invite me?" Tracey stood in the doorway, hands on her hips, scowl on her face as she took me in.

That scowl flipped into a flirtatious smile as soon as she noticed the men surrounding me.

And they were definitely surrounding me. I'd been overly optimistic when I thought we could all eat at the circular table. In my defense, it seemed plenty large when I sat at it, or when Caroline and I worked on her payroll together.

I hadn't quite taken into account the size of Graham and his friends. Their shoulder width and long legs had left me scrunched in the back corner, and with all of our food and drinks, there wasn't a free spot at the table.

"It wasn't quite a party," I told Tracey.

She texted me an hour ago and asked if I was busy. I told her the truth, that I wasn't, but I hadn't expected her to show up, too.

"Campus must be really boring tonight," I said.

Next to me, Graham bumped my shoulder. I wasn't sure if it was a tease or for lack of space until he muttered, "We've already been over this."

I rolled my eyes and leaned back against him, a move Tracey didn't miss because she skipped into the office, closing the door behind her.

"No worries. Now..." She tapped her lips with her long and sharply pointed hot pink fingernail. Those things should be registered as assault weapons. "Where do I get to sit?"

Tanner and Eli both widened their spread legs, but it was Tanner who pushed Eli out of the way and patted his thigh. "Got room for you right here."

"Huh. We've met, right?"

"Yeah, Tracey, we've met." Sounded to me like not many girls forgot meeting Tanner, and he wasn't all that happy about it.

"Huh," she said again and then plopped her tiny little behind right down on his thigh. His arm had to drape over her back to hold her in place, and he settled his hand on top of her leg.

Guess Tanner didn't like women forgetting him, but he didn't mind the second chance.

"What are you doing here?" I asked and swirled my now-cold fry into a pile of mustard, something that had already earned me relentless teasing.

"You said you weren't busy, I was bored, ergo..." She flipped her hand in the air. Like that explained anything.

"Asher busy tonight?"

"You dating someone?" Tanner asked. There was grit in his voice.

"Talking," she drawled. "So much *talking*..."

"What's wrong with talking?" Eli asked, which reminded me.

"Tracey meet Eli. Eli...Tracey," I introduced them, and once again Tracey's smile turned stunning. Man, the girl knew how to work a crowd. If I had half her confidence, I'd have three times as much as I had now.

"Talking is fine," Tracey said and stole one of my fries as I popped another into my mouth. She flinched, probably from the cold potatoes. "It's just that, after the talking part, I'd prefer to do other things with my mouth."

I choked on my fry.

Graham chuckled and patted my back while I grabbed my water and washed it down.

"You can't just say things like that."

"I don't mind." Eli shrugged and smirked.

"Me either," Tanner quipped. "What kinds of things are we talking about?"

"Eating. I love eating." To prove it, she grabbed an onion ring off his plate and crunched down on it. "Mmm. So much better than your fry, Holly. So, what are we really doing back here? Who are we hiding from tonight?"

The fact she knew this was my hiding place was pathetic enough.

"So I take it that happens often?" Eli asked.

Weirdly enough, as soon as I suggested the guys come back and hang with me in the office, none of them mentioned a thing about the girls. The looks or what they'd said before.

"It's not uncommon," I admitted.

"Why?"

Tracey tossed a chip at him. "Because they're small-town people with small minds."

"I'm from the small town," I said to Tracey.

"Yeah, but you're not small-minded. That's the difference. Who was it this time?"

"Hannah and them."

"Ugh. Good Lord. You'd think those girls would be so focused on the Spring Fling they wouldn't have time to do anything else."

Great. I'd totally forgotten that was coming up.

"Spring Fling?" Graham chuckled as he asked. "Isn't that a dance?"

"At schools, yeah," I answered. "But in Deer Creek it's a town thing. There's a parade, a carnival, all the things."

"It's a big deal," Tracey confirmed.

"It's unbearable," I groaned.

All the people. The looks. Last year I'd hid at Tracey's apartment all weekend. Considering my dad had only gotten arrested ten weeks earlier, there was no way I was going to it. Hatred for Marvin Jones was at its full height, my dad being blamed for the sudden death of our winter tourism. Considering all the rich city people canceled their reservations following the accident, I couldn't blame them.

Wild how the bartenders who had served him that night got off with a slap on the wrist and no lingering hatred. If someone had cut him off...

His court-appointed attorney had tried that route to shift the blame.

No one went for it.

Especially the judge, who happened to be friends with the governor. He should have recused himself considering he knew the governor personally. Our attorney had fought for that until we realized *every* judge in North Carolina knew the governor. My dad had no shot at a fair trial anywhere he went, but that didn't really matter in the end.

He'd killed the governor's daughter, and now he was paying the price.

"Aw. Come on. It used to be fun," Tracey said. She grinned at the guys. "She's dragged me to this both our freshman and sophomore years. For a small town, they do it *up*. You get free rein to spend the entire weekend being a little kid again. But this year we can also hang out at the beer garden."

"Right." I gave her a face. "That'd be fun."

Her face paled, but fortunately, she kept her mouth shut. Frankly, I was surprised none of these guys had put two and two together yet. They seemed awfully smart. And monied. Definitely Tanner and Graham. Eli came off as a little rougher, a little less Daddy's *money would have paid for my college if I wasn't playing hockey,* and more like he'd be taking out loans with the rest of us.

"Fine. Anyway, you guys in?"

"I like carnival rides," Tanner said.

Eli smirked at Tracey. "I like all kinds of rides."

She smirked right back. "I think I like you."

Tanner abruptly shifted his leg, and Tracey crashed to the floor, shrieking in surprise.

I laughed loudly and freely for the first time in months.

"IT'S LATE, and I'm guessing you won't invite me back to your place."

Graham's gloved hands were on my cheeks. We were standing outside The Premier Grille, and Tracey and his friends were out at their cars. After most of the customers left, Caroline asked me to come back out and help her close up. To my utter astonishment, Graham and his friends and Tracey all chipped in.

They cranked up music on the sound system, and then they threw Graham under the bus with all sorts of stories of things he did on hockey trips, and in less than an hour, The Premier Grille was spotless, the silverware all wrapped in napkins for the morning shift. The dishes were washed and dried and put away, and everything in our salad bar was prepped and back in the refrigerator for the next day.

Graham and I had even had time to go to the back and chop extra vegetables for morning omelets.

Caroline had locked up and waved goodbye with a relieved smile on her face. "You guys can come visit anytime. Next time I might even give you some tips."

The guys thanked her for allowing them to hang out, and said the help was no problem.

We'd saved her hours of morning work, which meant she wouldn't have to show up until nine, giving her precious hours of sleep.

"Not tonight," I whispered, but man, I wished things were different.

"I'm guessing your dad's not the kind of guy to allow you sleepovers."

My dad. Right. Of course that's what he assumed. My dad wouldn't have ever noticed if I had company, much less sleepovers in the last few years, but that wasn't why I wouldn't let him see where I lived.

My trailer was rotten compared to his own apartment. The only thing we had in common with our living arrangements was that we lived alone.

"You guys need to get back to school," I said so I didn't have to mention my dad. He was a topic I wasn't ready to approach.

"Someday, you're going to open up more, aren't you?" His eyes scanned mine, dark pools with tiny flecks of gold I could barely see in the darkness. They peered straight into my soul, like by looking at me this way he'd discover everything.

"Opening up isn't easy for me."

"I know, and I get it, I do, but I feel like you have one foot ready to leave, and the other isn't exactly standing on steady ground."

I chuckled. "That's kind of my entire life at the moment, Graham."

He grinned, but it vanished quickly, and there was no warmth in it. "It's been a long time since I've felt like this, Holly. Just...be honest with me? Don't screw with me."

A sarcastic retort filled my throat, but I choked it down. This was the time to walk away, free and clear. I couldn't. His expression was too earnest. His words too honest. I should have...right then. I should have pulled out my phone and blocked him and sent him on his way.

I didn't *want* to, despite all the signs being there that I should.

"I'll be honest," I finally said. "And I'm sorry. I'm interested. I like you, but we're also graduating, and who knows where life will take us."

"Good thing teachers and finance majors can get jobs anywhere, then, huh?"

Oh God. He meant that, too. My heart squeezed with the thoughts of it. That he was thinking of this...our future. "We've known each other for two months, Graham."

I meant it to come out as a tease, but my tone was flat, and there was a bite to it I didn't expect.

His hands fell from my cheeks, and his jaw worked back and forth. "Right. Good night, then."

Damn it. I was screwing this up.

"I'm sorry," I said, and then said it again, louder, loud enough that Tanner and Eli arched their brows in our direction, and Tracey turned to face me. She was frowning, like she knew I was messing this up. Of course I'd mess it up.

I was a Jones. It's what we did with our lives.

"I didn't mean it like that," I said and reached for his arm. Graham turned, and his sad expression made me flinch. "I mean, it *is* true, I guess...I don't know. I was surprised you were thinking that way."

"I don't really like messing around. I tend to be the kind of guy who sees what he wants and goes for it."

"And that's what you want."

Me. Him. And man, I could see it, too. A hazy dream flashed in my mind of him teaching kids hockey lessons, me enjoying watching while sipping on hot chocolate in the stands. Us playing house. Living in the suburbs somewhere where my past and my parents weren't a part of my life.

For the first time in my life, dreaming wasn't terrifying.

"Yeah, Holly. I think I might."

"Oh." It fell from my lips on a heavy exhale, and I shifted on my feet. "Well...that's a surprise. What do we do now?"

His lips curled at the corners. "Now, you kiss me good night. Like you mean it. Like you hate the idea of me walking away."

Now that he mentioned it and gave me that speck of a dream to hope for, I kind of did hate that idea. I rolled to my toes and gave him exactly what he wanted.

"Don't get lost or arrested." I slapped at the bill of Graham's NCWU hat.

His smile matched mine as he laughed. "Funny. We'll see the hotel and the hockey arena. That's about it."

"You'll sneak out."

"I'll leave that one to Tanner. You gonna miss me?"

Graham had taken to asking that question every night we went our separate ways after the night at The Grille, which was most of them. We spent most of the nights curled on his couch watching movies until I had to head back to Deer Creek. Sometimes we spent the night with his friends and Tracey.

He was getting ready to leave for the team's trip to Pennsylvania for spring break, where they were finishing the regular season games before playoffs began. We were waiting outside the science building for Eli's last class to finish up so they could head out together. This was always his longest trip of the season, and he wouldn't get back to school until late Saturday night before classes resumed after break. We had plans to spend Sunday together. Probably at his place, catching up on all his laundry.

He'd be playing the game he loved and doing it with his friends. I'd be slaving away at The Grille and meeting with a career counselor to start applying for jobs post-graduation.

"I might," I teased, because we both knew it was a lie. I'd taken to texting Graham as much as he reached out to me.

"You'll miss me. I know it." Graham bent down, swiveled his hat around backward, and kissed me. Like every time his lips pressed to mine, my bones turned to jelly and my heart turned to a puddle of mush. If this was what falling for someone felt like, it was all warm and gooey and comfortable and terrifying at the same time, and yet that ship had sailed.

I was falling, starting to dream those dreams he'd put in my mind weeks ago.

Maybe we *could* do this.

My phone buzzed in my coat pocket, and I ignored it, focusing on the way his mouth pressed to mine, the way his tongue teased at the seam of my lips.

"Gross," Eli groaned. "You're supposed to keep it PG around me."

He flung his arm across my shoulders and yanked me away from Graham. Before I could get too far away, Graham grabbed my arm and pulled me back until I was facing Eli and tucked securely to Graham's side. "And she's mine," he grunted. "Hands off."

"Jealous?" I rolled to my toes and kissed the side of his neck.

"Yes." There wasn't a hint of that teasing tone I liked so much.

What a silly man. Eli was his best friend. "How was the test?" I asked him.

"A killer," Eli groaned. "It's a good thing I love science, or I'd be rethinking my dreams of med school."

I'd recently learned Eli was heading to Chapel Hill in the fall for medical school.

He traveled constantly for hockey. He was graduating with a 4.0 in chemistry, treated life like it was one giant game of fun, never seemed stressed, and beneath all his jokes and laughter, was also one of the nicest guys I'd ever met in my life. At least, outside Graham, anyway. I'd also learned he was only playing hockey in order to keep a scholarship after being raised by a single dad most of his life. Eli Howell was impressive indeed.

"That bad?" I asked, because the man had to be close to genius IQ levels, if not surpassing them.

He groaned again. "If I hear the word immunopathology again, I'm going to stab someone."

"Yeah, pretty sure you'll never hear that word around me."

Both guys laughed at me.

"And that's why we like you," Eli said. "When we need a nap, you put us to sleep with all the fun talk about amortization schedules and the economic growth and development of third world countries."

I snorted. "That was one time."

In my defense, he'd started it by asking about my major and what I was learning.

"Besides, won't you study immunology in medical school?" I asked.

He turned around and started walking backward ahead of us and jabbed a finger in my direction. "Didn't I just say if I heard that word again I'd stab someone?"

"Better me than a med student. Or a patient," I joked.

"Nah." Graham squeezed me tight to his side. "The world can live with one less doctor. Not sure you're replaceable."

"Gross." Eli coughed and made a gagging noise to punctuate it.

"Yeah, 'cause it definitely needs more bankers."

"No." Graham grinned down at me, and the softness in those gold flecks of his made my knees wobble. "Just needs you."

Heat burned my cheeks. He was often complimentary, always polite. Definitely always sexy and patient, but this... this tenderness was new.

My phone buzzed again, this time getting Graham's attention since it was in my pocket by his hip. "That's been going wild. Does Tracey have an emergency?"

"With Tracey, you never know."

I doubted it was Tracey. She was packing to leave tomorrow to go on a cruise with her family. I'd offered to take her to the airport, since I didn't really have anything else to do, but instead, she was hitching a ride with another student to Charlotte and getting dropped off at a hotel near the airport.

"Probably Caroline wondering when I'll be in."

It could have been, but I doubted it.

"Hey, G!" He stopped, and a friendly smile swept over his face as Piper waved her arm.

"Hey, P. Thought you already went home."

"No." She grinned at him, and I noticed she made a studious attempt not to glance at me as she neared us. "Don't you remember when we talked last night? Mom's coming to get me later."

She looked at me then, and if she thought I'd be upset

hearing that they talked, she was wrong. Graham had taken to telling me every time Piper reached out to him.

"Right," Graham mumbled, but his brows tugged in. "So what's up?"

"I just wanted to wish you good luck on your trip. I know how nervous you always get flying."

She held out her hand. In her palm was a small, square box wrapped in neon yellow wrapping paper with a hot pink bow on top.

Whatever was inside, Graham knew, because he scowled at the box and then at Piper. "Are you serious?"

For the first time, Piper stopped hiding the hatred she had for me in her eyes before nodding and smiling up at Graham. "Yeah. Of course I am. You know Fee would want you to have it. She had it made for you. Engraved and everything. I found it last week when I was visiting her parents."

"Fee made you something engraved?" I'd tried...I'd tried so hard to stay out of their conversation. This wasn't the first time Piper had shown up when Graham and I were together and took little jabs at how well she knew him or when they talked. What she didn't know was that Graham usually shared them with me first, and yeah, I didn't like it.

But mostly because there was a secret there. Something was brewing, and Piper's presence always seemed to bring it simmering to the surface. Someday, it'd all come out, and I was trying to be brave enough to weather the storm.

"Yeah, our friend Sophie. She's gone, died actually. Well, really she was killed last year by some loser of a drunk near here, but Graham and me and her were like best friends. They were going to get married..."

Water stormed my body, my ears, making everything else she said a giant blur. I barely heard a thing until she mentioned the worried "married," and I stumbled back a step, out of Graham's reach. "Married?" It came out as a rasp, and I took another step back as Graham tried to reach for me. Eli looked on, and humiliation and horror washed over me at the exact same time.

Eli had *known*.

"Of course." Piper grinned, and there was nothing kind about the venom in her tone. "Graham told you, right? I mean, he told me he told you about our friend who was killed, so I just assumed that he told you they were engaged—"

"That's enough, Pipe," Graham snapped and put himself between me and her, but the damage was done.

"But Graham," she whined.

"Eli, get her out of here," he demanded, and then he was in front of me, blocking my view of everything.

"She had to know, G. You know Fee would be so ticked about this. She *loved* you!" As she shouted, her voice turned shrill but quieter. I imagined Eli picking her up and throwing her over his shoulder to do what Graham had told him to do, and I would have laughed, but there was absolutely nothing to laugh about.

Sophie Alston was killed by a drunk driver.

Sophie Alston was the governor's daughter.

Sophie was also the girl my father ran off the road.

My father was the loser drunk driver who killed Sophie.

And Graham was going to marry her.

"I have to go." I sputtered the words, and as Graham reached for me, I shook my head. "Don't. I have to go."

"I'm sorry," Graham whispered. "That's not...please... listen to me for a second."

I'd listen to him for hours. I'd let him explain everything. But it wouldn't change a thing.

Because once I opened my mouth and explained everything back, whatever we had growing between us would be lost forever.

"Bye, Graham."

"IT COULD BE A COINCIDENCE," Tracey whispered.

Her arms were wrapped around me as we sat in her small living room she shared with three other girls.

"How many other Sophies were killed by a drunk driver in the last year?"

Man, my throat hurt. My eyes did too. My lips were cracked and dry, but it was my throat that hurt the most.

No, my chest. Definitely the pain crushing my chest like an elephant was stomping on my sternum was the worst of it.

And my damn phone kept buzzing. It'd been going off and on all day long, and I should have answered it just to shut him up and get him to leave me alone, but I couldn't bring myself to hear his voice.

Not after what I'd just learned.

It wasn't just my dad calling, either. It was the calls and texts that started coming in from Graham that made me toss my phone into my bedroom and shut the door as soon as I called Tracey.

I'd barely gotten a word out, more like a single sob before she said, "On my way."

That felt like hours ago. A lifetime. How could everything change so quickly?

I was already dreading having to tell him about my dad eventually and the guilt I felt that I hadn't yet, not when he'd been so honest. But this?

How did I recover from this?

And had he been as honest as I thought?

"Okay, maybe not a coincidence, but maybe there's an explanation? I mean...how did he not recognize you? And being engaged? That was *never* mentioned in the trial. You'd think the lawyer would have used that in opening or closing arguments, or *something*. And Graham was never there. I feel like we would have seen Piper too, you know?"

"I only went to court once," I reminded Tracey. She'd followed it online, but the three-day trial hadn't exactly been national news. It was all over the local television, though, but my dad didn't have much of a defense.

He was drunk.

She was the governor's daughter on a weekend ski trip with her family over the New Year's holiday weekend.

One day she was there. That night she went into town to grab some snacks for her family to take back to their Airbnb mountain rental home, and then she was dead.

I went on the day of the opening arguments, sat in the far back corner, and left as soon as I could. My father never knew I was there and didn't seem to care either way.

He was sentenced immediately following his trial, and I'd met him at the courthouse in the holding area before he was taken away to the prison near Durham. He hadn't bothered to give me a hug, not that he really could with his hands and ankles handcuffed, but I hadn't expected it. Nope. After telling me this was all a bunch of bullshit, his parting words to me were, "Make sure you put money in my account."

"What do I do?" I asked her and got up to get some water. I could guzzle the entire town's water supply, and my throat would still hurt. My chest would still feel the weight of everything that was coming.

"Talk to him," Tracey suggested.

Laughable. "Sure. I'll do that. That sounds like a fun time. 'Hey, you know that girl you were friends with your whole life? Yeah, well she's dead because of my dad, so... wanna make out?'"

Tracey sighed. "Maybe leave the make out part out of it?"

"It doesn't matter, Trace. Whatever we had was gone."

"It doesn't have to be. He really likes you, Holly. You've never opened up to someone the way I've seen you do with him. Maybe he'll understand."

Such optimism. I almost felt bad crushing it.

"He was *engaged* to her, Tracey."

Engaged or not didn't matter. He still knew her.

He'd still cared about her.

Nothing I could do would change that, and once I told him the truth, nothing I could do would keep him.

THIRTEEN
HOLLY

I scrolled through my phone. It seemed I liked inflicting as much pain on myself as possible. Graham had left a dozen messages, more voicemails that I deleted immediately because I figured they said the same things as his texts.

It's not what you think.

Damn it. Text me back.

I'll explain.

Piper was wrong. She lied. And I've already yelled at her.

We were not engaged, Holly, I swear it.

Don't block me over this.

That text had included a winking emoji after. I couldn't bring myself to smile. After the first handful of texts, they trailed off to daily ones sent horrifically early in the morning.

My daily text to make sure I'm not blocked...

He was joking. He was worried about me and needed to be focused on his games and his life, and he had absolutely no idea what was waiting for him when he returned, and still, he was cracking jokes.

By Thursday, I caved. He'd be back in two days, and we had to have this conversation whether I wanted to or not, whether I was ready or not. I'd spent the week making my own decisions. It was better to end this now, quickly.

It was after his early morning text that I got as soon as it came because I'd barely slept all week, when I finally texted him back.

We'll talk when you get back.

Thank God. Finally. Seriously, Holly, we weren't engaged. U okay? Is your week okay?

How's work?

I should have known that'd open the floodgates, and tears blurred my vision as I texted back.

It doesn't matter if you were. We'll talk when you get back.

As soon as he saw, as soon as he heard, I had no doubt he'd do everything he possibly could to forget my schedule and go far out of his way to ignore me on campus for the rest of the year.

Only six more weeks to graduation. I had to make it through, and then I wouldn't have to worry about seeing him anyway.

I turned Do Not Disturb on my phone so I wouldn't get alerts from him and climbed out of bed. I'd planned on spending all week at the diner, working as many hours as I could to stock up on tips, but Caroline took one look at me on Sunday morning before the brunch crowd rolled in and declared me off-limits to the customers.

Apparently, I looked horrific.

Her exact words? "You look like you got stomped on by a pack of buffalo."

I'd never seen a buffalo, but her point was clear. I was raw, broken down, and definitely beaten up.

Sleep would help, if only I could manage to do it for longer than twenty minutes at a time.

Instead, I spent the rest of the week finalizing her taxes. Then more time reorganizing her office. It was such a disaster that I worked two eight-hour shifts and still had more work to do. Then I was planning on setting up a new inventory system for her. She *had* to stop using scrap pieces of paper and backs of receipts to take stock of her refrigerator items. I was finding them balled up in all corners of her desk drawers. It was no wonder why the restaurant consistently ran low on important items like onions and tomatoes.

Caroline loved people and serving and helping cook good food and making sure people had a good time, but when it came to numbers and planning? From the looks of it, the systems hadn't been updated since my grandparents were alive. I was hoping to make something simple so her life would be easier once I left.

At least I could do something good for someone.

I showered, cleaned my room, and washed the dishes I'd been too tired to take care of the night before. By the time I got to The Grille, I'd missed most of the breakfast rush. Business was already slowing down. We'd get some traffic during the elementary through high school spring break next month, but that always fell at a hard time of year. It was usually too warm to ski and tube, but not warm enough to enjoy a long day of hiking. Which was a bummer. A restaurant packed full of tourists could have kept me too busy to think about the conversation that would soon come.

Instead, that was all I spent my time doing once I got tucked away in Caroline's office.

Her office door opened, and she appeared like I'd conjured her up. "You doing okay?"

"Splendid."

She stepped into the office and closed the door behind her. "I know you probably don't *want* to talk about it, but I'm guessing it involves that boy?"

"Graham. And yes."

Caroline didn't immediately respond, and I glanced up at her. She had her lips pushed to one side, and while she was silent, she said a hundred things with her look. She did this often, torn between being the fun aunt and wanting to be a mother figure, and since I'd gone to college, that struggle had only increased.

I sat back in my chair and pushed away from her desk. "Say it."

"He was really cute. And he seemed smart."

"And he's a hockey player," I filled in for her. "Do you know the last name Marchese?"

Her brows wrinkled. "No, not off the top of my head. Why? Should I?"

"Apparently, he was close with Sophie."

"Sophie..." She trailed off. It didn't take her long. A blink of her eyes, and then her shoulders drooped. "Crap. That Sophie?"

"He has another friend who doesn't like me so much, or rather, doesn't like that he's with me. She freaked out last week. Mentioned Sophie being killed by a drunk driver near here and that they were engaged."

"Engaged?"

"Not really the point, Care."

"What'd you say to him?"

"Nothing. I bolted, and he's been on a trip with his team."

"Damn. That's tough." Her shoulders heaved. She lifted her head. "He seemed like a really good guy..."

"He is." Which made this all harder, because for the

first time since I could remember, I'd started *dreaming*. Not chasing practicality and safety, but I'd started collecting hopes and dreams of the images he'd planted in my mind. I'd started wanting things, believing I could have something more than survival and a comfortable income.

But luck had never shined my way, and I never should have gotten my hopes up.

"Maybe he won't—"

"Don't." I shook my head. "Tracey already tried that. No one can be close to someone and then date the killer's daughter. That crap only happens in movies."

While my life definitely could have been a made-for-TV special on the dangers of drug addictions and alcoholism, this story wasn't that kind of movie. And there was no happy ending here.

"Okay, no platitudes, but I'll still hope. In the meantime, if you can handle it, I have other news that isn't so great."

"My dad called you."

"No." She shook her head. "Lydia did."

I stared at my lap and then closed my eyes. Caroline quit calling her my mom years ago, before I was a teenager. I hadn't heard from her since I was eighteen years old. She'd showed up a week after my birthday, which was a day after my high school graduation. For the briefest moment I'd hoped she came to congratulate me.

I couldn't have been more wrong. Her teeth were yellow, her hair stringy and greasy. Her clothes were two sizes too big, but that was more due to the fact that she was all skin and bones and scarred cheeks. Dad hadn't been home then. He'd still managed to hold down jobs, and that was the only thing I was thankful for. He hadn't seen how horrifically ruined she'd become. She'd stumbled into the trailer, saw me, and instantly went to the kitchen cupboard where they'd always kept spare cash in a coffee can. When she found the can gone, *then* she'd remembered I was there.

"*Where's my money?*"

"*Gone. You took it when you left, a decade ago.*" She didn't notice her daughter standing right in front of her. I wasn't sure she knew who I was. If a grenade went off nearby, threw me thirty feet into a pile of lumber, would that hurt more than my mom standing in front of me, treating me like I was nothing?

"*There's always money here.*"

"*We don't have any.*"

"*You probably do. Probably working at that restaurant, doing the right thing, being the good girl you always were.*"

Good girl. So she did know who I was. She just didn't care. I imagined a mom calling me that for years, and now I wanted to vomit. Her eyes were glassy, and she couldn't stand straight. I should probably give her coffee to sober up or a bed to sleep it off, but there was no way I could let Dad see her like this. He'd go on a bender, and I'd have to hunt him down. Or he'd beg her to return and based on the way she kept looking to the door, she had no intention of that.

I went to my room, closed and locked the door, and rummaged through a small hole I'd made in my closet wall. When I opened my door, she was standing in the same spot, now leaning against the cupboard like the effort to stand was too much for her.

"*One hundred dollars. It's all I have.*"

I said a quick prayer that she didn't go looking for more. She was right. I did have plenty. I worked long hours, every second I could, but I had college to pay for and a car I wanted to buy to get me there.

She took it from my hand and left the trailer Dad and I

had to move to the last time he went months without working.

She never once looked back. Or said thank you. Or said goodbye...just like the first time she left.

"So she *is* alive."

"Seems that way." Caroline nodded and then swiped her hands over her mouth as she sighed.

"What'd she want?" I asked, as the memory washed through me, making my pulse race, my fingertips shake, and my voice tremble.

"She asked where your dad was working."

"What'd you tell her?"

"Nothing. Said I didn't know, which isn't a lie because if he does have a job at the prison, I don't know what it is."

She quirked a half-smile, but the joke fell flat.

"She'll come here looking for him." It'd been almost four years since she showed up. She probably needed money again.

"She also asked about you."

That was worse. "Considering I gave her money all those years ago, that doesn't surprise me entirely."

"Yeah. I'm torn between being glad she's still alive, hopeful I can maybe convince her into rehab if she does show up and wanting to move to Alaska so she can't find us and tear out our hearts again."

All valid feelings.

"Alaska feels extreme," I quipped. Caroline and I didn't have much, but we had each other. She had this restaurant, I had my future, and we both had our sarcasm.

She chuckled. "I just thought you should know, in case she does show up and asks about your dad. I wouldn't have figured she knew about the accident, but I also have no idea where she's been, so she could still learn if she tried hard enough."

"She wouldn't even have to try. All she has to do is stumble into Golden Eye, and she'd hear it all."

"And find Mick," she suggested.

"And find Mick," I agreed. And that would bring its own set of problems. The man had wanted her, but he beat his wife and son. In a dream world, Lydia would go to rehab, discover the error of her ways, get sober, come back here and help Caroline run The Grille, and then stay far, *far* away from Mick.

But I'd given up dreams a long time ago, and this mess with Graham only confirmed why there was no point in having any anyway.

FOURTEEN
HOLLY

Shoot me your address. I'll be there as soon as we get in.

I stared at the text for far too long after it came in. Graham had already landed, and while I'd planned for him to come to my place so we could talk, I changed my mind.

Being able to leave his place would be easier than trying to kick him out of mine, so I sent him a text a half hour before he was supposed to get back in town.

I'll meet you at yours.

So you can run when you want?

His response came almost instantaneously, which meant he'd been staring at his phone. I didn't bother responding. He'd learn soon enough.

The air had a warm thickness to it, odd for late March, but it was nice enough I didn't have to cage myself in my Jimmy. Instead, when a newer model black Honda pulled up, I was already pacing back and forth on the sidewalk in front of his building.

"Hey," he called as he climbed out of the back seat.

The trunk popped open at the same time the driver's window rolled down, and Tanner poked his head out. "You should listen to him, Holly! Piper's lying, and I never liked her anyway."

"Shut up, Tan," Graham grumbled and slapped the button to close the door, although he did it with a ferociousness, like he was pissed he couldn't slam it closed or shut Tanner's mouth.

"I speak the truth!" Tanner called out as his window started to rise, and he drove away.

"I was worried you'd stand me up." Graham had a large green duffel bag flung over his shoulder. He held the small hand strap of his backpack loosely at his side.

"I said I'd be here."

"And yet you don't look thrilled about it." My eyes widened in surprise at the anger in his tone. I couldn't exactly blame him considering how I treated him this last week. "Sorry," he mumbled. "It was a crappy week, and thinking about you was only part of it."

I cringed. "I'm sorry. I really am, but we should talk."

"Yeah. Never heard those words before and had a good outcome from it." He walked past me toward the stairs to his place. The landing was covered, and four apartment doors were at the top. He went to his, the first door on the right, and opened it.

Compared to all the other times I'd been here, when he'd stood in the doorway and held it open for me, this time was different. He walked in, flung his backpack to the floor, and barely held the door as he walked through. I skirted around it as it started to close on me, and once it did, he dumped his bag on the floor with a thud.

I tossed my purse on the kitchen counter and put as much space between us as I could.

Graham read the move too, because he flinched. "I have to tell you, I've been wrestling all week between feeling incredibly guilty for not being fully honest with you and pissed you took off and haven't let me explain. I've *called* you, Holly, and I've texted. And you practically ghosted me."

"I know, but..."

"You're a hard enough girl to get to know, you know? It feels like you have one arm stiff-armed out, only dropping it occasionally, but you know, when you do, it feels like I've won something special. And I get you were mad, hell, I don't blame you for that. But hell, I don't know..." He turned and shoved his hands through his hair. His ball cap flew off, and he spun, grabbing it at the last second.

Gone were his cocky smirks and disarming grins. There was pain on his face, and I was only going to make it worse.

"I needed to think." I swallowed, and as I did, my phone rang from my purse.

Dread curled my gut at the familiar sound.

"Is there a reason why every time your phone rings you look sick?" he asked.

Oh, the irony of the moment. The horrifically perfect timing. For the first time since this had happened, I actually answered. "Yeah. Let me show you."

I unzipped my phone, the ringer stopping, but it was my dad. He'd call right back. I hadn't answered his weekly call in months. No doubt the first words out of his mouth would be filled with venom.

"Who is it?" Graham asked. He was smart. He had to see the way my hand shook.

"Hold on. He'll call back."

"He?" Oh, there was jealousy in that tone, a hint of it, but it was there all the same.

Right as rain, my phone rang. Barely glancing away from Graham, I hit the call button and then the speaker button.

The tinny, computerized voice came through. "Collect call from Durham Maximum Security Prison from inmate—my dad's voice came through—Marvin Jones. Would you like to accept?"

"Holly," Graham whispered, his voice thready, like he was expecting a monster to jump through the phone. His face was pale, but there was no way he'd made the connection because his thick brows were tugged in, almost knitted together, and his hands were on his hips, fingers flexing.

He was mad, but not at me any longer, more *for* me. Oh, how that would change in a second.

"I'll accept," I said into the phone.

There was a beep. Then the familiar pause where I hoped he'd either hang up or become the dad I had when I was seven. But nope, he ended up being himself.

"'Bout time you answer the damn phone. You know how long I'm stuck in here? I've been waitin' for you to send me money."

"Hi, Dad." And because this was already bad enough, and because this had to end and end *now* so I could get out of there, I continued without taking my eyes off Graham. His lips had parted, and there was worry there, for me, sure. But I wasn't the only one who could feel the weight of the ticking time bomb. "I'll send some later tonight. But, Dad?"

"What?"

"You remember the name of the girl you killed? The one you ran off the road?"

A gasp and then a curse came from Graham. "No." He shook his head. "No...it's not...how could..."

"Stuck up rich little thing. That's the only reason I'm here. Governor's daughter. You think I forgot a name like that? Sophie. Damn stupid name haunts my dreams. Woulda gotten off with a slap on the wrist if her daddy didn't run the state. Bad luck for me."

Yeah...bad luck.

"Bye, Dad." I ended the call and grabbed my purse.

"I didn't know," I told Graham. "I didn't know until Piper said anything, but as soon as she did, I knew exactly who she was talking about. *That's* why I took off the way I did and why I haven't talked to you."

"Your dad...he..."

"He's a drunk and ran your fiancée or friend or whoever she was to you off the road and killed her. Now do you see why I said it didn't matter if you were engaged or not?"

He swallowed and shoved his hands over his face. "I can't believe it. I can't believe this is happening."

"I'm sorry." My chin shook, and tears burned my eyes, but I forced them down. "I'm sorry for everything he took from you."

I turned and opened the door.

Behind me, his croaked and tortured voice asked, "Where are you going? You're just leaving? After dropping that? We have to talk, Holly."

He closed the space between us in three long strides, but I held up my hand, shaking my head. "We don't."

"I have questions. Give me a damn minute to think, would you?"

I took a painful moment and memorized all his hard lines and muscles and that floppy curly hair I liked so much and the depths of his eyes. "What else do we have to talk about? Think this through, Graham. Are you going to tell

Piper who I am? Your *dad*? He's friends with Sophie's dad, right? That's what you said? You can't be with me and be honest with everyone else you know, and you've already been through enough. And you might not have put it together who I am, but somebody you love would."

His jaw dropped, like he hadn't considered. He probably hadn't since I hadn't given him time. But I'd spent the week moving pieces, trying to make the puzzle fit, and every time I did, I came up with a giant hole in the middle.

We would never fit. Never work together.

It was time we both accepted it.

"Goodbye, Graham."

The sound of the door shutting behind me paled in comparison to the pain of my breaking heart cracking in two.

Crappy luck had always been the card I drew in any game. I shouldn't have dared to hope this would end any differently.

ROARING THUNDER JOLTED me from where I'd somehow been able to fall asleep on my couch. I threw off the blanket, and it took a moment to realize where I was. What had happened. How I'd gotten back home. Hard to see with tears blurring my vision on the twisting and winding mountain roads, but somehow I'd made it.

Another rumble of thunder rocked the trailer, and I whipped my head toward the door.

No. Not thunder.

I jumped from the couch, catching my foot in the blanket I'd thrown over me when I got back home after shattering Graham's pretty illusion of what could have been between us. I stumbled at the thought, fell into the coffee table, and righted myself before I toppled over it as the furious pounding came again.

"Hold on!" I shouted at whoever was knocking on my door so loudly they could crack the glass.

The microwave clock showed it was one in the morning. Hopefully it was morning, and I hadn't slept through an entire night and day. The *last* thing I needed was to miss a shift at the diner.

It had to be Tracey. Graham probably called her, and she was coming to check on me.

It wouldn't be Graham. Tracey wouldn't tell him where I lived, and I doubted even his aunt would give him that information.

The pounding started again, and then another sound quickly followed it. Sounded like squawking chickens or screeching raccoons. Something feral.

"I said," I started to shout as I opened the door. "Stop —"

My voice froze in my throat. The squawking wasn't chickens. Or raccoons.

It was a baby. Red-faced and screaming.

The woman holding it had pockmarked scars on her cheeks. Stringy, greasy hair that not only looked like it hadn't been washed in weeks but also hadn't been cut since the last time I saw her. Her collarbone poked out from the worn and frayed collar of her sweater.

Her dark blue eyes had once been a warm, rich color, and now there appeared to be no life in them.

"Mom?"

She shoved her way past me, making me jump back before the baby in her arms slammed into me.

"What are you doing here?"

"Where's your father?"

She rocked back and forth as she asked, deadened, drug-addled eyes flicking every which way but at my face, at the daughter who stood in front of her.

"Prison," I said, before I could filter myself. Who would expect it?

What was she *doing* here?

She jolted, and at least she hadn't known. Caroline's earlier warning rushed back to me. She'd called. She'd been looking for us.

Looks like she found us. "Why do you have a baby?"

She flinched again and looked down, eyes widening like she'd forgotten she was holding anything in the first place. How could that happen when the baby's face was now a deep shade of red and screaming, filling the air in the trailer?

"Oh. Here." She shoved it at me so fast I almost dropped it before my arms grabbed for it on instinct.

"Can't take care of him. You do it. All this shit I have is here." She dropped a weathered, worn, and disgustingly dirty bag onto the floor. "Tell your dad I stopped by."

She skirted past me. My mind was still frozen. This baby was screaming. My addict of a mother was leaving?

"Mom? What are..."

"Don't got time. Ride's leaving. And I definitely don't have time to take care of that. Needs his family, though. So there...you and your dad can handle it."

"What?" I rushed after her, but for being high as a kite and frail, she moved quickly. "Mom!"

She didn't stop rushing down the stairs, out to the gravel drive. She wasn't joking about having a ride.

It was dark, and I couldn't see who was driving, but she climbed into the passenger seat of a rusted, maroon car, far older than me. It peeled out so fast that gravel kicked up and hit the side of my Jimmy before it turned and disappeared.

The baby screamed again, and my jaw dropped as I watched my mother take off, leaving me again...

With a *brother*?

FIFTEEN
HOLLY

He was so little. So tiny. He also wasn't very old. The first thing I figured out how to do was feed him, and thankfully in the wretched and dirty bag my mom had dropped on the floor, there'd been a dozen diapers, two empty bottles, and two small cans of formula.

My mind spun as I tried to bounce the baby and then feed him. My ears ached from the piercing scream he refused to let go of.

But finally—*finally*—I managed to read the can of formula, fill the bottle with water, add the powder, and as soon as the bottle was brought to his lips, the boy quieted.

"Holy crap," I whispered as he sucked on the bottle. I figured out how to prop him in my lap and dragged the bag over to me, where I pulled out everything inside I could find.

I found another, smaller pile of diapers, two small cloths I figured were for burping but looked like they needed a decent washing, and at the very bottom of the small bag was an envelope.

I tossed the wrinkled envelope onto the coffee table and

tried with all my might to figure out what in the world just happened. This had to be a dream. This was a nightmare. I was subconsciously feeling alone, needing someone for company, feeling despair over everything with Graham, and that my subconscious conjured up my mother and some random baby she threw at me before disappearing.

"Except I'm awake," I muttered and blew out a breath and closed my eyes. When I opened them, it was to the sound of the baby quietly sucking on the bottle, his tiny little face scrunched and pink. Tears were drying on his cheeks from all his crying. I reached out and tenderly brushed my fingertip along his cheek, wiping away wet tears. His eyes opened and closed again, but as he did, a tiny milk-filled sigh escaped the side of his mouth, and I swore he burrowed closer to me.

My chest went burning hot, and my lungs expanded. My heart swelled.

I had no idea who he was, but he was *mine*.

It took a breath, one tiny moment, and all the plans I'd worked so hard to make for my life irrevocably changed.

My only sole focus was now on this tiny little bundle so carelessly shoved into my arms.

"Crap," I whispered and reached for the envelope.

The little guy gurgled and tensed, but as I leaned back into the couch, he relaxed.

So he didn't like being scrunched up.

"Sorry, little guy," I whispered.

He peered up at me like he'd heard me and returned to sucking on his bottle, dismissing me for substance.

Couldn't blame the guy. I tended to ignore people when I was eating too.

My hand shook as I pried open the envelope with two fingers, resettling the baby in my arms for something more comfortable for him, and then pulled out a folded, wrinkled sheet of paper. It stuck on the envelope and looked like it'd been balled up before being flattened and folded.

My heart raced, and my fingers trembled as I leaned back on the couch and unfolded the thick page of paper. Something smaller fell out, and I ignored it, my gaze stuck on the printing at the top of the paper.

State of Florida was stamped at the top of a thin, dark blue line.

"Florida," I whispered, and my chin started wobbling. My mom lived in Florida. Or, at least, she'd been there for a time...since December, according to the date of birth.

"Jonah Hodges." I trailed my fingertip over the printed name on the official sheet of paper and then peered down at the little boy in my arm. "Hi, Jonah."

Tears rushed before I could stop them, dropping down my cheeks, off my chin, and onto the paper. December twenty-fifth. A Christmas baby, and my mom had cared for him enough to get his birth certificate before dropping him off here.

Had she wanted him? Had she hated that she was pregnant? She could have left him at the hospital. Given him up. She could have gotten rid of him, but she hadn't. She'd somehow wanted him enough to have him, to bring him here.

Can't take care of him. Don't have time to take care of that.

Had she tried? Had she gotten off drugs? Had she tried to stay clean and then fallen back into it? God, so many questions swirled through my mind, I couldn't think straight.

There was nothing else in the envelope, nothing else that would help me figure it out. I tossed both the envelope and the certificate to the table, and the smaller folded sheet fell to the floor. Settling the baby—Jonah—on the couch, I reached down and grabbed it.

Holly loved whales and that story.

"Oh, Mom." I cried harder and cradled Jonah in my arms. He finished his bottle, and I propped him to my shoulder to try to burp him. Thank God when I'd still had friends, some of them had little siblings, and I'd babysat when I was younger, so I wasn't entirely incompetent.

But I'd never done it on my own...

Now, he was all I had.

Jonah. I *had* loved whales. All from the story I'd learned in preschool back when my family was relatively normal and we went to church every weekend. That all stopped before Mom took off, but I used to have a book about Jonah and the whale. I'd sing songs about him. There was something so fascinating to me about a boy being swallowed by a whale and spit back out. A story about a boy who'd screwed up, gotten angry with God, and tried to run from him only to be found all over again.

I used to draw pictures of whales, sometimes with a tiny stick figure in the belly of it. They'd be plastered all over our refrigerator. If I searched through the pile of boxes in my closet from all the little-kid things I'd grown out of, there might still be a small orca whale in it.

Jonah. That was the name my mom gave him. She'd thought of me.

The realization hit hard and fast, and while I finished burping him and then changed his overly saturated diaper, I also got up and grabbed a pen and notebook from my school bag.

I was going to need things.

Lots of things.

All the baby things.

As the sun was starting to rise, my eyes were dry from lack of sleep. Jonah was sleeping soundly on the couch, bundled in his blanket and between pillows so he couldn't fall off.

There was no way I could go to class. I didn't have anywhere to take him, or any way to get him there safely.

Except...

It was early, but Caroline would be up. Probably getting my uncle breakfast and packing his lunch before he headed off to work.

I grabbed my phone and wasn't surprised when she answered after the first ring.

"What's wrong? Car won't work?"

I didn't blame her for assuming something was wrong. I rarely called her for anything.

My car not working would be a normal day worst-case scenario, but oh, how far off the mark she was.

"I need help. Can you come here?"

CAROLINE STOOD in my living room with her hands on her hips, gaping at the still sleeping baby. Jonah was so bundled up only his face was visible, and he'd wiggled a little so an edge of the blanket now covered his forehead.

"She just dropped him and ran off?"

"Yep." It was the sixth time she'd asked the question.

"I can't believe this." Her voice carried anger, but she said it quietly enough so as not to startle him, but I could feel her rage building. Her head whipped toward me. "Why wouldn't she tell me? When she called? And why call me at all? Why not ask—"

Her words broke at the end, and she shook her head. Caroline and my mom had been super close once. That relationship fractured when Mom started showing up high on pain meds and forgetting things and screwing up orders. While she and Caroline always planned on running the restaurant together, I long ago figured out that while the restaurant was Caroline's passion, it was Mom's duty. Caroline never fired Mom since she couldn't actually do it, but their closeness was gone long before Mom was.

"I don't know," I whispered, my voice raspy. Caroline and Uncle Paul couldn't have kids. They quit trying when I was ten, things I learned later when I spent time with Caroline and was older. "She only asked about Dad. Didn't even act like she cared I was here."

But she'd named him Jonah. In some way, that warmed me. She'd loved me once, and to this day still remembered something important about me. Maybe in her own way, she still did love me.

It wasn't enough, it never would be. But it was better than nothing.

"What kind of car was it?"

"I don't know, Care. The bumper was falling off, and it was rusty. Was definitely older than my Jimmy, though."

"Did you get a license plate?"

"No." I shook my head. "It was dark. Why?"

"She's only been on the road a few hours. We could find her and get to her."

"Get...what?"

Caroline gazed at Jonah. "She loved him enough to get the birth certificate. That takes time. She loved him enough to bring him here instead of ditching him somewhere. She... Lydia is still there, somewhere. If I can get to her..."

"Caroline." I went to her and wrapped my hand around

her bicep and leaned against her. "I know what you're saying, but she's gone. You at least have the county she delivered in. If you want to find her, you can start there."

"Right now I'm so ticked at her, I want her arrested for child abandonment. I mean, what the hell, Holly? What are *you* supposed to do with him?"

"I think one parent in prison is enough for me."

She snorted and smirked at me. "It could also get her free of drugs. Get her some help. You can't raise him, Holly. You have college and a life to start living."

"I can't leave him. Outside of you, he's now the only family I have."

Like any little girl growing up alone, I'd always wanted a sibling. I begged for one for years once I realized other kids had brothers and sisters. I didn't want to be twenty-two with one, but there were worse things.

I'd already survived them.

"I could..." she started, but I shook her head.

"You have the restaurant. And your life. I'll figure it out."

She drew her arm from my grasp and wrapped her arms around me. "*We'll* figure it out, Holly. We'll figure it out together."

My phone rang, and I went to the kitchen to get it, only to get sidetracked by a loud pounding at the door. The noise was so similar to what I woke up to in the middle of the night, I jumped so high I almost dove right out of my skin.

"Is it her?" Caroline asked.

I hurried to it and glanced out the side window. Probably should have thought to do that last night, too. "No. It's just Tracey."

"Just Tracey," she called from the other side. "Nice. I

feel loved. Now let me in. I've got breakfast and all the fixings for a broken heart."

She held up a bag of donuts.

I opened the door. "I could use breakfast, but breakups are the last thing on my mind."

"Hi, Caroline." She glanced at me. "What's bigger than that?" she asked, helping herself inside, dropping the bag on the kitchen table. She dug through the bag, and Jonah chose that time to wake up with a pitiful little squawk I was already starting to get used to.

Tracey froze, her hand deep in the bag of donuts, and her eyes widened. "What was that?"

"Come see."

I took her hand and pulled her to the couch, where Caroline was starting to bend down to mess with Jonah's bottle.

"What the heck?" she shrieked. "Holly. There's a baby. On your couch."

"Not just any baby," I told her. "That's my brother."

SIXTEEN
HOLLY

It was after I had to retell the story of Jonah's abrupt middle-of-the-night arrival to Caroline. After I fed him, changed him, dressed him in the only other decently looking clean outfit he had, and after Caroline left to go to the nearest store to get me some baby things.

She came back an hour and a half later and walked into me making breakfast, donuts not nearly satisfying enough. We all got caught up on the miserable ending of things with Graham, something which Tracey already knew because Tanner had called her last night to get my number and my address.

It was after I thanked her for not giving that to him, and it was after I told Caroline to get to work.

Tracey stayed with me, and we managed to figure out how to install the car seat, but an internet search told us to go to the firehouse to make sure it was installed correctly, and it was after Tracey asked me a gazillion times if I was sure I was going to do this.

Technically, he wasn't mine. My mom was listed on the birth certificate, the father wasn't even though I was assuming that's where his last name Hodges came from. I had no idea *how to* get legal custody, or even if I could. I had no idea how I was supposed to learn how to do any of it, but I knew exactly where to start.

Which was why Tracey decided to skip her classes for the day like I was doing and join me on a trip to the Deer Creek's Women and Pregnancy Center. It was opened a couple of years ago when Trina Mills returned to town, fell in love with her high school sweetheart for a second time, and then got married. They actually got married on the night my dad caused the car wreck. Almost everyone in the department had been at the wedding, so it had not only taken longer to get a response team to the scene, but half of them showed up in suits.

Then they were at my house immediately afterward to tell me what was going on. Being questioned by an officer in a sharply fitted suit was something I'd never forget. But Cole's new wife, Trina, was a sweetheart. She'd apparently always been one, and her dad wasn't only a pastor in town, he was the pastor at the church where I'd gone when I was little. Every time he saw me in town or at the restaurant, he was kind to me. One of the few good ones who didn't let my parents' problems determine how they treated me.

Trina opened up the center shortly after her arrival back in town, and now, with Jonah strapped into his car seat in the back seat, Tracey in the passenger seat next to me, my hands white-knuckle gripped the steering wheel as we pulled into the parking lot. Two other cars were there, and since I'd called to make sure they were open and had already spoken to her, Trina's car was one of them. I was guessing it was the mammoth-sized, sparkling clean, white Suburban.

"I'll support you," Tracey said. "I swear I will. Anything

you want to do, I'll be there for you, but are you *sure* this is what you want? There are foster families. Or your aunt. You're in your last semester and..."

"Tracey."

"I know. I'm rambling."

I reached out and squeezed her hands that were knotted together in her lap. "I'm sure. I'm not the first college kid to have a baby. I might have had less time to prepare for his arrival, but I can *do* this. I *want* to do this."

"What about leaving after graduation? Starting a life on your own? Getting out of this town? Raising a baby and starting a new career will be so freaking difficult."

"We'll figure that out as we go."

"What about Graham?"

I huffed and opened my door. "That's done. You know it, I know it, and he knows it."

"It didn't sound—"

"I've already blocked him, Tracey. If it wasn't done before last night, it was done the moment Jonah was crying in my arms."

I'd blocked him around four in the morning. He'd know what that meant. It was the worst ending to something that had the potential to be beautiful, but even if Sophie's death wouldn't be forever between us, I now had other responsibilities. Dating college guys who were gone half the time playing hockey and wanted to start their own lives and own families no longer factored into my future.

"Okay." She sighed and climbed out her door. I walked around the car and reached into the back seat and grabbed the car seat handle.

Okay. Done. Moving on. Nothing else mattered except for taking care of Jonah, making sure he was okay, and graduating college.

The rest would come with time.

I walked up the short walkway to the building's front door, took a deep breath, opened the door, and stepped into a whole new world. A whole new life I wasn't sure I was ready for, but that didn't matter.

It was already here, and I had to figure out how to live it.

SEVENTEEN
HOLLY

Present Day - Six Years Later

"YOU OKAY?" Dr. Ellis Myers pushed away from the foot of the exam table.

"Great." I gritted my teeth together until she came back, moved my feet back to the paper sheet-lined exam table, and shoved the stirrups away.

"Let me help you up." She reached out and took my hand, pulling me back to a sitting position.

"You'll have some cramping later today, maybe for the next two or three. You can take ibuprofen, but if it becomes too unbearable, call the office, and I'll get a prescription sent in, okay?"

"Okay." I sighed as I pushed my gown down. My head spun, and it wasn't from lying down and letting her shove a needle up my hoo-ha and take a chunk of my flesh out with her.

Biopsy. Abnormal Pap smear. For the last two weeks my

head had swum with fears and possibilities. All the hours I'd spent googling my symptoms was a bad idea.

Here I was, twenty-eight years old, getting a biopsy done on my uterus.

Nothing good could come of it.

"Any questions?"

I blinked and realized the doctor had kept talking.

Such was life these days. I lived with my head in the clouds, trying to fight against all the worst-case scenarios.

"How long?" I swallowed and tried to fight through my fears and worries. "How long until the results come back?"

The doctor's expression told me she'd already said it, but she reached out and pressed her hand to my knee. "Up to two weeks at the latest, but I'll try to work to get them back earlier. *Rest*, Holly, okay? You're young. It's probably just a scare. *Don't* let your mind race to worst cases, okay? We'll cross those bridges when we get there."

I nodded, but my chin wobbled, and I closed my eyes.

"Jonah needs you strong and healthy, Holly. We'll do whatever it takes, whatever the results. That, I promise you."

"Thank you." My voice broke as the first tear fell.

Dr. Myers tugged some tissues out of a box and brought them to me, and she pressed them into my palm. "Take all the time you need before getting dressed. Everything you're feeling is totally normal, but don't lose yourself to the worst fears, okay?"

"I'll try." I laughed and then cried and as she left the office with a soft, understanding smile, I blew my nose.

The biopsy was painful enough, but it wasn't the beginning of the pain I'd suffered, and it wouldn't be the last. Not with the luck I'd had in my life.

Dr. Myers was right, though. Jonah needed me. And a

quick glance at my watch told me if I sat there crying and wallowing in my feels for too much longer, I'd be late picking him up.

Single mom life was a rocking life indeed.

I never regretted keeping Jonah and doing everything I had to do to work for us, but along the way, I lost all the rest of my hopes and dreams.

Getting cancer would truly be no surprise.

I slipped off the table and got dressed.

There was no time left for wallowing or thinking of the past.

What was done was done.

I stepped out of Dr. Myers's office and headed down the hall. Dr. Myers had been my gynecologist for as long as I had been getting female exams. The shock in her eyes when I walked in with a six-month-old baby in my arms had been one amusing conversation.

"Um... did we miss a few appointments?"

She'd eased the awkwardness with perfect comedic timing and had been encouraging ever since. At least I had a doctor who truly cared. I couldn't imagine going through this with someone who was cold and clinical.

I hit the button for the elevator and stepped back to wait.

"Holly? Holly Jones?"

My spine straightened as a man called my name. I only came to Boone when I had to, but it'd been years since I worried about running into someone I knew.

I turned, and all the blood in my face fell to my toes.

His face broke out in a wide smile. "Holly freaking Jones. You're really here! How's it going?"

As he asked, he came rushing toward me. Decked out in blue scrubs and a long white coat with a stethoscope draped around his neck, Eli was no less handsome than he'd always been. In fact, age, and it appeared, med school, had been kind to him.

"Hi, Eli." I barely got it out before his arms were wrapped around me, hugging me tight. It took me by surprise, the fact that one of Graham's friends would dare to speak to me, much less touch me, after the way everything with us ended all those years ago, but there he was, hugging me like he'd seen me yesterday.

After tensing for a second, I returned his hug.

"I can't believe it's you," he said and pulled back. "How are you? You look great."

"Um..." I glanced down the hall and back to him. This was one of Graham's friends. A guy I'd hurt and hadn't done it kindly. He was the first guy, the only guy, I could have really seen myself having a life with. Everything crashed and exploded to the ground when I learned my own father had been responsible for killing one of Graham's friends.

It was Eli who warned me to stay away from Graham if I wasn't serious about him in the first place. I should have heeded that advice the moment he said it. I didn't, which was why I was surprised that he was being so kind.

"I should go," I told him. "It was good seeing you."

"Don't." He reached out his arm to stop me from moving toward the elevator. "Catch up for a second, would you? I hardly get to leave this building, and it's good to see someone I know. I just...I can't believe you're here. I thought you would have taken off after graduation."

His brow furrowed, like he was trying to remember the past, and he was slowly working to put the pieces together.

"We all thought you left. You vanished."

"Things changed." I shrugged and shuffled on my feet.

And still, even all the years later, I couldn't bring myself to tell him what happened. Didn't want to risk it getting back to Graham. But that was silly. It'd been *years*. My best friend Tracey still kept in contact with Graham's friend, Tanner, and I knew he'd never said anything.

Still, I couldn't open my mouth to say anything.

"You were here?" He shook his head. "Or in Deer Creek this whole time? Does Graham—"

"Don't." I held up my hand. "It was really great seeing you, Eli. But I need to go."

Jonah was at a hockey camp. The day he told me he wanted to learn to play, my heart broke a little bit. I'd do anything for him, though, even sitting through all his Mini-Mite games, cheering him on with my whole heart, while half my mind was on the past. The past that was now standing in front of me.

I needed to *go*.

"Miss Jones?"

I turned at the sound of my name. One of Dr. Myers's nurses headed toward me. She gave Eli a cursory glance before holding out a card for me.

My heart stalled. Not for what she was about to say, but for who was listening.

"Yes?"

"Dr. Myers wanted you to have this." She held out a small card.

I took it like a snake waiting to strike my inner wrist. "Okay..."

"It has her cell. She said to tell you if you need to talk, or if you're worried, call her personal phone while you wait for your biopsy results to come in."

"Biopsy?" Eli asked. His glance at the nurse or me wasn't cursory. "What's going on, Holly?"

His tone was too thick, suddenly too worrisome.

If only there was a bridge nearby, one with a large amount of space between water and cement.

Thank you," I managed to mumble.

I shoved past Eli and rushed toward the stairs. Screw the elevator.

I needed to get out of there. Away from Eli, away from the past that haunted me every day, and away from the fear of the future that was coming.

Fortunately, footsteps didn't follow me.

Just the constant thumping in my own brain reminding me that for me, life would always suck, always be hard, and there was nothing I could do to escape it.

EIGHTEEN

GRAHAM

Man, I hated being back in this place. It'd been over six years since I stepped foot into the skating arena at NWCU, but there I was, skating across the ice and spending the last of a three-day hockey camp helping kids ages five to twelve work on their hockey playing skills. Dribbling the puck, shooting, and playing defense, we were doing it all, and while I always felt at peace on the ice, being back on campus brought the opposite.

After hearing some of the attitudes of the older kids when we first got started, their cocky little backtalk that bordered on completely disrespectful to adults, I'd chosen to spend my time with the younger group of kids. Which was why I was currently working with a small group of five- and six-year-olds on their passing drills. They skated to the front of the line and passed me the puck. The second time through, I was moving, and they had to pass it to me, guessing where I'd be.

One of the boys skated to the front. I'd had my eye on him for a full three days. He was always smiling behind his cage guard and encouraged every other kid who did something well. He had a great attitude, large dark eyes, and gear that had most likely come from a secondhand store or had been handed down through a handful of kids. His skates were old, laces fraying, and from the way his ankles kept turning in when he skated, it was clear they'd lost strength.

He was good, though. And quick. If he had the proper skates he'd be even better.

"Nice pass, kid," I told him as he smacked it right into my stick. "That was really good."

"Thank you, sir." He skated back to the line, and I passed the puck to the next kid in line.

"Graham!" I stood as Jackson called to me and lifted my hand out to the kid who now had the puck. "Give me one second, little guy, all right?"

Jackson had been a player on our college team and now ran an athletic training facility nearby. He started putting on hockey camps for low-income kids two years ago to build attention for the sport. Every summer he'd called and asked if I could come help him, but until this summer, I'd declined. I wasn't even sure why I'd agreed to come back now, but maybe it'd been long enough. Six years had to be far past long enough to get over the girl who broke my heart before I truly realized I'd given it to her. But now that I was here, I was counting down the hours until I could leave and head back to Denver. A small town northwest of Charlotte, it'd been the first school district to hire me for a coaching position when I was right out of school. I'd had to substitute teach for two full years before a permanent science teacher position opened up, but I didn't regret a single minute of those first two years. My dad helped me financially, and I couldn't have done it without him, even if deep down I knew he wanted me closer to Raleigh.

Denver was also hours away from the college campus,

the girl, and the time in my life where everything that I thought I knew and felt turned out to be a complete disaster. Being back on campus made me think of her constantly. I couldn't stop it. We'd spent a few months together, a mere blink in the span of time, but it wasn't just the time we had together that made Holly difficult to forget. It was the bomb she tossed in my lap and then walked away, practically vanishing without a trace, that I always came back to.

All these years later, and I was still pissed she didn't give me the respect of a conversation. Didn't give me a *chance* to come to grips with what her father had done and who she was. It all made being back in Boone frustrating, but I wouldn't take it out on the kids.

It wasn't their fault I'd had my heart broken by a girl and couldn't stop thinking about her.

Jackson skated to me, coming to a quick stop and spraying ice into the air. "What's up?"

"Nothing, you looked tired, and I wanted to make sure you were okay."

"Yeah. I'm fine. Why?"

"Nothing. It's...look, I know it took a lot for you to be here. I get it. I just...I appreciate you being here, is all, but if it's too much..."

He tapped his glove against the side of his thigh. Jackson and I were teammates, but we hadn't been close. Not like I'd been with Eli and Tanner. He knew about Holly, though. Hell, everyone knew. After I found out about Holly and her dad and then she blocked me and Tracey adamantly refused to give me her address, everyone knew what happened. Things might spread in a small town, but things blew up on a hockey team. Especially when I played like crap for three weeks and almost cost my team a run at the playoffs.

"I'm not going to be a di—jerk," I corrected. Little ears and all. "To kids, Jackson. And there's only a couple hours to go, so I'm good."

"Yeah, well, a couple of guys were talking about getting out of here for the night and going out before everyone heads home tomorrow. You wanna come?"

"That'd depend on where you're going."

There were places I would always avoid.

"I heard a place in Deer Creek is pretty cool."

And that was one of them. "Yeah, I'm out."

"You sure? We've got Ubers planned and everything. There's a restaurant by a ski slope that sounded pretty cool."

I swiped sweat off my cheek and tasted dirt and sweat. "It'd take an act of God to get me back in Deer Creek, Jackson. I'm good. Y'all have fun."

"Oh shit. That's where...damn, man. I'm sorry. Really. We can change."

"Don't." I was already walking away. "It's my issue I can't put to bed. Y'all have fun, and if you're lucky, I'll see you here next summer."

Deer Creek. Damn. Every time I heard the name, which was often considering the tourism and location and the fact it was on my local news's weather forecast every damn day, my gut still tightened.

Holly was out there. Somewhere. Living her life. Probably killing it at some massive corporation as a finance rep or whatever she'd be doing. She'd be making good money, setting up her own apartment or home. And she'd be miserable. Still locked behind all the walls she never gave me the chance to scale.

Which was what sucked in all of this. If I ever saw her again, even with the past a difficult hurdle to jump between us, I still wanted to try.

"All right, kids!" I slapped my stick on the ice to get their attention. "Ready for some more?"

Tiny cheers went up on bodies barely large enough to skate with all that gear on.

Soon, another area of ice was open where we could practice shooting. I needed something else to think about for a while. Shooting always cleared my mind. "Follow me, guys."

The kid with the worn skates was at the front of the line. He was adorable. His blue eyes were enormous, round, and bright, and there was a tiny divot in the middle of his chin. He called every coach he saw *sir* like it'd been so drilled into him it was the first word he spoke, and his r's sometimes came out as w's. I taught and coached high schoolers who were all attitude and trying to find themselves and thinking rebelling was cool. Spending my days around high schools was eye-opening. They acted all tough and cool and like they knew everything, but inside, they were tiny adults who needed acceptance as they explored the world and themselves and the future. There was so much to them, so much stress in their lives they needed to navigate. I was glad I could be a part of it.

But there was something so special about the kids I'd spent the last few days with.

It was their innocence and kindness and excitement over the smallest things. It was in the encouraging others when they had a good play during a scrimmage and the way their faces scrunched up in concentration when learning something. Parents joked about kids ruining their lives, and older teachers I knew grew grumpy as the years went on at how much things changed, how disrespectful the youth was.

But I figured that's because they were focused on it. I saw a lot of good in the world, in school, and on the ice. I saw a lot of goodness in the pint-sized kiddo standing in front of me, already wrapping his fingers around the stick in the exact same place I'd coached him on yesterday.

"Hey kid, what's your name?"

"Jonah, sir. It's Jonah."

"Cool name for a cool kid."

He grinned at me. "My mom used to love whales."

I chuckled as the connection hit. Odd thing to name a kid over, but whatever. "All right, Jonah." I tapped my stick to his and skated in front of the goal. "Let's see what you've got."

Immediately, I saw his weakness. Jonah might have been able to pass and dribble the puck well for his age, but shooting was his downfall. He either pulled up too soon so the puck hit the tip of his stick or he dropped his back shoulder, hitting the puck on the stick's heel. It didn't matter how many times we tried, how much I coached him, he just could *not* get his body to stay in the right position long enough to hit the puck toward the goal with any good strength of direction.

"You've got this, Jonah. You can do it."

He squinted and gripped the stick harder.

I passed the puck to him.

He pulled back...and dropped his shoulder. The puck went five feet to the right of the goal. Not even close.

He dropped his head toward the ice and skated to the back of the line, dragging his stick behind him like he'd cost his team the college championship game.

"Hey, Luke!" I called out another coach's name. His son was now playing in the minor hockey league along with Tanner on opposing teams. "Can you take over?"

He was at the water coolers on one of the team's benches and didn't have a group of kids around.

"Just for a minute?"

"You got it." He downed a plastic cup of water, tossed it to the floor and grabbed his helmet and stick.

I went off to grab Jonah from the back of the line.

"Come here, Jonah." I steered him away with my hands on his shoulders, pushing him toward an open area on the ice before he could argue. There was something about that sad face he made I couldn't shake.

The dejection in it, like if he wasn't good enough to score, he sucked at everything, and that simply wasn't true. For one, he was six, for crying out loud. But man, it made my heart squeeze tight.

Maybe this was the downfall of teaching kids how to play the game versus coaching kids who thought they were all the best. There was *failure* in learning.

Without the stress of other players around the pressure to score a puck, I dropped my stick to the ice and skated behind Jonah. "Here's what we're going to do."

I walked him through the movements, keeping my hands on his arms and shoulders while he practiced shooting. "It's just like passing," I reminded him. "And you did that perfectly every time."

"I get nervous to miss," he said after we took a break, and I asked if this was helping. "I don't want my team to lose."

"Well." I crouched down on my skates in front of him until we were eye level. "You're going to lose sometimes. When the kids on your team miss, do you get mad at them?"

"I mean...sometimes." He shuffled on his skates, mumbling like he was afraid to admit the truth.

I couldn't keep in my chuckle. "Okay. I hear you there. I'm going to go to the bench and write some things down, okay? You show it to your dad, and he can help you."

He looked up at me behind his cage guard. "I don't have a dad."

"Oh..." Well, shoot.

"But I have a Papa Paul." He grinned. I playfully pushed against his helmet.

"Papa Paul will help then, I'm sure of it. And soon you won't be nervous at all."

I skated off to the bench as the buzzer rang, signaling the end of camp. I had to check my watch to make sure. Working with Jonah had made the afternoon fly by.

We were done now. Tomorrow, I'd head home and go back to Denver.

I should have been happy about it. Instead, as I skated to the crowd of kids stepping off the ice and starting to strip out of their skates, there was a heavy sinking feeling in my stomach.

I was leaving Boone. Leaving Deer Creek. Leaving the memories of Holly behind again.

None of it felt right.

While the kids went to the locker rooms and changed, I finished writing down some instructions and helpful tips for Jonah.

He dashed out of the locker room, straight toward me, worn shoes on his feet in almost the same condition as his skates, but his smile was as large as Texas. His hockey gear bag slammed against his legs and hit the floor as he ran.

"Hey, Mr. Coach."

I squatted down to get to him at eye level and handed him the paper. "This is what I have, okay? It's what we worked on earlier, but you can do it in a garage or anywhere with a flat, smooth surface. You don't need ice to practice. Got it?"

"I got it."

"Jonah!"

His grin grew larger. "That's my mom. Thanks, sir, for everything."

He bent to grab his gear bag near his feet, and when he stood again, I settled my hand on his head and ruffled his hair. "Good meeting you, Jonah."

He turned and called out, "Mommy! Mr. Coach says I'm a great passer!"

"That's great, kiddo..."

Her voice came to a halt. Something sparked in the air. In my memory.

I *knew* that voice, but it couldn't be. It couldn't be her.

Still, I found myself pushing from a squat...turning...

And I came face-to-face with a ghost.

The world stopped. I was pretty sure I stopped breathing. I shook my head to clear it. Blinked to make sure I wasn't mistaken, but when I opened my eyes, she was standing there, reaching out for Jonah.

She had...a son? My brain didn't work fast enough to do the math, but if he was six...and I saw her....

"What the hell?" I muttered. It didn't make sense. We'd barely done anything more than kissing. She hadn't seemed ready. I hadn't rushed...hadn't felt the need to when every time I was near her I felt like I had forever in my hands and arms. Boy, was I wrong about that.

"Holly," I breathed out.

The kid...no, Jonah...grinned up at me. "You know my mom?"

Her face went white as snow, and her jaw dropped. "Graham."

My name fell from her full, pink lips with a raspy gasp, drawing it out. At least she was as surprised as I was.

We stood there, both of us gaping at each other, at a loss

for words. I was completely unable to move, to say anything more but her name.

Holly blinked first. "Hey, Jonah. We need to get going, kiddo."

She took his hand and reached down to grab his bag. That got me moving, and I got to the bag first.

"You're not going to say hi?" I asked and hated the twinge of sadness in my voice.

Holly's eyes said everything. They always had. It was how I knew she wanted me even when she tried to fight it. It was the interest in her eyes, the way they beckoned me closer and could so easily freeze me in place.

Right then, she was terrified. I didn't blame her, but man...even confused and shocked to my toes, I wanted those eyes on me. That rich gaze that could turn so angry she could set the world on fire.

She'd definitely done that to mine.

"Hi, Graham," she muttered. "Thanks for taking care of him."

"Your son." I glanced at Jonah, who'd found a puck to take an interest in, and he was tossing it into the air. "You have a son."

She snatched the bag from my hand. "Goodbye, Graham."

I stood and stepped back.

She was still *here*. In the area of the state she once couldn't wait to run from, and hell if I wasn't prepared to go with her. Anywhere. I would have followed her to Alaska if she'd asked.

Something happened. Something changed everything, and there was no doubt in my mind that it was all due to Jonah. I was going to figure it out.

"Someday you're going to end a conversation with me and those words won't be the last thing you say."

"Yeah, well, that day isn't today." There was a smirk on her face, though. Like she couldn't resist the sarcastic banter we always had. "Come on, kiddo, Papa Paul's waiting for us. I need to get back to work."

Jonah grinned up at me. "Don't worry, sir. I'll tell him everything."

I tipped my chin toward him. "Good job today, Jonah."

He slipped his hand in Holly's, and she headed off out of the arena without looking back, but Jonah did and waved.

I waved back. *Paul.*

Her aunt Caroline's husband's name was Paul.

At least this time, finding her would be easy.

Jackson glanced at the two walking away, brows pinched together and then faced me. "Is that who I thought it was?"

"Yep." I rocked back on my heels.

"Well, I didn't see that coming."

I hadn't either, but a smile broke out on my face. Of all the sports, all the games her kid could play, she'd put him in hockey.

She could act unaffected by me all she wanted, but that said enough. I wasn't any farther from her mind in the last six plus years than she'd been on mine.

I glanced at him. "Think I'll head to Deer Creek tonight after all."

NINETEEN
HOLLY

How in the world? What in the world? Of all the places. At all the camps. How in the heck did I walk into that fiasco with Graham freaking Marchese smiling down at my kid?

After just running into Eli? The world was playing a sick, sick joke on me I couldn't afford.

The day Jonah was tossed in my arms, my life changed in ways I never foresaw at the time. With only Caroline and Tracey to help out, Caroline needing to be at the restaurant at all hours and Tracey juggling her own last semester of classes, getting to school had been impossible. Fortunately, most of my classes were offered as online options, and due to extenuating circumstances, I was able to get all but one moved over. The one I couldn't move meant I was only on campus on Tuesday nights for three hours.

That last semester had been horrific. Jonah cried all the time. I practically lived at the women's center in town with Trina and a handful of other volunteers, helping me work through colic, infant classes, and preparing to have a toddler.

Eli had been right. I did vanish, but not in the way he assumed.

But I'd done it. Definitely not alone. The worst moment after that came when Tracey graduated and moved to Tampa to get her masters in software engineering. Saying goodbye to her had been the hardest goodbye I'd ever had to say.

Looking for a job as a single mom became next to impossible. I had help in Deer Creek. Tracey was right about that objection from the beginning. I decided to stay for two years, find what jobs I could in Boone or in surrounding towns, attempt to build a résumé, and wait until Jonah was a little bit easier to manage on my own.

Then Caroline had a stroke. It happened one night when Jonah and I were at the restaurant with her. One moment she was busing tables, and the next, she couldn't speak. Before I figured out what was happening, she'd collapsed.

My dream of a stable finance job went up in smoke, and thus began my life being stuck in Deer Creek.

There were days I despised it. Days where knowing everyone made leaving the house dreadful. Those days came when Jonah wasn't allowed to play with certain kids or when he was excluded from events like birthday parties altogether. Then there were days where I felt wrapped in a village. Between Trina and Cole slowly becoming friends, and then their friends, even though they were a couple of years older, I'd somehow acquired a life filled with girls' nights outs and girls' days, and I now had a plethora of babysitters for when I simply needed a break.

Through all the pain and tears and fighting, through all of the struggles and constant streams of bad luck being thrown in my direction, I had *never* expected to run into

Graham or Eli. Definitely not in Boone. Certainly not on the same day.

In those first few weeks after our split, he hounded Tracey for my address. Begged her to borrow her phone. He'd even shown up at The Grille and pleaded with Caroline to talk to me.

I never caved. Had never had a second thought that what I did wasn't the right thing, even if I *did* have regrets on how cruelly I'd handled it over the years.

He was the guy I always cared about. The only one I thought of.

And he was *here*. Far too close to home. Far too close to me.

"He was really nice, Mommy. He said Papa Paul could help me shoot better too and told me what to tell him. He even wrote it down!"

"That's great, kiddo," I murmured, doing my best to keep my eyes on the winding roads, my hands on the wheel, and my racing heart and trembling hands in check. "I'm glad you had fun."

"I did. So much fun. Mister Graham even said I was a great passer like you tell me all the time."

Fantastic. Freaking hockey. I worked really hard to be a present mom and an involved single mom. The small nest egg of funds I was able to save over the years meant I could put Jonah in almost any activity he desired. I tried putting him in safer sports, but he kept going back to skating and hockey. I loved him so much I couldn't deny him.

"How do you know him? My coach? He said he doesn't live here, and we never go anywhere, Mommy."

"Yeah, we don't really travel, do we?" We'd taken weekend vacations here and there. I once took him to the zoo in Georgia, and we tried to get to the beach every fall.

That was harder now with him in school, but it was cheaper to rent a place at the end of the main season, heading into the offseason.

I hoped the mention of travel would switch topics, but unfortunately for me, Jonah was too smart. Too determined.

"So how do you know him?"

"He was a friend in school."

"In Deer Creek? He lived here?"

"No, kiddo. When I went to the big school, Northwest Carolina, where you just were. I knew him then."

"He said he played hockey there. He must have been so great."

He was. I knew that even if I didn't go to all the games. But I'd read his stats and articles written on him and his team. They'd come in second place that spring all those years ago in their division. His friend Tanner was still in the hockey minor league somewhere in Iowa.

I knew that from Tracey, who occasionally kept in touch with Tanner over the years. They'd stayed friends, and she'd caught a few of his games when he played close enough in Florida for her to get to.

"Yeah, Jonah. He was a pretty great player, I think. You hungry?"

"Starving. Hitting a puck around is a lot of work, and I did it so many times my arms are tired."

"I bet they are." I chuckled. My kid was cute.

"So tired I might not be able to lift a fork."

"Then we can get you soup, and you can drink from a bowl."

"Like a puppy!" Jonah shrieked. Not exactly what I meant, but the visual had us both dissolving into laughter.

Being a single parent wasn't always easy, especially with the route I'd taken, but man...Jonah was awesome. And

I'd had a hand in it. There was nothing more satisfying. Nothing I wouldn't give up to ensure that *he* would thrive.

I tried to brush off running into Graham. He was most likely in town to help out with the camp. He'd be gone again, out of our lives. And that was for the best.

I didn't have anything to offer him anymore, and that was assuming he wanted anything from me in the first place. So I ran into not one but two blasts from the past. Those things happened, and then they went away. That's all it was.

The same as the last time I'd met Graham, I had larger things to think of. Jonah. Taking care of The Grille, Caroline...

And what I'd do if my most recent doctor visit brought back the results I was dreading to hear.

"HE'S TIRED TODAY," Caroline said, grinning at Jonah scrunched up in the booth, reading through a stack of books we kept in the restaurant.

He'd been practically raised in this place like I'd once been, and he knew he had to stay out of the way, so we'd stocked a basket with books and card games and activities that would keep him seated. When it was slow, he'd help me fold silverware into napkins or clear tables, but I didn't want him dreading the work in this place like I'd once done.

"Camp wore him out for sure."

By now, he was usually bored and whining and wanting to run laps around the empty tables. Long gone was the divider wall between the old smoking and non-smoking sections. I'd spent time over the years renovating and updating the restaurant. I came in one weekend and painted all the walls a bright cream color. Trina and Cole had sent their friend, Robbie and some of his friends over to help tear down the dividing glass walls. After, I patched up holes and painted the beams an even lighter shade. It made the restaurant feel ten times bigger and gave me a better view of all the tables from a single spot at the serving station outside the kitchen.

"I need to tell you something," I told Caroline.

She paused at where she was refilling the salad fixing bins to prepare for the dinner rush.

"Did you get a call?"

"No." I shook my head. "The doctor said it would take up to two weeks for results to come back." Results I was refusing to consider or believe for a moment.

"What else could make you look so constipated?"

I barked out a laugh. "Gross, Care. Thanks for that."

She shrugged and started slicing cherry tomatoes in two. Her hands worked so quickly the tomato was there and gone, and I'd barely seen it before it was sliced. "Well, you get this look…"

"Yeah, yeah. I get it."

Jonah busted through the door. "Mommy, Mommy! Your friend is here!"

"What?" I spun, jolted at the banging of the doors and the excitement on Jonah's face. "What?"

"Your friend. The one from the big school? My coach!"

"Oh no," I groaned before I could stop myself.

Caroline didn't miss a thing. "Friend?" she teased with a gleam in her eye she'd soon lose. "I want to meet your friend." She might have some lingering left-sided paralysis from her stroke, and it'd taken her a good six months to speak clearly again, but it hadn't short-circuited her brain. She was still too damn smart.

She moved and pushed at the door before I could stop her.

"Don't," I cried out, but I was too late. She pushed through the doors and then stopped so abruptly they swung back and smacked her in the backside.

"It's good to have friends, right, Mommy? That's what you always say. That we need to be nice to them."

"We should, Jonah. Definitely. Always be kind to everyone. It's important."

"Then why don't you want to talk to your friend?"

I folded and refolded a towel. Slapped it down onto the counter and picked it up again. "It's..."

"Won't that hurt his feelings?"

Jonah peered up at me with those large eyes. They had to have come from his dad, because while our coloring was similar and he definitely had my hair, his eyes saw *everything*. They were large, round orbs of gold that absorbed every single thing he saw and somehow understood nuances that adults still had trouble getting. It wasn't a surprise he caught my reservations.

"Jonah, it's not about hurting his feelings." It was about protecting mine.

This was the worst timing possible. I wasn't even surprised he tracked me down despite my wishes he'd leave town without doing this very thing.

It was Graham. He was always chasing after me. But had he talked to Eli? Was that why he was here?

"But Mommy..."

"Enough, Jonah!" I snapped and then flinched. I *rarely* raised my voice at him. His face puckered, and his tiny chin wobbled. I crouched down and pulled him into my arms before his tears started falling. "I'm sorry, honey. I'm so very sorry for raising my voice. You're trying to help, and you're happy your coach is here, and I'm well...it's been a hard day for Mommy."

"Are you sick?" He sniffed and pulled back, those perceptive eyes scanned mine, and I hoped he *couldn't* see the truth. "You don't look sick."

He had no idea how close he might be.

"I'm not sick." I kissed his cheek and stood. It wasn't a full lie. I wasn't the kind of sick he was talking about, like an upset stomach or a sore throat.

I peeked out the small rectangular window to find Graham's profile, grinning down at Caroline like it'd been yesterday when we'd all hidden in her office or the night he helped me close.

"Let's go say hi," I told Jonah.

I reached for his hand. Pathetic that I needed the little guy's strength to do this, but again he took off like a rocket. He was out the doors before I could blow out a breath.

Time to say goodbye to Graham Marchese once and for all. Only this time, I'd be more polite about it.

TWENTY
GRAHAM

"Not sure it's a good time for you to be here."

I'd missed this woman. She was sweet and southern and everything you pictured if you imagined a woman running a business in the South on her own. Her hair was curled but pulled back with more gray in it than there was six years ago. She was more rounded, but it was the way the left side of her mouth drooped a bit when she talked. And the way her arm hung loosely at her side that grabbed my attention more than the worry piercing her golden-brown eyes.

"I had Jonah in my camp this week. I have questions, you know?"

"Not sure how you can when you darn well know he's not yours."

If I were younger, I'd be embarrassed if someone close to who could have been my mother's age knew about my sex life.

"That doesn't mean I don't have questions, and frankly, you owe me this, Caroline. You kept me away from her."

She huffed out a laugh. "I didn't do anything except protect my own, and like I said, now's not a good time."

I scanned the restaurant, where only a couple of tables were taken. It'd fill up soon, though, hopefully. "Because she's so busy?"

I couldn't keep my sarcasm hidden, and Caroline scowled at me.

"Mr. Graham!" The door slammed open, and Caroline jumped out of the way as the cute little kid I'd spent practically all day with ran up to me. "You should eat dinner with me! It's so boring here when Mommy has to work. You like onion strings? Aunty Caroline makes the best."

"I know, Jonah. I've had them before."

"You have?" he asked like I'd told him Santa was coming tonight. "When?"

"Back when we were friends at the big school, Jonah," Holly said. She stepped through the doors, looking at me like she was dreading every step she took.

Jonah smiled wide, and I glimpsed the similarity between them, along with the differences. Same eyes. Same shape and color and everything. No wonder why I'd been drawn to this little guy. She wasn't smiling, but that wasn't anything new. Every time I pulled a smile or laugh from Holly, it felt like I'd won a battle. Now that I knew more about her life, I understood.

Knowing what I learned before she ran from me, I now understood a lot from our time together back then. The way she guarded herself, the way simple gestures like how dinner seemed to mean everything to her. The fact that the first time she'd melted into me meant so much more to her and her ability to let someone in than it had to me at the time.

Questions raced and fought themselves for first place in my mind, but there were so many, and she was standing in front of me, guarded all over again.

She was dressed in the same clothes she had on earlier. The only new addition was the apron she used to wear when she worked. Another question flared.

Here? She worked *here*? Still?

"I shouldn't even be surprised you're here," she finally said, scanning the restaurant. "You always were tenacious."

There was a slight tease in her tone, which gave me hope she wasn't going to kick me out.

"Can we talk?"

"Yes!" Jonah bounced on his toes. "Mommy, I told Coach he could have dinner with me. He said he loves Aunty Care's onion strings."

"Rings," Holly corrected. "They're rings."

"They're so tiny like my shoestrings, though. And delicious." He grinned up at all of us.

"How about you help me go make them, then?" Caroline said and held out her hand. "Let's give your mom a chance to get caught up with her friend."

"But..."

"No buts, Jonah," Holly said. She smiled down at him, but her tone was firm. "Go with Caroline. We'll eat later."

She was a *mom*. How had this happened?

"Fine," he muttered and slinked back through the kitchen. The door swung slowly back and forth behind him.

Caroline tossed me a small smile over her shoulder. "You look good, Graham. Hope you're well."

"I am, ma'am. Thank you."

At least I *was*. Before today. Before everything went ass over teakettle, like my grandmother used to say when describing how everything fell apart.

"We can go sit," Holly said. She moved toward a table piled with crayons and markers and books, and I imagined it was Jonah's table when he had to be here.

I followed her to the table and shoved some of the books to the side when she sat down on one side, staying at the edge. She was ready to jump and bolt, and I couldn't blame her.

"I didn't expect to see you here," I admitted, and it probably wasn't the best first thing to say.

She shrugged one shoulder. "I didn't expect to see you at Jonah's camp."

"Touché. So...hockey, huh?"

A pink glow rose on her cheeks, and she looked out the window toward the parking lot. "He likes it, and I want him to have the things he likes."

There was a soft smile curling her lips, and my chest squeezed.

In my youth and stupidity and thinking I could crack through her walls with patience and time, I'd dreamed of being the one to give her that.

We were older now, though, and I'd spent the last few hours trying to figure out what to say to her. Hell, I'd spent the last six years thinking about it.

Which was probably why I broke the silence and blurted, "I understand, you know, why you left. You were right back then. Sophie, Piper, our families..." I shook my head and shrugged. It was so easy to see why she assumed the mountains between us back then were insurmountable. They weren't, not really. But from her perspective, I could see why she thought it. "That would have made things really difficult."

Holly's lips pressed together, and her shoulders heaved as she sucked in a breath. "I always felt bad for letting you know so cruelly. I could have found a better way."

"Well, your dad calling from prison wasn't the best time,

but I get it. We were young, and you did what you thought was best."

She reached for a set of rolled up silverware, removed the paper wrap, and unfolded the napkin.

"So, you're here now? You stayed."

She was still so pretty, even with her sad eyes that seemed to get sadder when I asked the question. There had always been something so enthralling about Holly. Maybe some of it had to do with the mysteries she cloaked herself in, but the rest was all her. Beneath the exterior she'd had to grow, there was a softness I'd craved to discover.

It appeared at random times, in the smallest moments, but there were enough flashes of it to keep me hooked.

"Things happened, life changed. I needed Caroline's help with Jonah, and she needed mine."

There was a wistful expression on her face, telling me it wasn't all bad, but she still had dreams.

"Can I ask? About Jonah?"

"I don't know his father, if that's what you're asking." There was a bite in her tone.

I had the sense I should tread carefully, but that wasn't really my style, and it never was when it came to Holly. "He's the same age, Holly...and we never..."

She picked at the napkin and stayed looking at the table where she was peeling the napkin apart. "He's not mine. At least, I didn't give birth to him, but he is my son."

"I don't understand."

She lifted her head, and the coldness in her eyes made me lean into the booth's back behind me.

"You don't have to. Why are you here, Graham?"

"Because I saw you and knew I'd regret it if I didn't come and find you. Pretend we were nothing more than friends, if you have to, but I wanted to catch up. See how you were."

"And figure out if I was with Jonah's dad when we were together? If I cheated?" She shook her head back with force. "I'm past the days of letting people create their own versions of me. The day Jonah was handed to me was the day I stopped living in fear and irritation of what everyone else thought of me. He became the only one that mattered, and he still is."

"Easy." I lifted my hands, palms facing her in surrender. "I'm not here to get the dirt, Holly. Have you considered the fact that maybe I've thought of you over the years, wondered about you? Maybe I came here tonight for the closure I should have gotten all those years ago."

I didn't even think about her cheating. She wouldn't do something like that. It took me thirty seconds to clock her character, and she didn't have that kind of betrayal in her. It was one of the few things I was certain of.

Ire spiked, and that same pain returned, the pain of watching her leave, the horrible truth she'd flung at my feet. I'd been nothing but *good to her*. Sure, I told her it was in the past. That I understood. All those things were true, but now she was sitting across from me. Angry. Frankly, I hadn't done anything to deserve it except start to fall in love with her.

She sucked in a breath and her shoulders fell, the fight left her in a gentle wave. "Tell me about you. The camp. What you're doing now. Are you teaching?"

"Northwest of Charlotte, in Denver. I had to substitute teach for a while, but I was hired to coach right away. I took a teaching job once one opened."

"That's good." She smiled. It was soft, but there was

genuine happiness in it, too. "You're doing everything you wanted. Is that why you were at the camp?"

"An old teammate puts it on every year, and this was the first year it worked for me to get here and help out. It's summer break, and my own school's season is over, so I thought it'd be fun."

"You always loved the game. Jonah talked my ear off about you all the way home."

"He seems like a good kid. You've done well with him, Holly. I hope you're proud of that."

"Raising Jonah is the best thing I've ever done. The only thing I care about."

"Tell me, then, tell me the truth. How is he yours?"

I leaned forward and rested my forearms on the table. I needed to know. Was it a guy before me? A guy right after? But she'd said she didn't give birth to him...

Her tongue poked at the inside of her cheek. I gave her time. Giving Holly time came as naturally as breathing.

"He's my half-brother."

TWENTY-ONE
HOLLY

I couldn't believe I was here. Couldn't believe Graham was sitting across from me, prying into my life, telling me about his. I'd wanted more information from him than only if he was working. Maybe he wasn't the only one who needed to know if the other was dating or seeing someone. Maybe *he* had kids of his own by now. A cute little wife who wore her baby in a carrier and cheered him on as he coached his games.

The smartest thing I could do was leave without ripping open the rest of my secrets, but I was stuck in that booth.

"He's...what? But..."

His confusion matched the same expression I wore for the first three months of Jonah's existence. I swear, every day I walked around the trailer, bouncing him, rocking him, crying right along with him, and thinking...what? How is he mine? How did this happen?

Graham recovered quicker than most. "Your mom...she came back?"

"A few hours after I got back from your place that last night." I was already spilling my secrets, might as well give him the rest. "She showed up high, practically tossed him at me, and then took off."

Tears burned my eyes, but it was no longer in anger. It was sadness. It was pain, at how she never bothered to try to learn how great her little boy was. How smart he was and how sweet he could be. He'd slept with me until he was two, even though I'd gotten a crib for him and then a toddler bed, but he went straight from my bed to a full-size bed donated by someone to the women's center.

My mom walked away from both of her kids, and while I might have been okay, Jonah was a gift. She'd never been sober long enough to realize what she had.

I no longer hated my mom. She lost her tools to care about anything but her next high years ago, and I'd spent enough time at a local Al-Anon to forgive her. But Jonah would someday ask questions. Someday he'd know the truth, and I despised the day I became the person who made him have all the questions I'd had when it came to our mother.

Across from me, Graham gaped in silence. I'd opened the honesty valve and couldn't seem to shut it.

"It took me a few years to be able to adopt him, but I was awarded custody immediately. I had some help with that. There's a women's center in town that takes donations, teaches classes, and helps women with things like pregnancy tests. Trina, the owner of it, was there for me a lot in the beginning. The court had to give Mom time to show up and reclaim him, that kind of thing, but eventually, after she never came back or reached out or anything, enough time went by, and I was able to plead for her rights to be terminated. Now he's mine."

Graham's gaping silence turned him into looking like a fish out of water, like words were forming in his throat, but he couldn't find the right ones to say, so he kept stuffing them down.

"Anyway, it was hard. I *did* graduate but switched to mostly online classes. Caroline and Paul helped out a lot, but then, when I wanted to leave, it was too hard. The job market wasn't great, every place I looked at was so expensive. Daycare costs absolutely blew my mind. I hadn't planned for those."

"And so you stayed."

I tore at the napkin, the paper that had been wrapped around it. Those first couple of years had been the hardest. All my dreams went up in smoke, but I'd been given something—someone—so much better than I could have ever dreamed of, too. It was the strangest thing, feeling the loss of a life you'd fought for for so long, but loving the surprise that had come into your life.

"It wasn't only the expenses," I told him. "Caroline had a stroke when Jonah was two. She had a long, difficult recovery and still isn't one hundred percent." I glanced at him and felt embarrassment creep up my neck. "I never told you this, but this restaurant is half mine."

"Really?" Two brows rose into perfect points on his forehead.

"Yeah. My grandparents put it in their will to Caroline and my mom. Mom left, and Caroline always hoped she'd return, but well, obviously you know how that turned out. After Jonah showed up, Caroline had a lawyer change the ownership from my mom to me. I couldn't ever figure out how to leave Caroline after her stroke, leaving her with all the work of this place. And then there was Jonah..."

It'd been a perfect storm of changes that had leveled my last remaining hopes of freedom.

"So you stayed," Graham said again. This time he wore

a soft smile full of understanding. It was a look I knew well. A look I vividly remembered.

A look I was once certain I'd never see again and wasn't sure I was thrilled to be doing so then.

"So I stayed."

He looked out the window and blinked, running his three main fingers back and forth across his forehead. "You were here all this time. I looked for you. I *came* here looking for you. For weeks after. Banged down Tracey's door so many times she almost had me arrested."

"I know."

"You knew." He laughed, but it lacked the warmth all his old laughs used to have, and I cringed.

I was the cause of it this time. That didn't surprise me. What surprised me was the devastation stamped all over him.

"I would have helped, Holly. I would have been here for you."

"Sophie was still between us." I shook my head. "You wouldn't have."

"No...I *would* have. You just wouldn't let me be there for you. You didn't even give me the chance."

Sadness crept into my bones and my veins, making me cold. He was still so naive, but he hadn't lived a life with whispers and gossip and people looking at you with disgust. Like you were poisoned because of who you came from. Those were mostly gone now. Enough time had passed that most locals seemed to have forgotten why I was alone in the first place, but there were a few that remained.

"I did what I thought was right at the time. You would have still left eventually, and I needed to learn how to do it on my own. And I did have help. Tracey and Caroline were lifesavers."

Along with Trina and Cole. Their friends Sarah and Robbie were foster parents and frequently had kids of all ages in their home, so they were prepared for everything. We were friends now, and Jonah enjoyed playing with Cole's girls, Ella and June, from his first marriage.

Others in town had come around to help too, some from the church I grew up in, some were older women from Caroline's occasional sewing club.

"You were here, though. And maybe you had help, but I know how the people treated you."

He sounded so broken, and that empathetic part of him broke me a little.

"People change and grow, Graham. It hasn't been all bad. In fact, most of it's been pretty great considering how wonderful Jonah is."

His fingers tapped on the table, and his jaw worked back and forth.

Food would be ready any minute knowing Jonah and Caroline, and I'd have to get up and get working. "Tell me more about you, Graham. What have you been up to?"

"There's not a lot to say. I teach, I coach. I try to get to Tanner's games every once in a while."

"He's doing well, it sounds like."

"You've heard?" It took him a beat, and then he sighed. "Tracey. They still keep in touch."

"Yeah. She lets it slip every so often."

He sighed and dropped his head. "I was hoping I could come tonight and see you and realize we had nothing in common and realize that everything I once felt for you was gone, but you're making it really damn hard, Holly."

"I'm not doing anything."

He lifted his head, and his eyes pierced mine, and not

for the first time, it seemed like he saw straight into my soul. "You're being you, and that's always been enough."

My heart stuttered in my chest, and my cheeks burned. "Graham—"

"Onion strings!" Jonah shouted. Behind him, Caroline pushed through the doors with the plate of onion rings piled high and three glasses of water.

"Onion strings," Graham muttered. "Kid's cute."

"He's the best thing to ever happen to me."

Caroline delivered the dish and drinks without asking Graham if he wanted anything else and left us alone.

It hurt, only a little, when Jonah shoved his little body into Graham's side of the booth instead of mine and dug into the onion rings like I hadn't fed him for days.

"Try one!" Jonah practically shoved the onion into Graham's face.

He scanned the table. "No mustard?"

Man, he really had remembered so much. "Not with the onions. I save that masterpiece for the fries."

"I think it's gross," Jonah said, munching on a mouthful of snacks. "Ketchup is the bestest."

"I agree, Jonah," Graham said. "Mustard on fries is gross."

I resisted the urge to toss an onion at his face and dug into the plate.

I didn't stay because I still had that comfortable feeling around him.

I didn't stay because the thought of walking away again hurt.

I stayed because it was rare I got to see Jonah interact with many good men, and I wanted to soak it up for as long as he was allowed to have it.

"I SHOULD GET GOING." Graham was at the hostess stand.

Behind him was a buzz of activity. I'd sat with them for as long as I could, loath to walk away, but in the end, customers started coming in, and I needed to get to work. I stopped by and checked on them when time allowed, eventually bringing Graham a French dip sandwich and Jonah a bowl of ice cream, but it was late. My feet and lower back ached, Jonah was restless, and our nighttime servers were here to handle the late-night crowd and close up.

When I started working with Caroline, that was one of the things I insisted on. I handled mornings and would happily stay through dinner, but neither of us was going to kill ourselves working fourteen-hour days again. Not after her stroke.

She was already gone, trusting me and the assistant night manager, Cain, to take care of the rest.

"Heading home tomorrow?" I asked.

"Camp's done, so yeah, I was planning on it."

He stressed the *was* like maybe now he had options. I had to ensure one of those wouldn't be me. "Okay."

He shuffled on his feet and didn't take his eyes off mine. "I'm finding it hard to think about leaving, Holly."

"Don't, Graham..." I shook my head. "We saw each other, we got caught up. Leave it at that."

"I should. Shouldn't I?" He tapped the side of his wallet onto the stand before slipping it into his back pocket. "The problem is walking away from you isn't something that's ever come easy for me, even when I know I should."

I pressed my lips together harshly to stave off the sob

clawing its way up my throat. This wasn't fair. Not to me or to Jonah.

It definitely wasn't fair to Graham.

"I think maybe it's time you try a little bit harder," I told him honestly. "I'm not at that place to give you anything."

He frowned, taking it as the rejection it was intended to be. "Can I at least have a hug goodbye this time, then?"

I shook my head again. I couldn't. If he had his arms around me, it was possible I could cave, let him draw me in all over again, and this time, the stakes were much higher. "I don't think so."

"All right then." He sighed and glanced around the restaurant. "Place looks really good. Not sure if I said that yet, but to me it looks like a really nice life you're building, Holly. I'm glad you have that."

"Thanks," I said, as tears swam in my eyes. I couldn't even blink them back. "You should go."

He saw the tears. He opened his mouth and then thought better of it. "Take care, Holly."

"Bye, Graham."

The sad smile he gave me as he turned and left the restaurant was a look I wouldn't forget anytime soon.

It hurt almost as much as the last time he left, but just like last time, I was still confident it was the right decision.

"YOU GOOD, LITTLE MAN?"

Jonah dragged his hockey bag out of my Honda Pilot, an upgrade from my Jimmy by twelve years, and dumped it on the garage floor. He had to walk over it to get into the house, and tomorrow, he'd still probably forget where he put it.

"Tired," he grumbled. "So tired my eyes hurt."

"We'll get you in bed as soon as you get a bath."

"Ugh. A bath?" His little body shivered with revulsion, and I opened the door to the house.

The trailer was gone, and we now lived in a small, three-bedroom townhome. The small neighborhood had a pool for summers and a playground where dozens of kids could always be found. It was tucked back off the main roads and far enough away there weren't many tourists outside the two or three townhomes that went up for winter rentals, but even then it usually attracted families with small kids.

I suppose it was better for me as well, too. I had a nice home that I gave Jonah entirely on my own, but there were days I missed the quiet land around the trailer and the peace that came from seclusion...something I never thought I'd say, but I'd started finally falling in love with my run-down trailer when it was the place Jonah crawled for the first time and took his first steps.

His sudden arrival in my life flipped a switch, and my entire life perspective afterward changed. Where I'd once despised the rundown trailer, I started looking forward to cooking healthy meals in it. I smiled as I paced back and forth on the worn carpeting, rocking him while he cried himself to sleep. I smiled and felt a peace the first two years I decorated for Christmas, and then Jonah was old enough to help hang ornaments on the lowest branches.

The townhome was safer and cleaner and larger and newer and everything a parent wanted to provide for their kids, but when I looked back on the days he and I spent learning how to do this life thing together, my heart ached at the memories we'd created there.

"Come on." I dropped my purse onto my kitchen island,

scowled at the breakfast mess I'd left on the counter, and guided Jonah upstairs to his bathroom.

I started the water, grabbed him a fresh towel out of his bathroom closet, and set it on the counter. "Shout if you need help."

I grabbed his dirty clothes and towels and dumped them on the floor of the laundry room at the top of the stairs right outside all three bedrooms.

Laundry. Between the two of us, it was somehow never-ending. Along with sweeping and vacuuming and cleaning the kitchen. Had I known the majority of my days would be spent thinking about meals and cleaning after meals and planning for the next meal and writing grocery lists for more meals outside what I already thought of for the restaurant, I wasn't always sure I would have agreed to keep him.

But then he smiled or caught a baseball. He learned to skate and scored his first goal or read a book all on his own, and every painful amount of energy that went into thinking about food vanished.

I kept the bathroom door open for Jonah while he bathed and busied myself in my bedroom. I put away clothes, started a load of laundry, and cleaned up my own bathroom counter, and when I couldn't find anything else to do to keep busy while he bathed, I plopped down on my bed and dropped my head into my hands.

Graham Marchese. Time had only made him more attractive. His hair was shorter but still had that curl to it, and his eyes bore the same intensity they used to when he focused on me. He still had the body of a college athlete, not surprising given that he was a coach, but man...

I shook my head and blew out a breath. What a day. What a wild freaking day.

If I were a different woman, with smaller problems and

fewer complications, I would have taken that hug from him. Who was I kidding?

I would have taken everything he had to give me.

But I wasn't. I wasn't that woman. Which meant for the second time in my life, I had to figure out a way to forget Graham and move on.

"Mom! I'm done!"

I shoved off the bed, blew out another breath, and got back to my life.

One where Graham didn't fit. He never had and never would.

Just my luck.

TWENTY-TWO
GRAHAM

The walls of my hotel were closing in on me. I'd already racked up thousands of steps in the small space. It was time to check out, time to go back home. The camp was over, and I had six more weeks before my own year started.

Yet I couldn't stop thinking about Holly. Or Jonah. How cute he was and how silly and also how smart. I couldn't stop thinking of the way Holly tensed and stepped back when I asked for a hug. I had a hundred reasons to stay away from her and take her warning that we wouldn't work to heart, go back to Denver, and restart my own life, but every time I reached for my suitcase, my hand froze.

Walking away from Holly again, or rather, letting Holly walk away from me again, felt like the biggest mistake. Everyone in her life left her.

What would it take for me to convince her I would stay?

"This." I decided. "This right here. Staying. Right here."

Screw the life I had in Denver and the summer break that would involve hanging out on some friends' boats and jet skis. I had six weeks before I needed to start thinking about the school year.

My lips twitched as I fought a grin, and I looked out the window at NCWU's campus and the mountains beyond.

"I have six weeks."

I grabbed my wallet and phone, tucked both into my pocket, and grabbed my suitcase. If I only had six weeks to get Holly to open up to me, try one last time to see what could happen between us despite her warnings, I couldn't be in Boone.

I needed to be in Deer Creek.

By the time I got to my truck and tossed my luggage into the back seat of the crew cab, my plan was forming.

There were still things that had to be said. We were far from over.

I started my truck and pulled out my phone, quickly going to a vacation rental site. I didn't need much, but I had to be close, and this time of year, rental prices dropped, so I found a long-term rental available, booked it, and then I finally pulled out of the hotel's parking lot, leaving Boone behind. I was grinning, fingers tapping on the steering wheel, cementing the rest of my plan.

Six weeks to scale Holly's impenetrable walls.

Six weeks to dig my way into Jonah's sweet little heart—which might be the easiest of all.

Six weeks to convince her we could do this.

The drive to Deer Creek had me restless, and I forced myself not to speed through the windy mountain roads. I had to slow down, be diligent and intentional, and I also had to take the biggest risk of my life one more time.

Twenty minutes later, I pulled into The Premier Grille's parking lot, among a dozen other trucks and SUVs.

Due to the last-minute booking, I couldn't get in until the late afternoon, so with nothing else to do, exploring Deer Creek became my new mission.

Starting with lunch.

A smiling brunette with her hair pulled back into a low ponytail, wearing a polo-style shirt with The Grille's logo on it, greeted me with a smile.

"Good afternoon. One today? Or are you expecting more?"

I wasn't expecting anything, but I had a load of hope bursting inside my chest. "One. And is Holly working?"

"She's in the office," the hostess said. "Follow me."

As she led me across the restaurant to an empty booth, she glanced back and asked, "Can I tell her you're here for her?"

"No, thank you." I slid into the side of the booth that gave me a better view of the restaurant and the doors to the kitchen and checked her name tag. "At least, not yet, Annie. Maybe after I've eaten. Thank you."

"No problem. Enjoy your meal. Your server will be right with you."

I'd shown up last night after the dinner rush, not wanting to surprise or interrupt Holly while she was busy, but today's visit was completely different. Over half of the tables were filled, and in a far corner were four local cops. Easy to spot since they were all decked out in uniform. I'd driven past the police station on the way here, although it wasn't the first time I'd been in it. The station was close enough the officers could walk over for a meal. I figured they were frequent visitors.

I tucked into the menu and scanned it even though the few times I'd come to eat here, everything had been great. I went with the Homemade Smokehouse burger that boasted of those crispy fried onion rings that were so damn good and an in-house-made Carolina barbecue sauce.

"Hi there, I'm Emma." Another young girl appeared at the table. "Here's some water for you. Can I get you anything to get started? Or are you ready to order?"

I placed my order, complete with an appetizer of onion rings, fries on the side of my burger.

"Anything to drink?" The server didn't write down anything I requested but held her pen to a tablet.

"No, thanks, I'm good with water. Oh, but can you make sure I have a side of mustard with my fries?"

Personally, I thought it was wretched, but I also knew Holly loved it.

"Mustard?" She shook off the surprise request. "Sure, sir."

I handed her my menu, and when she was gone, I tapped on my phone's screen.

If I were staying, there were calls that needed to be made.

I put a temporary hold on my mail, not that I got much more than advertising fliers and coupon pamphlets, and sent a few texts to friends asking them to keep an eye on my place.

Tanner and my dad were on my need-to-call list, but the conversations I needed to have with them would be done later.

For one, Tanner *knew*. He'd kept in touch with Tracey, and while I knew that because it came up occasionally, he never said a word about Holly. Granted, I didn't ask, although I had to bite my tongue not to. But he could have told me. I had not one single doubt he'd known about Jonah this whole time and where Holly was.

My dad would be a different story. He was still good friends with Sophie's family, and eight years later, they were still understandably reeling from the loss of their youngest daughter. But things changed.

People changed.

At least I hoped so.

MY ONION RINGS CAME OUT, and I dug in, closing my eyes with each glorious bite. More customers came in until the restaurant was almost full, and the teenage girls worked like a well-oiled machine. I had yet to catch a single glimpse of either Caroline or Holly, but I tried to be patient as I played a hockey game on my phone and enjoyed my onion rings.

A shred of hope came when Holly walked out of the silver doors that led to the restaurant. Since I'd been keeping an eye out, I saw her immediately and then grinned down at my phone.

She had a serving platter in one hand, and if I'd been a betting man, I would have already known it was my lunch.

I didn't look up from my phone when she stepped to the edge of my table. The plate was flung down harder than necessary, and I slowly glanced up.

"Good afternoon."

She scowled at me, and she looked so frustrated with me I bit back a grin. "Mustard with fries? Really?"

"Maybe it's growing on me."

I slid the plate closer to me and chomped on a crisp onion sticking out from the bun. It smelled incredible, and the small bit of barbecue sauce on the onion hit my tongue with the mix of vinegar and tang.

"No one but me likes mustard on fries."

"Not true." To prove it, I dunked my own fry into the mustard and took a bite. Man, that was horrible. I had no idea what she ever saw with that. "Did the waitress tell you?"

"No. Caroline did when Emma told her that someone ordered mustard with a side of fries. Caroline knew it was you right away."

"She's a smart cookie. I like her."

I could do this all day long, but Holly scanned the restaurant and sighed. "I thought you were leaving today."

"I was. Change of plans."

Another quick look from Holly around the restaurant. With the way her eyes narrowed, I assumed she was taking in every table, making sure all their needs were met, maybe seeing if she knew anyone. When her gaze hesitantly reached mine, she dropped into the booth across from me, sliding her serving tray into the booth next to her.

Without asking, she stole a fry and dipped it in the mustard.

I pushed the plate closer to her and grabbed my burger.

Before I could take a bite, Holly asked, "What are you really doing here?"

I bit. Chewed my food. Took my time. Holly rolled her eyes, but she appeared tired of this game already.

So was I. I was so tired of playing games.

"I have six weeks until I think about heading back to start getting ready for the school year. I've decided I'm spending it here."

That wasn't fully true. I would need to either go home for a day and grab my computer and some other things, and I would need to spend time doing some professional development learning and reading. I typically spent the summer making lesson plans for the following year, figuring out what worked the previous one when things were still fresh so I didn't have to take time to do it during the school year. Sure, things changed, but doing the bulk of the work over the summer kept my school year less stressed, especially during the hockey season. Fortunately, that didn't start until October, so hockey season was only a drop in the bucket of items I'd need to worry about.

"Why?" Her shoulders dropped, almost like she was defeated and exhausted. Didn't blame her. I was a lot to deal with.

She'd have to suck it up, because while I was tired of playing games, I had one last one to start, and this time, I intended to win.

"For you," I told her, and I wasn't surprised when she blinked and her lips parted. "You said you didn't think we had a chance of working out. I intend to prove you wrong."

"I CAN'T BELIEVE you didn't tell me." I didn't introduce myself, and I skipped the niceties altogether when Tanner's voice said hello through my AirPods.

"Graham?"

"Yeah, it's me. How could you not tell me about Jonah?"

"Oh crap." There was a beat of silence, and then he said, "Tracey said she didn't want you to know. Sorry, man, but you were going through a hard enough time. I didn't want to make it worse."

I wasn't sure if it made it worse or better if he knew this *entire* time or not. "You've known since the beginning?"

"Called Tracey one night to hang out, and he was screaming in the background. Then she and Holly got into an argument about how to calm him down. It all happened so fast it took me a minute to figure it out, but yeah. Listen, I'm sorry. But she was adamant she didn't want you to know. It was senior year. You'd already gone through the Sophie stuff...you know?"

The Sophie stuff. Like my best childhood friend dying was a *thing* to be managed. My lip curled, and I bit back the anger before it came across. "I can't freaking believe it."

"Wait. How do *you* know? Oh...you found her, didn't you? You're still looking? After all these years?" He sounded part shocked, part disgusted.

"I'm not hunting her down," I drawled and rolled my eyes. Not like he could see that part. "I'm at Jackson's hockey camp, and guess who showed up to pick up their *kid* while I was helping him with skates after his drills?"

"Who? Oh...oh dang." He coughed and then laughed, and then I wasn't sure if it was a cough or a laugh, but it irritated my senses. "That's wild. She walked back into your life after all this time, huh? That's kind of cool. Kismet or whatever that's called."

"Yeah, Tanner. Kismet." This guy. He might have been hit in the head with too many hockey pucks this season. Swore he kept getting dumber by the week.

"So what'd you say?"

"I said hi. She said goodbye."

"That's it? After all this time?"

I scratched at the scruff on my jaw. "And then I showed up at The Grille and told her I was staying in Deer Creek for six weeks."

It was a definite laugh this time that filled my ears. Tanner howled like there was a full moon. I shook my head and checked the kitchen cabinets in my rental until he composed himself. There were basic seasonings I could use and some coffee for a Keurig. The small two-bedroom place wasn't much, but it was mostly used as a winter ski chalet. From the back patio, I could potentially ski right out the backdoor and down to the lift. Probably why it costs more than the upper two floors.

"That's *wild*, G. You're not actually considering it, are you?"

I couldn't tell if he thought it was a good thing or not. Probably wasn't. There was a chance the high schoolers over the years had hurt my brain too much. Maybe I was the one getting dumber by the minute.

"In the rental now. Only packed for three days, so I need to head home and get some stuff, but yeah. I'm pretty serious. You going to tell me this is the dumbest thing I've ever done?"

"Not the *dumbest*. But maybe the riskiest?" He coughed and cleared his throat. "Listen, Tracey and I are friends, right? We don't see each other much, but we talk every couple of weeks. And she's been worried about Holly for a long time. There's a lot going on there, with her folks, her aunt, the restaurant...Jonah. I just...don't screw with her, you know? And give her time? Frankly, I'm not sure six weeks is enough."

"Has to be enough to start a foundation. What's going on with her folks?"

I'd assumed she had no contact with either of them, but was I wrong?

"Not helping. I'm staying out of this and not giving you anything."

"Well, I know about Caroline's stroke and that she half-owns the restaurant." The fact she never shared that had hurt in the moment, but that was always how getting to know Holly had been. Tiny, quick jabs of pain in between the times I'd never felt happier.

"Huh. So you're there and staying. Can't *wait* for Tracey to find out. That'll be fun. Maybe I should come down."

"Stay far away." Tanner turned everything into a joke and a good time. He was good to have around, definitely, but not now. "How's the offseason going anyway?"

He was in Iowa, working hard to get his big shot. His team had lost in the playoffs in the last series before the finals, fighting for the Calder Cup, the AHL's Championship. He had two more years on his current contract, but he was also getting older. He either got called up soon and given his shot, or he'd soon have to join me in teaching. He was only twenty-seven, but even now he was running out of time. Not that I'd ever tell him that, but it was hard to watch nineteen—and twenty-year-olds getting to play when you were still down below, fighting it in the trenches.

"It's all right. My body is sore, like *always*. But I've been healthy for the most part, so I'm working with a trainer on my agility and flexibility to help with some of that. The guys and I are going down to the Keys in a few weeks for a long weekend, but I was thinking of coming to see you."

"Give me time alone with her. Let me see what progress I can make on my own."

"All right, G. Man, this is wild. Glad you're not pissed at me or anything, but I do think it's cool you found her. Just move carefully, right? From what Tracey said, she's not going to leap into your arms and declare it love at first sight."

"Trust me, I know. Talk soon, Tanner. Keep your chin up."

"You too, man."

I hung up the phone, tossed it to the corner, and then picked it back up again.

Holly might not want much to do with me, but she wanted the best life for her son.

And he needed new skates.

TWENTY-THREE
HOLLY

"What am I supposed to do?!" I cried into the phone and imagined Tracey flinching from my shrill voice in her AirPods.

After Graham dropped that bomb in my lap, he went back to eating his lunch like he hadn't rocked my world, stolen my breath, and given me a knockout punch all at the same time.

It shouldn't have come as such a shock, not with how we left things the day before, not with the things he'd said to me —*I'm finding it hard to think about leaving*—I'd thought of those words on a near constant loop since I put Jonah to bed last night.

I should have known then that he'd stay. It was naive of me to assume that goodbye would be our last. Graham enjoyed the chase, he always had. Now that he was in my town, I had nowhere to run.

"I can come up there and play defense," Tracey said. She meant it. She'd do it, too. She'd dropped everything and driven overnight to get to me before, once when Jonah and I had the flu so bad I was certain we would both die.

"I can't believe this." I was pacing outside at the back of the restaurant. I'd waited until I knew Graham left, had watched him get into a gray Toyota Tundra, and then I waited another half an hour, busying myself by pretending to prepare the payroll until I gave up and called Tracey. "I can't believe I saw him yesterday. I can't believe he knows about Jonah. And now he's here. He said he's staying for six weeks, Tracey. I can't *avoid* him."

There was a thick silence as I stared up at the blue sky. It was gorgeous, and I was starting to roast in my black pants and white short-sleeve shirt I always wore to work.

"I don't think you should avoid him," she finally said, and it was done so hesitantly, with such worry in her tone, I flinched.

"You can't be serious."

"He's the only guy I've ever seen you attracted to, Holly. He's the only guy you've cared about, and you haven't even *tried* to date since Jonah."

"Not true," I muttered and kicked at loose mulch that had escaped our landscaping on the sidewalk. "I tried."

"You've had two dates."

"So." If I'd had any doubts before, I now knew where Jonah got his pouty voice from.

"Listen, I'll come there. I'll kick his butt back to Charlotte or wherever he is. Heck, if you need me to, I'll shoot him and bury the body. I'll do anything you need, but right now, I think you have to consider this. He's *back*, and you've always missed him. It wouldn't hurt you to give this a shot. Maybe it'll go nowhere."

"Yeah, and then Jonah will be devastated."

"And maybe it'll end up being everything, and Jonah will have the father you've always wished he had."

"If my test results come back..."

"If they come and we can celebrate, then you don't have to mention it. If they come back poorly, you'll have help. And more, Holly...Jonah would have someone if..."

"That's enough," I whispered, but it was harsh enough to stop Tracey in her tracks.

I knew the chances. Words like survival rate, terminal, and reoccurrence had lived rent-free in my mind for the last two weeks ever since my annual exam came back with inconclusive results. Now I was spending my free time researching oncologists and treatments.

As much as I wanted to hope for the best and keep a positive spirit like Caroline, Tracey, and my doctors have said, I'd never had a run of good luck in my life.

"I know, and I'm sorry. Of course you don't bring Graham into this because of that."

"That's why I want him to stay far away." I laughed coldly.

"He's a big boy, Holly. He's going to do what he wants. Take the time to figure out what it is you want."

I wanted my health. My happiness. I wanted freedom, and most of all, I wanted to give Jonah a life better than I ever bothered possibly imagining.

I'd tried dreaming before, and the shattered glass shards of them being broken still scarred my heart. I wasn't all that revved up to give it another shot.

"ALL RIGHT. What are we doing today?" I squirted dishwasher detergent into the machine, closed the door, and pressed the start button.

Jonah was at the kitchen table, done eating, reading a comic book about a famous baseball player Paul had bought him. I'd hated reading when I was little, numbers and facts were more my thing, along with running outside and biking, but Jonah loved to read. He soaked up every age-appropriate book I gave him, and his teacher had started recommending books for him much higher than his grade level. For now, we were sticking with books about sports or fictional stories based on real-life players. He gravitated toward baseball and hockey players, though the hockey ones were harder to find.

I tossed and turned all night long trying *not* to think of Graham and his purpose for being here. Maybe he'd run off after I jumped out of the booth yesterday and told him to go home. That there wasn't anything for him there.

Unlikely. Graham giving up on something wasn't a strength he possessed.

"Park!" Jonah slapped his book closed and jumped off the kitchen chair. It scraped along the tiled floor, but his feet thundering to the front door made the screeching sound inconsequential.

I had the morning and afternoon off from the diner, but I would go in before the dinner rush and stay until we closed. Saturdays were our busiest days, and I couldn't even stay hidden back in the office working on payroll and scheduling and ordering. It was also the day I insisted Caroline take off, so while our morning workers could handle breakfast and lunch without me, one of us had to be there for dinner and beyond.

Thank *God* for Emma and Annie. They were lifesavers. Heading into their junior year of high school, they begged for as many hours as possible to save up for college tuition, and Caroline and I quickly complied. Fortunately, the summer weather had been perfect for tourists, and we'd had a steady stream of locals with a slight uptick in visitors. I attributed that to my recent foray into strengthening our social media presence and working with the city to get our name out there more with marketing fliers and catalogs that got sent out all over the state.

The old adage was true: you had to spend money to make money, but I'd done most of it with very little upfront cost.

I was seeing it on the back end, though, for certain.

All things that I could think of at work, and not while I was spending the beginning of my day with Jonah.

"Neighborhood park or city park?" I asked and slipped into my knockoff Birkenstock sandals.

"City! 'Cause then we can get ice cream after and run through the splash pad."

"Sounds like a perfect plan. Maybe we can invite Ella and June?"

Ella and June were Cole and Trina's daughters. Ella was his age, although in a different classroom at school, and June was a year behind. They were all young enough that it didn't matter to Jonah that most of his friends were girls.

"Yes!" He was tugging on his tennis shoes at the door to the garage, and his little brows puckered. "Does Mr. Robbie have kids at his house?"

Robbie and Ashley were friends with Cole and Trina, so I also knew them well. They were also foster parents, so while they had a few long-term placement children in their home, they occasionally had short-term ones.

"I haven't heard," I told him. "And Carlie and Addison are probably too old or busy."

At twelve and fourteen, they'd been with Robbie and Sarah the longest. Sarah desperately wanted to adopt them, but their mom kept making the minimal effort with long stretches of absences in between, so the courts kept hesitating to allow the adoption to go through. Due to my own issues with my parents, especially my mom, I'd been able to relate to the girls when I first met them.

"Maybe they can watch me later."

"We'll see. I don't have any plans tonight." Babysitters were an expense my budget didn't always allow for.

"Fine." He slapped down the Velcro on his last shoe and jumped to his feet. "Last one to the truck is a rotten egg!"

The door slammed shut behind him right before the quiet hum of our garage door opening kicked on.

I pressed the lock button on my key fob and hoped it worked before I followed him outside. I had nothing wrong with letting Jonah win occasionally, but I'd always win this game no matter how many times he tried to win by closing the door in my face.

"Hey!" he shouted at me, laughing while he tugged on the door handle. "Unfair!"

I ruffled his hair as I scooted by him. "So was closing the door. Second try. You ready?"

I stood at my side of the Pilot, key fob in the air, other hand raised in the air. "Hands up, kiddo, lemme see 'em." Once he did, I grinned at him. "Last one to buckle is the rotten egg, got it?"

He nodded seriously. "Yup."

I hit the unlock button, and we both dove to the handle and into our seats. My purse got caught in the door, losing precious nanoseconds, and Jonah's click and then squeal erupted through the back seat. "I win! You stink, Mommy!"

"Yeah, yeah." I laughed. "I stink."

"Pee-you!" He pinched his nose together and scrunched up his face. "Guh-ross."

Laughing, I started the SUV, backed out, and once the garage door was closed, we headed off to town, where I'd spent the day with Jonah, thinking about him and playing and getting ice cream and doing all the things he thought were cool to do with his mom before taking him to see Paul for a while.

And I wouldn't spend a single second thinking of Graham. Or that he was in town, probably looking for me. Tracey had been right last night.

Until I knew what I wanted, or what I hoped for in having him around, I intended to avoid him at all costs.

I'd only been to Deer Creek a handful of times, and since most of the times I was there, I only went to The Grille, I hadn't spent much time checking out the other areas.

The only two exceptions to that were a few days after Sophie's death, and I went to the police station to get some answers to questions the family had since I was closest. The second time I'd been to Deer Creek it was to say goodbye to Sophie. That happened to be the night Tanner and I met Holly and Tracey for the first time. We'd stopped at a bar in town for a couple of drinks so I could calm down before heading back to school. It'd been a year later, then, and after living with grief and sadness for so long, the new year had given me a desire to move on.

Crazy that a few hours later I was running into a girl I was still hung up on all these years later.

But Sophie wasn't Holly, never had been and never would have been, despite the lies Piper had once spewed.

As much as I wanted to see Holly again and prove to her I wasn't going anywhere, I stayed away from the main area of downtown Deer Creek. My rental was a condo at the base of one of the ski slopes, giving me incredible views of the mountains in the distance. There was a small area that looked to be a local golf course, and I made a mental note to grab my clubs when I went back for my teaching gear.

Clothes, too, would be needed considering I'd only planned on being gone for a couple of days.

Just off the ski slope, there was a mini golf area, and around the corner was a small market that had local foods and wines and beers, along with tourist-type clothing with Deer Creek stamped across in bold letters. There was a small section remaining, or recently in, of winter and ski gear, including gloves and hats and hand warmer pouches.

"Mornin'." Behind a long counter that was built like a log cabin, there was an older gentleman standing next to the cash register.

"Morning. How's it goin'?"

"Well, I woke up, so I can't complain. You visitin'?"

I chuckled at the lame joke he probably made every day. "Here for a few weeks. Any recommendations on things I need to see while I'm here?"

"You the huntin' and fishin' type?"

"I could be." I shrugged. "Golf and hockey are more my thing."

"Well, we got Lake Winona nearby. Not a bad place to do some shore fishin', and they rent out boats for the day too if you wanna give that a shot. Golf courses all over the place if you don't mind a fair bit of a drive. Best thing about town, though, is the food. We got some darn good homemade food in town."

"I've been to The Grille. Definitely know that."

"Ahh...Caroline. She's a good egg. Runs a good ship, too. Her food is top tier, but if you want somethin' else, check out Sorento's Italian or Scalecki's Pizza. He's right around the corner. Best pizza pie you'll ever taste. So good it'll make you want to move."

Again, I chuckled at his joke. The man was older, missing a tooth or two, and the ones he had were turning yellow. His gray hair was shining, right along with his beard, and the lines around his mouth and eyes said he'd lived a hard life, but maybe a happy one, too, given his mood.

"Thanks." I grabbed the fishing and boat pamphlets. "I'll check it all out."

A day out on a boat wouldn't be a bad thing by any means. Better if I could convince Holly and Jonah to join me. "What about breakfast? Outside of The Grille, any good place?"

"You're darn right. Head back to Main, turn right on Ansel Road, and there's a place right there. Britta's Café. The sign just says The Café, though. Right next to Mellie's Cakes if you got yourself a sweet tooth."

"Thanks." I reached forward with my hand extended. "I'm Graham. Renting a place at the ski slope, so I'm sure we'll talk more."

"Billy." He shook my hand with his weathered and liver-spotted one and squeezed tight. "Enjoy your time. I've been around longer than most of the homes on these hills, so you need anything, don't hesitate."

"Thanks, Billy."

I turned and left with a smile on my face. Small-town people. Man, they were friendly.

I climbed into my truck and headed to Britta's. After, I'd head back home, take a couple of hours and pack, get some groceries, and I could still do all of it and be back before nightfall.

I'd give Holly the day to think, but then it was game on.

BRITTA'S CAFÉ was as easy to find as Billy said. Attached to other places like the bakery and an insurance office, the entire building had multiple dark wood peaks, making it seem perfectly at home in the mountain town.

There was nothing mountainy about the inside of the café, though. Done in all whites and hot pinks and lime greens, the small restaurant felt more like I'd walked into a bubble gum shop. It was bright and happy, and I caught a sight stapled to a beam in front of me just beyond the entrance that said *Make yourself at home. Seat yourself.*

I did just that and slipped into a two-seater table at the front window. There were five older gentlemen at a small semi-circle table, sitting on chair-height stools, just off where a waitress was standing, pouring coffee. In front of the men were opened Bibles.

"Be right there," she called to me as we made eye contact.

She slipped the coffees to the men at the semi-circle table, and I reached for the menu stacked on its side behind the salt and pepper and sugar packets at the table. The menu was only one page, front side only, but boasted of buttermilk fried chicken and waffles, eggs Benedict, and all the common breakfast options. There was a small section of sandwiches and soups, or combos of both, for lunch.

I was sold on the chicken and waffles as soon as I read buttermilk, and I slipped my menu back to where it belonged.

"Mornin'." The same server came to me holding a tray with a glass of water and a coffee mug and had a carafe in her hand. "Need some coffee?"

"Please. Thanks."

"No problem, sugar. You know what you want?"

"Buttermilk chicken and waffles, please."

"Anything else?" She finished pouring the coffee and hugged the tray to her chest. "Eggs? Bacon?"

I shook my head. "Think the chicken will be plenty."

"Sounds good. Be right out with that."

After she walked away, my gaze went to the outside. My family had never gone skiing on Crystal Mountain. My dad took us to the beach and to bigger cities like New York and Chicago. Before my mom's death, we did family trips like the Grand Canyon and Disney World. Once we went skiing in Breckenridge. Sophie's family hadn't been that much different either, and it'd been a last-minute weekend getaway with all their kids home from college and visiting for Christmas that had led them to Deer Creek the night she died.

Was killed.

Run off the road.

Like always when I thought of Sophie, my chest ached, and the familiar gut punch of pain returned. It'd been eight years, but the pain of missing someone never truly went away. While shocked to learn that Holly's dad had been responsible, what Holly needed was to give me the chance to tell her that I didn't blame *her*. She had nothing to do with that night, and it was obviously clear before that night she hadn't grown up in a stable home.

It'd hurt to hear. It'd taken me a few days to think it through, but what Holly didn't know was after that night, I'd called my dad and talked to him. I told him everything.

He'd left the choice to pursue her up to me. Said we only had one life, and I was grown enough to make my own choices.

Would it have been awkward and hard for them to meet? Definitely.

Would it have smoothed out eventually? I had wanted to think so.

But now, I had no idea how to convince Holly that it truly didn't matter. I had no idea how to scale that wall she'd resurrected and reinforced over the years.

"Ice cream!"

The words were shouted so loudly from outside, it grabbed my attention. I turned to find the source and then laughed as Jonah ran across the parking lot, arms flailing in the air like one of those marketing blow-up tube guys.

Holly followed behind him. Her smile was wide and carefree, something so rarely seen from our history I couldn't take my eyes off her. Her hair was down, shining from the bright sun. She was dressed so much like a *mom* in cutoff denim shorts that went halfway to her knees and a fitted, simple pink T-shirt with a small backpack strapped over her shoulders. I still couldn't believe she was a mom. It still struck me how poorly her mother had treated her. Who dropped off a baby and *ran* like that, and never once reached out to ensure they were okay after?

A woman riddled with drug abuse—that was who.

I leaned back in the booth, crossed my arms over my chest, and enjoyed the gift of watching Holly with her son, with her walls down like they wouldn't be resurrected the moment she saw me.

"Mommy!" Jonah shouted.

He'd stopped in the parking lot and then threw his arm out in my direction. "My coach is here! From camp! Can I say hi?"

As predicted, her smile fell. She followed where Jonah's arm was gesturing to, and her shoulders slumped a fraction.

Dang. I didn't want to cause her stress. I wanted her to know I was there to make her life easier. Not harder.

I lifted my hand as our gazes met and smirked. *Come on, come sit with me. You know you want to.* I silently pleaded with my eyes, *daring* her to take the risk.

She said something to Jonah, and his arm fell. Together, the two of them headed straight for the bakery, Mellie's Cakes, next door.

Right before I lost them from sight, she looked back and smiled at me, shaking her head like I was ridiculous.

Now *that* look, I was used to. Typical Holly. She might have walls, and she might try to act tough, but deep down, she was as tenderhearted as they came.

I took it as a small win that she didn't ignore me completely.

My food would come. If they hadn't come out by the time I was done eating, I'd go after them. Scratch that. If they came out while I was still eating or waiting, I'd go say hi.

Wouldn't want to disappoint Jonah, after all.

TWENTY-FIVE
HOLLY

"What's he doing here?" Jonah asked, peppering me with this thousandth question of the day as he scanned the large menu board in front of us and drooled over all the cupcakes, beignets, donuts in the cases. "Camp is done, and he doesn't live here. That's weird, right, Mommy?"

Not so weird, actually. I should have known he wouldn't leave. Should have known hoping he would leave would make my hopes come true.

He'd said he was staying. He was staying.

So much for avoiding him.

"Promise we can go say hi when we get our treats?" He bounced on the balls of his feet as he asked.

"I promised, Jonah, and you know I keep my promises."

"It's the right thing to do," he sang.

I closed my eyes and shook my head. What a great kid. Sometimes I wondered how much I was actually teaching him, how good of a person I was raising, but then he said things like that in his sweet little voice, and I wanted to trap him at this age forever.

Although I was pretty sure *every* age he hit so far was my favorite.

I said a quick prayer I'd keep feeling that way as he grew and turned into a preteen and then a teenager.

"Well hi, friends!" Millie pushed through the back door, her blond hair pulled back into a bun, her eyes glimmering with excitement. To date, I wasn't sure I'd ever seen her frown. She had that perpetual happiness about her that made me envious. "Early for treats today, isn't it, Jonah? You must have been a *very* good boy."

He gave her a serious nod. "Yup. I was. Made my bed without being asked and everything."

He flung out his arms as wide as they went.

"Well." Millie laughed. "Sounds like you definitely earned a treat. How can I help?"

"Only two and some ice cream, Jonah," I reminded him.

The extra two treats were bribes. Our friends couldn't join us at the park, and he'd been so disappointed. Maybe it wasn't the best parenting strategy, but it worked in a pinch.

"And *two* scoops of ice cream in a bowl. Superman and bubble gum."

"I'm on it. Anything for you, Holly?"

"I'm good."

The downfall to letting him pick treats was I didn't have enough money for my own, but I didn't mind. It was only ten in the morning. I'd save my treat for when I could dive into the ice cream already in my freezer.

"All right, then." She gathered our things, rang us up, and as we were leaving and Jonah was merrily sucking a spoonful of Superman ice cream, I hoped he forgot all about Graham.

"Now can I see my coach?" He slurped off the rest of

his spoon and grinned at me. His teeth were bright blue, and he had a ring of pink growing around his lips.

I held back my sigh. "Sure."

Some days, I really wished his memory wasn't so great.

I didn't hesitate to go next door. This time, my arrival would surprise Graham instead of the other way around. Just once, I'd like to see him thrown off-kilter like he made me feel.

Britta's and Millie's were owned by a grandmother and granddaughter. Millie went to a culinary arts and sciences program after high school and returned wanting to open up her own bakery. There wasn't a lot of property available at the time, and she'd had little funds. To help, Britta cut back the size of her restaurant, renovated it so Millie could have her own space, and then slashed her hours to only serve breakfast and lunch.

Aunt Caroline had been thrilled with this news, and for a few years until more restaurants were built and opened, the only place in town to get any decent dinner was The Grille. Max's Tavern was around, but they served mostly burgers and bar food, so Caroline practically ran a monopoly on serving locals and tourists dinner. Sales and profits soared for Caroline. I'd never seen her happier.

Because of the connection between Britta and Millie, it was a locally-kept secret that you could take your food from one establishment to another, so I pushed through the front door, and with my shoes weighed down by my lead weights of hesitation, we entered Britta's.

Graham had a bite of fried chicken at his mouth. As I caught his eye at my arrival, he froze.

A slow, smirking grin stretched across his face, and it was that look that made my heart skip a beat. That stupid, attractive smirk.

"Hi, Mr. Coach!" Jonah cried. He slipped past me and hustled to the table, sliding into a chair across from Graham like he'd been invited.

I rolled my eyes at him and then followed.

"This is a surprise." Graham set his fork down and leaned back in his chair. "What brings you two here?"

"It's *my* town," I drawled, but it lacked heat. Somehow, Graham slithered past the weakest spots in my defenses. "Why are you still here?"

Next to me, Jonah happily slurped on his ice cream.

Graham glanced at Jonah, and then his eyes pierced mine, freezing me in my chair. "One, you don't own the town, so I can be anywhere I'd like, and two"—he leaned in closer and lowered his voice—"I think you know exactly why I'm here."

Warmth flooded me from my chest to my toes. I shook it off before the heat reached my brain and burned my common sense. "You shouldn't be. There's no point."

"And I think you're worth fighting for."

"We're fighting?" Jonah asked, and Graham chuckled, smiling at him.

"No, buddy. Your mom and I aren't fighting. Fighting *for* something is trying to win."

"You want to win my mommy?"

A slow, sleek smile stretched across Graham's face that made my toes curl in my faux Birks. "You bet I am."

"If you win, what's the prize?" He slurped a spoon of bubble gum ice cream. Bless the innocence of little kids.

I reached across his bowl and grabbed a napkin. "Wipe your chin," I told him before glaring back at Graham. "There *is* no prize."

He smirked right back. "Oh...I think there is."

"SO, what are you two doing today?" Graham slipped his hands to his hips and tipped his chin to the sky. He and Jonah talked about hockey, and Graham finished and paid for his meal.

I should have left sooner, but once Jonah got started on something, it was hard to get him to redirect. Also, there was a part of me who enjoyed watching him light up talking about something he enjoyed with a man who understood it. I was trying to learn and definitely knew more than I did in those few games I saw in college, but there were some things that I still couldn't help him with.

And God bless the person who ever saw *me* on a pair of ice skates. After the first few attempts of trying to teach Graham to skate, I gave up and put him in lessons. I spent more time falling and sliding than Graham, and he'd been three.

"We're going home," I said. It was the one place where he couldn't follow, unless he'd done more stalking. Someone in town would tell him what neighborhood I lived in.

"We are?" Jonah whined. "I wanted to see Paul. Or *maybe*, Mr. Graham could take me skating?"

His eyes lit up with excitement. I sucked in a breath. *This* was why I didn't want Graham here. Jonah would latch on to him, Graham would someday leave, and then my boy would know the pain of watching someone you care about walk away.

Graham watched me like he saw every fear flicker through my brain and gave Jonah a soft smile. "Maybe another day, Jonah. I have to head back home today."

"You're *leaving?*" Jonah cried.

"Oh darn," I quipped. "So soon?" I snapped my fingers together in an *aw-shucks* gesture.

Graham's chest shook with laughter, something that wasn't hard to miss since his shirt could have been painted on to him.

"Don't get too disappointed. I only packed for camp. I'm heading home to grab clothes and work things."

Shoot. I should have already considered that.

"But you'll be back, right, Mr. Graham? And then you can take me skating and help me?" Jonah's tone was so pleading even as his little chin wobbled. He'd been around Graham for a few hours, and already he was getting attached.

I couldn't bring myself to stop it even seeing the ending play out.

"Of course. As soon as it's okay with your mom. Just not today."

"All right." His shoulders slumped, and he glanced up at me. "Can I go back to the park?"

"Look for cars and stay where I can see you." The park was right across the empty street, less than fifty yards away.

"Sweet!" He held out his tiny fist to Graham, who returned the fist pump and then took off running.

"Cars!" I shouted, cupping my hands around my mouth before he could run into the street.

He pulled to an abrupt stop at the curb, looked back at me, grinned and waved, and then looked both ways. My eyes followed the movement, and once he was across the road safely, I turned back to Graham. "I don't want you here."

"I plan to change your mind. We still have things to talk about, and until you can give me a few hours to do that, I have no plans to leave."

"And if I give you that time?"

"I intend to use every second to convince you that taking a chance on me isn't a risk."

He was so cocky, so sure of himself. It irritated me and drew me in with equal measure. He'd always done that to me. Made my head spin and made my feet feel firmly planted and secure.

I had my eyes on Jonah at the park and didn't *dare* look at Graham to see the smirk he'd proudly wear.

"When?" I finally muttered. Best to get this conversation done and out of the way.

"When's the slowest night at work, or when can you get away?"

It was Saturday, by far our busiest day.

"Tomorrow," I admitted. Maybe Graham would give up this foolish notion that he could find all those missing puzzle pieces from years ago and make us fit.

"Tomorrow then." He grabbed his keys from his pocket and spun the ring around his thumb. "And do me a favor?"

"I thought I already was."

He chuckled. "You've gotten sassier since college. I like it. Unblock my number."

"How do you know I haven't deleted it?"

"You haven't." He rocked back on his heels.

"How very presumptuous of you."

Graham's grin continued to grow larger. "Maybe, but I know you have it. You might have done what you thought was right, but that doesn't mean you wanted to say goodbye to me completely."

I glared at him.

He smirked. "Tell me you deleted it, then, and be honest about it."

I was a lot of things, but I wasn't a liar. "How do you get that large head through the neck hole of your shirts?"

His hands went to the bottom hem of his shirt and curled around it. "Want me to show you?"

"No," I cried and yanked my gaze back on Jonah. But I was smiling, and it seemed stuck there. No matter how hard I tried, I couldn't wipe it away.

"Unblock me, Holly." I swore he'd moved closer. "And don't skip out on seeing me tomorrow. I won't give up nearly as easily as I did all those years ago."

With that parting threat, he turned and whistled as he headed back to his gray truck.

I hadn't seen it when we hurried up to Mellie's, but I wouldn't forget it.

If he was intent on sticking around, I still believed it was smarter for me to avoid him.

Maybe after tomorrow night, he'd finally see how beneficial that would be to both of us.

I slid the bill and folder onto the customer's table and cleared away their plates. "Thank you for stopping by tonight. Y'all have a great night."

"Thanks. You too." The woman smiled up at me while the gentleman with her pulled the bill folder toward him.

Dinner rush was insanity. I couldn't figure out what made tonight different than any other, and I certainly wasn't complaining, but for the first time in over a year, we still had people waiting outside on picnic tables for dinner, and it was well after seven. Usually we were winding down by now, but I couldn't move quick enough tonight to help bus tables and take orders and deliver food.

The bonus was that it made time go by faster, and while I swerved around tables and chairs to dump the plates in my hand into a bin, I didn't have time to think of Graham or tomorrow night.

I dumped the plates and took the cleaner and cloth to tables in the old smoking section that needed to be cleaned. The sooner I got the tables cleaned and cleared, the sooner diners could get their food and then eventually, give me a minute to breathe. Luckily for me, since I insisted Caroline take Saturdays off, she and Paul kept Jonah for a sleepover. He was taken care of.

Graham was gone, at least for tonight, and all I had left were the worries I was trying not to think about until Dr. Myers called.

It had all started with stomach pain. At first it was worsening cramps around my cycle. Then the cramps lingered. My stomach swelled slightly, but not really enough for anyone but me to notice due to the fit of most of my clothes. I'd thought I was retaining water. Maybe eating too many fries. But when I started working out, substituting fries for salad, and things continued to worsen, I figured it was time for a visit. I'd convinced myself it was all in my mind for a while. Things in my life weren't typically good, and since I was actually settled and Jonah was mostly happy and doing well in school, I was just creating a problem in my mind because I didn't know how to relax and be at peace.

But then my bloodwork came back a little *off*, according to my doctor. My Pap smear showed inconclusive results.

Now, I was waiting, but everything on Google told me what I'd already started to suspect. And the worry in my doctor's tone didn't help. I'd set to searching online, and all the results came back worse than the one before…

Something was most definitely wrong with me.

Cancer. It was the worst possible conclusion to jump to. I was far too young. And yet, it was there every time I searched, making my head spin with fear and worry, not for me, but for Jonah. Of course my life wouldn't be as pretty as everyone else's. Of course something else would go wrong just when I finally had my feet on firm footing. It was the way my life rolled.

"Hey, Holly." I jumped at hearing my name and spun.

"Hi, Emily. What's up." I quickly scanned the restaurant.

"Can I help finish cleaning the tables for you? All my customers are taken care of and getting ready to leave."

Oh, thank goodness. More people leaving meant a slow-down was coming.

And getting out of cleaning? I handed her the cloth. "Knock yourself out."

While she cleaned the tables, I cleared off the remainder of them. I swooped over to two tables that had moved their plates to the side, and soon I was carrying back an overly filled bin to get back to the dishwasher.

"Hi Jimmy, more work."

He swiped the back of his hand across his forehead. "Busy night."

"Don't worry, I won't keep you past quitting time."

"Thanks," the teenager muttered in that sullen way they perfected. After hiring so many, I knew it well.

After washing my hands and grabbing a quick drink of water, I headed back to the hostess stand. Fifteen minutes later, all the people waiting were seated. I let Emily and Annie handle the tables so they could earn the tips, and I helped with drink orders and cleaning the hostess stand.

"There you are!" Trina said, breathless as she hurried in. "I've been calling you. I'm *so* sorry we couldn't come hang out with you today."

I smiled. Trina was lovely. Older than me, sure, but since our kids were all the same ages, the age difference never really mattered. It was when she and Ashley prattled on about married life that I felt like a third wheel.

"What's up?" I continued wiping down the menus and tucking them in the basket next to me. "Are you alone?"

"No, Cole's parking the SUV and bringing the girls in.

He just got called in, and since I was just starting to cook dinner, I scrapped it. Figured the girls and I could hang out with you for a bit." She glanced at the restaurant behind me. "Unless you're too busy?"

"I'm never too busy for you. Everything okay?" Cole rarely got called in.

"Should be. I think someone got sick or something, I don't know. He'll tell me later."

She shrugged it off like it was no big deal, but every time I thought about his job, my stomach tightened into a tiny ball. They saw the worst, and they met people at their worst moments. I'd had a front-row seat to all of it once, and it was something you never forgot.

"All right. Let me get you girls a table."

"Thanks, Holly."

As I turned, Junie, and I knew it was her because her quiet voice was permanently stuck at level ten, shouted, "Mommy! We're here!"

I shook my head, chuckling at the wild one who was still only six, but man, was she a handful. Boys had their own energy about them for sure, and sometimes I didn't know if Jonah was calmer than most because it was just me and him most of the time, or if it was his personality, but Junie rolled through life like a tumbleweed with a tambourine stuck inside.

I set them out at a table where Junie's volume wouldn't pierce the eardrums of the closest customers and set down the children's menu, crayons, and Trina's menu.

"Hi, Miss Holly."

"Ella." I bent down and kissed her cheek. "How are you today?"

"Good. Mom and Mama Trina took us shopping today."

She held out her hands. Her fingertips were covered in tiny flower stickers. "Look what I got."

"Oh, that's so pretty. I like the yellow ones."

"They're my favorite, too." She slipped into the booth all the way to the edge, and Junie bounced into the one on the other side.

"Mama Trina?" I whispered, brows raised in surprise.

"It's a new thing. Marie seems okay with it, so we're letting the girls set that pace."

"It's sweet."

She grinned at her stepdaughters and shook her head, like she couldn't believe this was her life. "It's wonderful."

I didn't know all the specifics of Trina's life, but I gathered I knew more than most. Since Trina's ex-husband was abusive and was also now in prison, we didn't need a bingo card to determine which of our lives had been harder. We'd both had our own unique challenges. I always figured that was why she'd been so kind to me at first. As if the pain and loneliness in me called to some part of her.

Sometimes I was surprised at how kind and trusting she could still be. Although, she'd grown up with a kind and stable family. When she returned to Deer Creek, she had a loving support system, whereas I was still learning how to trust mine.

Other days, I saw the darkness that still lingered in her eyes and knew every moment for her was a battle.

She made me want to be stronger, be a fighter.

"Drinks?" I asked them all once Trina seated herself, slipped her purse strap off her shoulder, and settled it between her and Ella.

"Shirley Temple!" Junie shouted. "With extra cherries!"

"Junie," Trina warned, and pressed her finger to her lips.

"Please," she whisper-shouted.

"I can do that." Junie was the main reason why I had to double our maraschino cherry order.

"Me, too, please," Ella said, her voice sweet and serene.

"Lemonade," Trina requested, "and I think we know what we'd like to eat. You girls decided on the way here, right?"

"Wonderful."

I scribbled down their orders: a BLT for Ella, chicken nuggets with extra sauce for Junie, and the chicken fried steak special for Trina.

"Be right back with your drinks," I told them all. "And if I have a free minute, I'll come join you."

"Perfect," Trina said.

She reached across the table to open up the crayon box for Junie as I walked away.

I returned with their drinks, praised the girls' coloring sheets, and played a quick game of tic-tac-toe before checking the rest of the restaurant. There wasn't a menu in sight, so I took that as a good sign that all the orders were in. Some of the newer tables were already eating, and after checking with Emma and Annie, who assured me all was good, I went and took a quick break.

"Whew." I sighed as I plopped down next to Junie. Her little body bounced with the movement, and her coloring went sideways.

"Hey." She frowned at the smudge.

"Sorry, sweetie." To make it all better, I kissed her cheek.

"You're busy tonight," Trina said.

"I know. It was surprising, and I'm thankful, but trust me, I am *wiped*."

"I bet. How was the park?" There was a tone I wasn't sure I liked in her sweet little voice, but I shook it off.

"It was fine. Normal. Jonah was bummed y'all weren't there, but since you are *now*, any chance he can hang out at your place tomorrow for a couple hours?"

"Why?" She propped her elbows onto the table, lifted one arm, and dropped her chin onto one of her fists. "Need time to spend alone with the *friend* you were sitting with at Britta's."

So this was why she was here.

"I should have known. Who told you? Britta?"

Trina laughed, and it sounded like sunshine, light and airy and full of goodness. "Please. If you think Mellie wasn't spreading *all* the tea to everyone who loves you today, then you've forgotten what this town is like."

Heat burned my neck and rose to my cheeks. When I made the choice to try to knock Graham off his calm, steady demeanor this morning, I hadn't considered what people would say. "He's an old friend. That's it."

"But he is who you're seeing tomorrow?"

My shoulders fell. I took a peek around us to make sure it wasn't anyone who cared about my life enough to listen. "He's the friend from college, Trina. The one I told you about?"

"The *boy*?"

"Boys are gross," Junie chimed in around a mouthful of nuggets.

"Not Jonah, though," Ella said and glared at her sister. "He's nice. Fun, too."

"Thanks, girls." I turned back to Trina. "Yeah."

"How'd this happen?"

I told her the story about camp, Graham showing up to eat afterward, and his plans for the rest of the summer. Her eyes widened with every new fact until they were as large as salad bowls before she finally blinked.

"Do you want my advice?"

"I have a feeling I'll get it anyway."

She giggled, and her gaze flicked to the girls before coming back to mine. "Take the risk, Holly. Trust me, I get the fear. I understand the need for self-preservation. I do, truly. But *take* the risk. Not all of them end badly. I'm living proof that sometimes those risks end up with the greatest rewards."

She tipped her head to the side. As if I needed the reminder that Ella and Junie were the best things to happen to her.

"It's scary," I admitted. "So few things have gone right for me."

"I understand." She grabbed Ella's place mat, slipping it out from beneath the plate, and then grabbed a crayon. She scribbled something on the back and slid it toward me. "Trust me, Holly. I understand fear. I also know we can be afraid and do the scary thing anyway."

Her fingernail tapped on the paper, and I looked down.

I'm pregnant.

Immediately tears burned my eyes, and I sniffed, careful to keep my tears hidden from Ella's soulful gaze. Like Jonah, she saw too much and understood far more.

"Really?" I mouthed.

She pressed her lips together and smiled. There was a sheen in her own eyes as she nodded.

"Holly?" I jumped in surprise at Emma suddenly at the side of the table.

"Yes? What is it?"

"We need some help in the back. Jimmy's having a hard time with the washer."

"Okay." Okay. I breathed out a breath to settle myself from the surprise of Trina's announcement and all my fears swirling inside me. I slid out of the booth. "Guess it's back to work," I told Trina.

"Think about what I said."

I promised her I would and headed to the back. I hadn't meant to tell Trina everything, but a small whisper in my brain corrected me. *Didn't you?*

Maybe I had. Maybe it was because I knew exactly what she'd say. Sometimes it still felt like I needed someone's permission to try to have my life be more about surviving. That it was okay to want happiness.

The question was, was Graham the one who could help lead me there? Or was my upcoming doctor's appointment going to send it all crashing back to the ground?

Me: Taking a chance. Am I unblocked?

I sent the text late. When I got back into town, the parking lot to The Grille had been crammed full with trucks and cars and SUVs. Every part of me had screamed at me to turn in, to see her, to make her listen. Instead, I drove past. If she was busy, she wouldn't want me there.

Once I got inside the rental, though, nerves hit, and I spent the night far too restless. If there was a rink open, I would have spent the time burning off all the nervous energy collecting inside me. It was hours later, after ten, when I finally found my courage and sent the text.

Holly was a wild card and had her own set of rules for living. She opened up to very few and kept the others out with a ring of barbed wire at the top of a cement wall. But there were moments where she forgot to be angry and scared.

Moments where she laughed freely. Where eyes shone with true joy and where her body wasn't always tense and ready to flee. Where she actually relaxed and allowed herself to be in the moment.

All I wanted to do was give her more of those, without taking away or ignoring the trials she had to reach to get there.

I scrubbed my hands over my face and groaned. She could ghost me tomorrow, although it wasn't like I couldn't find her. And this town was small. It'd be easier to find her.

But I wanted her to *want* it. I needed her to open the door a crack, peer at me through something more than a peephole and a chained door.

To most it wouldn't be much, but to Holly, it'd be terrifying.

My phone buzzed on the couch, and I practically dove for it.

"Smooth," I muttered to myself and flipped it over so I could see the screen.

Holly: **Five-thirty, okay? I'll come to you and bring pizza.**

Like I'd let her pay for my food.

I shot her my address and then—

Me: **I'll order pizza. Send me your and Jonah's Scalecki's order.**

Thank goodness for the earlier conversation with Billy.

Holly: **Jonah will be at a friend's.**

I'd have her to myself for a few hours. Perfect.

My phone buzzed again with her pizza order, simple pepperoni and mushroom, like she'd eaten before. I should have known she wouldn't have changed it.

Me: **Thanks, Holly. I promise you won't regret it.**

A thumb appeared on the text, and my heart squeezed. A thumbs-up? Really?

Then...

Holly: **We'll see ;-)**

Ahh...there was her sass.

I grinned, and to be a smart aleck, I gave her post a thumbs-up and tossed my phone onto the coffee table. Let her stew on that stupid thumbs-up emoji like I thought she was going to make me do. Served the stubborn girl right.

Shoving off the couch, now that at least plans were set, I headed to the kitchen and grabbed a beer. Holly hadn't drank in college, and I doubted that had changed, but I still wanted to have drinks on hand. Maybe after-dinner snacks if I could get her to stay for a bit longer. There wasn't much in the rental as far as things to do, and I hadn't seen so much as a deck of cards for entertainment.

I'd go get those things in the morning, heading to Boone if I had to. It might be safer. I highly doubted Holly wanted people knowing about me, and spending too much time in town would make the whispers start.

I vividly remembered how she handled them before—with shame and fear and hiding in an office so she didn't have to deal with it.

Never again. Now, I understood, even if people's reactions were despicable, but the last thing I wanted was to make things harder for her.

Flipping open my laptop, I got to work. First a grocery order, and then I got nosy.

Surprisingly, there were a lot of school districts nearby. A lot of struggling districts.

It was probably *far* too soon. I was probably bordering on losing my mind.

That didn't stop me from looking for or realizing I was grinning when I found an open coaching position.

I hit apply before I could second-guess myself.

Who knows what could happen?

I could always say no if it amounted to anything.

THERE WAS *NOT* a lot to do in Deer Creek, especially when trying to avoid spending too much time in town. I spent the morning hiking around Crystal Mountain and then went to Boone for groceries. In addition, I was now the proud owner of some pretty lame board games and card games, and even though it wasn't exactly in my teacher budget, I upgraded the television in the rental and bought a larger TV. Theirs was so tiny I felt like my dad, wearing reader glasses while trying to watch it from the living room.

I told myself I'd take it home with me, I could use a new one anyway, or I could take it into my classroom. For what? Who knows. But six weeks without a lot to do but watch TV would drive me crazy if I had to keep watching it on something you could only see clearly from four feet away.

It was setup.

The pizza was ordered.

The fridge and pantry were stocked with drinks and snacks.

The only thing I had left to do was to figure out what to say to get Holly to give me a chance to rejoin her life, and let's face it. I'd never been great at that.

If I could figure out a way to stop sweating through my shirts and dry my clammy palms from nerves, that'd be nice, too.

If only this was happening in Denver. I'd be comfortable in my own home. I'd be more confident.

A laugh burst from me. That was a lie.

It was Holly. I'd always be nervous.

That she hadn't backed out at the last minute was a small miracle.

My phone rang, and I dove for it. "Maybe I spoke too

soon," I muttered and flipped it over. I expected to see Holly's name, and instead, a grin broke out.

I answered it. "Hey, Eli. You still alive?"

I'd called him when I was going to be in town for the camp, but he'd told me he was working three twelve-hour shifts and didn't see how he'd be able to get away.

"Barely," he groaned. "Crashed last night and was barely able to get out of bed today."

He was in his residency at Boone Community Hospital. The guy could have gone anywhere after finishing med school at Chapel Hill, but his first choice was to stay in North Carolina. Seemed the boy originally from the Upper Peninsula of Michigan, didn't want to go home and wanted to stay far away from brutal winters that could last up to eight months out of the year.

"Sucks, man."

School days were long, and I often worked on grading papers for an hour or two at night, and that was after hockey practice, but even then, I was getting to spend hours playing the sport I loved. Eli was investing every second of his day into saving lives and healing diseases and cancer.

"Listen, yeah...I've been debating this, and I can't say too much. I'm not even sure if I should tell you—"

"Spit it out, Eli."

"I saw Holly." My breath left in a heavy whoosh, and I fell onto the stool at the kitchen bar. "The hospital?"

I chuckled. I hadn't told him I'd also seen her. Had considered it, but I was waiting until he was off his shifts to give him the news that I was closer than he thought I was.

"Blew me away to see her. You okay? I mean, I know it's been years, but..."

"I actually saw her myself."

"No shit. Really?"

"Hockey camp. Turns out she has a son who was there."

"What the...? A son?" He paused, and it took him a minute to ask, "Yours?"

"Not a chance, and it's actually a long story that's not mine to share. But yeah, so I'm glad you called, because you should know I'm here. In Deer Creek."

Silence hit, and then Eli didn't say anything, and my pulse kicked up. The man had mastered the silent pause when shock hit. It wasn't exactly the excitement I thought he'd share.

"You don't...are you okay? That I'm here? It's not forever, but I figured since I saw her and we talked some—"

"Has she told you?"

"About her son, Jonah? Yeah, she told me all about that. Him," I quickly corrected. Jonah wasn't a *that* or a thing. He was a cute little kid.

"Not her son. Shit." He cursed again, and now that kicked up pulse started racing when I remembered what he said earlier. She was at the hospital. *Why?*

"Eli," I said with a warning tone.

"I can't...I can't say much, but well, shit. I saw her leaving her gynecology appointment." So she had a woman's exam. Big deal. "She didn't exactly seem happy to see me, Graham, and then a nurse came up to her, handed her a card, and said she could call if she had any questions before the biopsy results came back."

"What?" I was glad I was sitting. "Biopsy? What... *hers?*"

"It could be anything. Probably should be minding my own business, but yeah. I mean, I don't know what's going on, but I could find out."

"No." Absolutely not. "You're not breaking into a patient's files for me, Eli, and besides." I paused and cleared my throat. "She's going to be at my rental any minute for dinner, actually."

"Really?" He chuckled then, more surprised than amused. "I would *not* have imagined she would have given you the time of day again."

"I can be persuasive." Tenacious, actually, was what she called me, but my humor quickly faded. "What else could it be? Give me something other than the worst-case scenario that's running through my mind."

My mom died of cancer. For weeks before that diagnosis, I'd heard that whispered word when my parents didn't think I could hear.

"It could be a lot of things. Benign would mean not cancer. But that could still mean a growth of some sort." He sighed through the phone and then yawned. "It could come back as nothing, too. Scar tissue? Maybe an infection? It's hard to tell without knowing her symptoms or why she had it done. And even then, it's all guessing and hoping until the results come back."

"Yeah." Dammit. I didn't want to know this. I *shouldn't* know this. "I should go. I have to figure out what to do with this."

"I'm sorry, Graham. I probably should have kept my mouth shut, but I was so surprised, and then I didn't know if that was something you'd want to know anyway."

"It was. It *is*. I'm glad to know it." Would she tell me? Was it any of my business? And now that I knew...what did I do with it? "I'm just not sure if it's my business yet."

And wasn't that a hard thing to realize? Holly and I could have very different ideas of how we wanted this night to go. I definitely knew we had different ideas on how the next six weeks should go.

"So, you're in Deer Creek, then."

"Yeah." I laughed a little and looked down at the floor. "Figured I had six weeks with nothing to do, so why not?"

"Why not?" He chuckled with me and then sobered. "You talked to your dad? Told him?"

"Not yet."

I did, all those years ago when I was worked up about the fact her dad killed Sophie. My dad showed up at one of our games in Raleigh, something I'd expected and known was happening. Having my dad in the crowd supporting me, despite growing up in Raleigh, always meant the world to me. After Mom died, he was all I had. Thank God he hadn't fallen apart like Holly's dad had. It took him two minutes of watching that game to clock that something was wrong with me.

After the game, our coach gave me permission to go have dinner with my dad instead of the team. I met him at a restaurant across from our hotel. He hadn't let go of our hug on the sidewalk outside before he said, "Tell me what's going on."

I broke down in tears. Right there on the sidewalk in the city where I grew up, where anyone could see me. I couldn't hold it in. Not then. Not around my dad.

It all spilled out over drinks and appetizers, and by the end, all Dad said was, "I'm sorry, Son. Sorry you're going through something so difficult."

No judgment, at least not verbally. No anger or disappointment. Life was life, and we all got kicked in the teeth once in a while. He understood that more than most.

Now, if I told him where I was and what I was doing, I'm not sure he'd initially be so understanding and accepting, but my dad was a good man. One of the best. He'd come around eventually. What I knew for certain was that

Holly would never sense or feel a hint of his doubts if he had them. He'd keep that contained.

Eli sighed. "Be smart, Graham. I like the girl. But she put you through the wringer once before. Not sure I want to see it happen again."

"I appreciate that, but I'm a big boy."

"No kidding. I saw your last Instagram pic. You should work out more. Eat less fat or something."

"Shut up." I laughed. "I gotta go. She'll be here soon."

"We'll get together soon, yeah?"

"Send me your schedule. You're the busy one."

"Ain't that the truth."

We hung up.

I checked my phone to make sure I didn't miss any texts or calls and then glanced at the clock.

Great. I had five minutes to pace and wonder and worry.

Biopsy. Hadn't her life already been hard enough?

TWENTY-EIGHT
HOLLY

I pulled into the resort's guest parking, and my stomach dropped like I was going down the first hill on a roller coaster. Seeing Graham again was more difficult than I'd ever imagined, and I'd definitely imagined running into him on a street. But I imagined him married, maybe. With a child or two of his own. I'd imagined seeing him in the distance, holding his wife's hand, teasing her with that arrogant smirk of his, promising all the fun they'd have later. Perhaps I did it for my own self-preservation. If I imagined him having the life he was meant to have, it was easier to let him go.

That I ran into him in Boone was surprising enough. That he was insisting on staying in Deer Creek was completely unexpected.

Was it bad? It should be. I shouldn't have unblocked his number. I should have told him to leave.

Graham had a way of loosening all the bolts on my locked walls, and six plus years later I still hadn't fully found a way to keep him out. Worse, given the last day to consider it, I was having trouble remembering all the reasons why I should.

Goodness. The sheer audacity of him to even consider lifting his shirt yesterday. Who was I kidding? I'd thought about that moment, tried to remember from before what she looked like. He was older now, but stronger. He'd stayed on his workout regime, that was for sure.

I parked my car, turned it off, and climbed out.

With a heavy sigh, my shoulders fell. I was heading into the belly of the beast with no protection.

The condo Graham got was on the first floor, according to his text, but I didn't need to get it to know. This was one of the oldest resorts on the mountain, or at least it'd been around since I was born. While locals might not spend the nights at the resort, we'd all had our fair share of day trips to do some tubing and skiing. Cole and Trina took Jonah and me last winter, my first time being able to afford such a thing, and we'd had a blast zipping down the hills right by the string of condos where Graham was staying. A three-story building, you only had to go inside to get the elevator upstairs. The downstairs condos all had parking on one side, and then the view of the slopes on the other.

I headed up to Graham's door with trepidation taking over, slowing my steps and stealing the warmth from my fingers. I'd be in such a better position to see him if I knew what I wanted. If I'd thought anything I wanted was possible.

My hand lifted, and my knuckles barely grazed the door before it flung open. Warm air from the inside rushed toward me, and it took all my nerves and fears right along with it.

There he was, arm extended, same arrogant grin, same well-built body. All that caring expression and soft eyes plastered on his face for the entire world to see, and it was directed at me.

He reminded me of exactly how he used to look when I'd come to see him. Absolutely thrilled, with maybe a hint of honor. I'd never quite understood it, but man, it felt just as good now as it did then.

"Stalking me?" I teased.

"Anxiously pacing." He grinned right back and stepped aside. "Can't even lie about that. Half expected you to text me and cancel."

I shrugged and stepped inside, slipping out of my sandals as I did. "I half expected to do it myself."

The door closed behind me, forcing Graham to move closer. Man, he was tall. I wasn't short, but I'd always liked the fact I'd had to lift my chin to meet his gaze. Those dark eyes of his were richer, no less darker, and I was certain there were more gold flecks rimming the pupils. "It's good to see you."

I swallowed down the lump in my throat, but nothing could wash away the goose bumps at his admission.

Graham had always had a way of making me feel special. Worthy. Sure, I'd maybe gone to him with a hand extended in self-defense, ready for the shoe to drop, but I'd had a reason for it then. I had a reason for it. Now, as I looked around his condo, his laptop opened and on the coffee table, and a glass of water set next to it, I couldn't grasp *why*.

Why would I keep pushing away someone who wanted to be close to me? Hadn't I learned in the last six years that life required company and help? That friends and community made life *better*?

I cleared my throat and grinned at him. "You're still the same," I told him, and I meant it as a compliment.

His smirk grew. "In some ways, I'm even better."

"So arrogant."

He knocked me with his elbow. "You like it."

God help me, I did. I really did.

"Dinner should be here in a few minutes. I wanted us to have some time to talk first."

"What's first?" I asked and couldn't believe I was being so blithe about the whole thing. "My family drama or your perfect life?"

"Not perfect," he said, and while his grin flattened, his teasing tone didn't. "Well-adjusted and healthy, maybe."

Same thing, I figured, but what would I know?

"Want anything to drink? Water or tea?"

"Tea?" Back in college that was one of the first things I'd asked for.

Graham shrugged, like he wasn't ready to admit he remembered the conversation I was. "I know how to purchase more than condiments these days."

A soft laugh fell from my lips. "I'll take water, but thanks."

"Kettle's above the coffee pot if you change your mind." He reached into the fridge and proved his statement about purchasing more than ketchup correct. It was stocked with vegetables, drinks, and a variety of containers that looked like yogurt.

He came back with a bottled water and handed it to me. "Thank you."

"I'm assuming you still don't dhink..." He let that thought trail off.

I shook my head. "Not really, maybe something occasionally, but definitely not when I'm driving or when I have to pick up Jonah."

"Understood." He nodded. "Mind if I have a glass of wine?"

"Of course not." He turned and went to the kitchen. I opened my water while he grabbed a corkscrew. Halfway bringing the water to my mouth, I paused, watching him work.

How was it possible for so many muscles to *pop* using a corkscrew? I didn't even know if I'd seen that many arm muscles. Bottle open, he grabbed a wineglass, and while he filled it, I went and took a seat at one of the chairs.

Curling my feet up underneath me, my gaze drifted toward the ski slopes. It was early enough that the sun was still high, but it lit up the slopes and hills of the mountains for miles. In an hour or two, twilight would come, and the tops of the trees would turn everything to beautiful pinks and oranges and purples. Deer Creek had a lot of faults, and life there hadn't been easy, but there was no arguing that I'd grown up and spent my entire life in one of the most gorgeous areas a person could live.

"What are you thinking?" Graham asked as he took a seat in the middle of the couch and slapped his laptop closed.

"What?"

"You had your thinking face on."

I laughed. "I have a thinking face?"

"Yep." He leaned back on the couch, legs bent and spread. He cupped his glass of wine gently, like he'd learned how to hold a glass with perfected manners, and draped one arm over the back of the couch. A king on his throne came to mind.

He said no more. I bit my tongue so I didn't ask what it looked like.

"Huh," I said instead.

Graham laughed. "You still don't give anything away, either."

"Trust me," I drawled. "I've given away plenty."

It was meant as a joke, but it fell as flat as his expression. Pushing his lips out to the side, he nodded. Apparently I wasn't the only one with a thinking face.

"How long until the pizza is coming?"

"Why? In a hurry to get out of here?" There was no teasing glint in his eye, only narrowed eyes filled with worry.

"No. How'd you hear about Scalecki's?"

"Met Billy at the store across the street yesterday morning."

"Ah...he's a good man. He give you any other tips?"

"Said Caroline's food isn't too shabby, but I already knew that. And to answer your question, pizza will be here any minute."

"So..."

"I never told you why Piper said Sophie and I were engaged."

"So we're just gonna jump into it all then."

Graham chuckled, like he thought my sarcasm was adorable, and sipped his wine. "If I'm only guaranteed a few hours, then yeah."

"All right." I tried to relax back into the chair but found it impossible. Not because of the furniture. It was worn and comfortable with large armrests. Any other day, I could sit curled up in the chair with a blanket, a cup of tea, and enjoy the view with a good book.

Tonight wasn't that night.

"Hit me with it," I said and leaned forward to set my water down.

"I told you that we all grew up as friends." At my nod,

he continued. "Sophie and I were obviously really close. I can hardly think of a time when I didn't know her. I'm pretty sure our moms became best friends when they were pregnant or something."

I smiled. It would have been so lovely to have been friends with someone for that long.

My heart thumped in my ears. He'd had such a different life than mine. Outside of losing our moms, we had practically nothing in common, and yet, what he had was what I always wanted. What I wanted to give Jonah.

I opened my mouth to tell him all of it, but the words stuck to my throat.

"Piper." Graham sighed. "Piper moved in later, around the time we were probably Jonah's age, now. All three of us were best friends for a long time."

"I remember."

"She didn't have an easy life, and all those years ago, I didn't think it was my story to share, but really, her family was a mess. She had an older brother who was in trouble all the time and a dad who really wasn't nice to her or her mom. He cheated a lot. I think he even hit or hurt her mom. She kind of clung to Sophie and me, especially our parents. She needed that stability, and when I lost my mom, all of that got worse. I told you once that she wasn't a bad person, just protective."

And then she lost Sophie...

It all made sense. The way she so rudely handled every-thing, tried to physically shove me out of the way at the first game of his I went to. Suddenly, I saw Piper in a whole new light, and she wasn't necessarily the villain I'd painted her as. "She was hurting and didn't want to lose you."

"Exactly." He leaned forward and brushed his hands

down his thighs. "When I grew up and started playing hockey and getting other friends"—he looked at me and blushed—"and girlfriends, Piper started seeing that shift. By then, my mom was sick. She got it in her head that since Sophie and I had known each other forever, we should be together. It wasn't that Sophie and I hadn't considered it. There might have been a kiss or two, and yeah, I loved her, but not that way."

"The box Piper handed you that day."

"So stupid." His nostrils flared, though, and there wasn't anything funny about it. "It was a plastic ring I won for Sophie when we were kids. In one of those gumball machines."

I nodded.

"Exactly. Sophie kept it because it was funny. That's all it was. Nothing more than kids joking, and I might have asked her to be my girlfriend that day or something. I don't remember. Piper was just starting shit that day on campus. To be honest, that's it. Piper was hurting. She had a crap family, lost her best friend, lost *my* mom who was a second mom to her, and she didn't want to lose me. I think after Sophie died, she thought she and I could have something, you know? I'd made it clear that wouldn't happen, but..." He shoved his hands through his hair and groaned. "It sounds ridiculous and childish."

"It's not." I uncurled my legs from the chair, losing the need to be in such a self-defensive mode. "Don't you think I get that? That after my mom left and my dad turned into one of the top two town drunks and I had *no one* but Caroline, that I wouldn't have given *anything* to have someone close to me? I would have fought to keep that, too, with everything I had."

He took a sip of his wine and sighed. "I know, Holly.

That was why I wanted the chance to explain everything that night. I *knew* you'd understand."

And I hadn't given him the chance. Hadn't tried. I still wasn't sure it would have done much good, but I at least could have taken the time to listen. I'd left him thinking that he and Sophie were engaged, even when I told him it didn't matter. I'd left him thinking that maybe had I listened, it would have. I cared about him a lot. I'd started imagining things with him I couldn't have ever thought I'd dream of, and I'd been so callous toward him.

The doorbell buzzed, a high-pitched ping sliced through the air making both of us jerk our heads toward the front door.

"Saved by the bell," Graham teased, but there was a coldness to his voice as he got up and answered the door.

So, apparently, he was still ticked about that night.

TWENTY-NINE
GRAHAM

There was so much else to get through, but a weight lifted at finally being heard. Granted, I'm not sure it would have changed anything back then, but there were things I'd needed to say and had spent weeks trying to be heard.

It felt good to finally have Holly sit and listen to me, to understand what had happened. I would never see Sophie again. I'd probably never see Piper again. What I hadn't gotten the chance to tell Holly was that after that day, about a week later, when Piper came over to try to console me, she'd not only done it so poorly, she'd thrown herself at me.

It had taken a split second of her lips on mine for me to shove her away and toss her out.

The last time I spoke to her was at our graduation parties, and that was only because her parents and my dad threw ours together. I'd avoided her then and had told her after that party to never speak to me again.

I'd held good on that promise.

I made my way to the door, the tip of my tongue burning to say more. To tell her everything I knew. To tell her about Eli and to tell her about my conversations with my dad. But it could wait.

At least through dinner. Holly already looked like she'd been smacked in the face, but I couldn't bring myself to apologize for the way I spoke either.

Telling her felt good, but reliving it also brought up old pain and anger.

I answered the door, grabbed the pizza, and thanked the delivery driver. When I turned, Holly was in the kitchen, taking plates out of the upper cupboard.

"Thank you," I said, and slid the two medium pizzas along with an order of garlic knots onto the counter.

"Thank you," she said. Her smile was soft, her eyes sad. I had a feeling that thank you meant a lot more than the pizza.

With a nod, I let her know I understood.

"Can we drop the heavy stuff for dinner?" she asked.

A dinner where I could simply enjoy my time with Holly after six years? A dinner where we didn't keep reliving everything that went wrong, and I could tease her, laugh as she sassed me back, and I got to see her smile?

There was no other answer except, "Absolutely."

She shook her head with her lips pressed together like she was fighting that smile I liked so much and flipped open a box. She instantly closed her eyes and inhaled. With a reverent tone, she whispered, "Scalecki's is the best pizza ever. Prepare to be amazed, Mr. Marchese."

I was every time I was around her, and knowing she'd stepped up to take care of Jonah only had me feeling that way more, but I had six weeks to let her know that.

Six weeks to calm down, take things slower, and try to see if we can make anything good that could be rebuilt from the ashes we left behind before.

"All right," I finally said. "Let's eat. Want to watch a show?"

"No." She slid a piece of pepperoni mushroom pizza onto her plate. The heavy scent of tomato and garlic and spices filled the condo. "I want to know what teaching's like. And coaching."

"You're on." I grabbed my own pizza, heavy on the meat, and Scalecki's looked like they definitely had a heavy hand with the cheese. It was thick, gooey, not overly greasy, and the crust wasn't too thick.

Nothing I hated more than biting into pizza and finding a mouthful of bread.

My first bite had me closing my eyes in wonder.

"Dang," I murmured around sausage and pepperoni and bacon and cheese. I might have groaned, too. "This is *good.*"

Holly hid her smile and mouthful of food behind her napkin. "Told you. Louie Scalecki's gift of cooking had to come straight from the hand of God." She patted the edges of her lips and grinned at me.

"I can't argue about that."

I polished off a slice and started working on my second. I should have ordered two larges. I could eat this every day. Fortunate for me that for the next six weeks, Scalecki's was a short walk away.

Louie and I were going to become good friends. He just didn't know it yet.

"Teaching," I finally said, after I raved for a few more minutes about the pizza. "It's a blast. So much harder than I imagined it would be, and also so much better."

"You're teaching chemistry?"

"I wish, but no. Not right now. I'm actually teaching biology. It's not my favorite, but things change, and I'm still young enough that I'm okay with the wait. I love my hockey team I coach. We made the playoffs last year, and it was the first time in the school's history they went that far."

Holly gave me a smile, like she was proud of me. "That's great, Graham. I can see you being a really good coach."

"Yeah?" My head tilted to the side. "Why?"

"Because you're patient and kind. Because you know how to get what you want from people. I can see you inspiring them, encouraging them to keep trying."

"Man, Holly." I leaned back on the couch. "That almost sounds like you like me."

She rolled her eyes, and I chuckled.

I let it go.

While we finished eating, I told her about some of the kids on the team and the difference between living in a smaller town than I'd grown up in around Raleigh. Because I was involved in the school and sports, every time I went to the store, I ran into either a parent, a fellow staff member or teacher, or a student. It'd made me nervous at first to do something simple like grabbing a bottle of wine or a six-pack of beer. It'd given me an appreciation for what Holly had grown up living with, really. That feeling of always being watched, everyone knowing you and your business. It'd faded with time, and maybe for Holly it had, too. She didn't really act like it bothered her anymore, and she had friends now.

A support system with Jonah.

As soon as I thought of him, I realized the funtime was over.

"Can I ask you something?"

The light faded from her eyes, and she chewed on the inside of her cheek. With a nod, she said, "Go ahead."

"Your dad. Do you still...?"

"I don't talk to him anymore."

She didn't make it sound like a good thing, and I gave her a moment.

Eventually she blew out a breath and scratched at the back of her neck. "I hated him. I was always so mad at him after Mom left and he fell apart, but I also kept hoping he'd do better, you know?"

She didn't ask like she really expected an answer, and since I didn't know anything about having a parent like that, I stayed silent. Not that she gave me time to answer before she continued.

"He only called for money, that was why I never answered. I mean, God"—she laughed—"you didn't even know where I lived, but it was such a crappy place. It reeked like spilled beer and smoke. We had to move into it when I was in high school when he lost the house."

My stomach plummeted, both in anger *for* her and realization of how much she kept hidden from me. We'd been together for months, and I didn't even know where she lived.

"It was this nasty trailer, and I was working two jobs, and every time he got access to the phone, he called me collect—which only cost me more money—to ask for more." She sniffed and stared at the blacked-out television screen, like she couldn't bear to look at me. "That was why I didn't answer when he called around you. I couldn't handle it, and I didn't want you to know that part about me."

"What part? The part where you are kind and hopeful? The part where you admitted you wanted a decent parent?"

A tear slipped down her cheek. It took everything in me to stay in my spot, to not lunge to hold her.

She sniffed and wiped at her cheeks with her napkin. "I talked to him once after Mom dropped off Jonah. I mentioned Mom coming, and he got so excited thinking she was back. That she'd take care of him or something, which was stupid. I told him what she did, and he blamed me for it. Said if I'd been better, she never would have left. Told me it was all my fault because I made her get hurt."

Screw staying in my seat. I moved as close as I could since she was in the chair and set my hand on her arm. "It wasn't. You know that."

She shrugged, barely listening to me, so lost in the guilt that wasn't hers to bear.

"Anyway, he got pissed she'd already left, and then when I told her about Jonah, he lost his mind. He told me he wanted nothing to do with him, but that I still owed him for being in prison in the first place. Caroline finally convinced me I didn't need him, but it didn't take much. I looked at Jonah, and even though he wasn't mine, he *was* mine, you know?"

She glanced at me, and I nodded. Of course I understood that.

"He was five months old when that happened. I stared at Jonah, his tiny little face, his pudgy little body, and knew without a doubt I would *never* treat him like that, regardless of what happened. That made me realize how bad my dad was for me. I called the prison and was able to get myself removed as an approved visitor or someone he could speak to."

"I'm really proud of you." I squeezed her arm until she looked at me. "That took a lot of courage. You should be proud of yourself for that."

"I didn't want Jonah to grow up seeing it." She cried as she said it. "And then I thought, why did I have to grow up like that? Ugh." She swiped at her cheeks and smiled through her tears. "It was years ago, and it's stupid for it to still make me cry."

It wasn't at all. Hell, I had a ball of emotion clogging my own throat.

It was time to rip the rest of the past away, and so squeezing her arm, I said, "I told my dad about you. All those years ago. I told him everything."

She whipped her head so quickly toward me I was surprised she didn't snap her neck.

"What? Why!?"

THE CONDO WAS SILENT. Holly had jumped from the chair, stared at me like I'd personally slapped her, and then ran off to the bathroom. The door slammed. The lock clicked.

I'd gaped at her reaction and then resettled myself on the couch.

I figured it would take her a minute to gather herself, but ten minutes later, she was still in there. I was just about to get up and check on her when the lock clicked again and the door squeaked as it opened.

"I'm sorry," she said, and it was clear she'd been washing and drying her face. "I think about that night and how I handled it, and I think about everything your family had gone through because of mine. And I just..."

She came back, and shocking me, she didn't take a seat on the chair. She sat at the other end of the couch opposite me, curling her legs beneath her so she was sitting criss-cross and put her hands in her lap. "I just...your dad. Sophie's dad was a friend of his, right?"

"Yeah, we were really close with the governor."

The November before Sophie's death, he'd been re-elected governor for a second term. He immediately stepped down to take the time to be with his family and his two other daughters. They moved away from North Carolina shortly after and now lived in Connecticut, where his wife had grown up. My dad and he still kept in touch, and Dad made annual trips up north to see him. Whether Dad ever told him or not about my connection to the man who killed his daughter, I didn't actually know. But I think the fact that they didn't still live in our neighborhood was a part of why it was easier for my dad to accept Holly and me meeting.

I gave her that quick rundown, leaving out the end. "You know, he doesn't blame you, Holly. He never did. He was shocked for sure, but he saw how worked up about it I was, and he listened. He's a fair man. Your dad was at fault, and that means your dad's actions left you alone. The only one to blame in any of this is him. People in Deer Creek might have warped your view of that, but it doesn't change my dad's opinion."

She scoffed, like she couldn't believe it. I was learning that Holly simply had a hard time believing there were purely good people in the world. I couldn't fault her for it, fully. I hoped that the time would come, though, where she wouldn't view everyone who came into her life as if preparing to hurt her.

"So if I showed up at dinner with your dad, he'd welcome me with open arms?"

"He's not much of a hugger, so the arms wouldn't be open."

"Shut up." She chuckled. "How do you do this?"

"Do what?"

"Make everything a joke. You make life sound so easy, and it's just...that's not my experience."

"Maybe because you're always waiting for the shoe to drop, and I'm looking to see the good."

Her face scrunched in displeasure, but before she could argue, I leaned toward her.

"You have to realize that *everyone* has something bad happen to them. Piper had crappy parents. I lost my mom. You lost yours in a different way. There are few people who escape their life unscathed from trauma, Holly. My dad's a good man. Was he shocked? Yes. Was he upset? Yeah, because it brought up his memories of Sophie, and it's absolutely shitty she was taken away from all of us so soon. Is he still pissed at your dad? Probably. Does he forgive him? I have no clue. I didn't ask my dad where he stands on that. But what my dad does understand is that *you* are not your dad. You didn't give him alcohol. You didn't tell him to drive away. You didn't even stand there and support him, and I know that because while I wasn't at the trial, my dad was. He would have known if you would have been sitting there. As far as he's concerned, you were dealt a shitty hand, and you kept working to create a better one for yourself. That doesn't make you weak or not worthy of knowing, it makes you honorable and strong."

If I had to keep hitting her over the head with truth, I would. Some day she'd look at herself in the mirror and believe it all.

She rubbed her hands down her thighs and shook her head. "Are you suggesting that if I would have stayed that night, everything would have been fine? It would have been a little blip, and then life would have moved on?"

Since she sounded like she honestly wanted to know,

like maybe she'd thought of that question a dozen times over the years, I gave her an honest answer.

"I have no idea. I don't care about what *could* have happened six years ago. I care about what's happening now."

Her lips parted, and she stared at me. Her hands balled into a fist, and she licked her lips.

"Six years ago, you didn't give me the chance to help you or to be there for you and Jonah. I want that chance now."

She blinked rapidly several times, and the color drained from her face. "What do you—?"

"I talked to Eli."

THIRTY

HOLLY

He knew. He knew, he knew, he knew.

My knowledge of the English language was quickly reduced to those two words, and I opened my mouth to speak, but nothing came out.

"I...uh...you..."

There was pain in his eyes, and his chest rose and fell rapidly. His heart had to match my racing one. "You talked to Eli." I finally managed to be able to repeat it.

"He didn't tell me anything but what he heard." Graham scooted closer to me on the couch. Not quite to the center, but closer. A brief hint of his cologne hit my nose, and I squeezed my eyes close to fight back my fears.

"Give me that chance to be there for you now," he said. "If it's..." He paused and cleared his throat. "If it's not good news, you'll need help."

"I have help," I muttered. I hadn't expected him to know. I'd debated all day and last night how honest I was going to be with him, what I was going to tell him, *if* there was any point in telling him.

"Everyone can always use more help."

"You're...stop this."

"I'm what?" he asked, and his hand reached out and tugged at the ends of my hair. "What am I, Holly?"

"You're scaring me." The admission was out before I gave thought to it. But now that it was there, a living, breathing truth between us, I couldn't stop. "You've always scared me."

"Don't you think I didn't know that?"

He huffed a laugh, and that laugh cracked through the tension and my fears like it always did.

One laugh or joke from Graham, and things never seemed as scary as I built them up to be.

He was a magician in that sense. He spoke, and my worries vanished, but only for as long as he was close to me.

"I'm scared," I admitted. "And I'm worried about Jonah, what will happen if..."

"Don't," Graham whispered, his voice thick and scratchy. "Talk to me. Tell me what's going on."

I shook my head and pressed my tongue to the roof of my mouth. I couldn't tell him. Tracey and Caroline were the only ones who knew, and I'd barely been able to tell them. Still, it was Graham, and he hadn't just slithered through the cracks in my walls—he was sitting in front of me, blowing them all to dust and crumbling the rest.

So I opened my mouth, and it all spilled out. I gave him every gory detail and symptom, not bothering to think he might be grossed out about hearing how my stomach swelled up or the heaviness of my periods.

He just kept running his hand through the ends of my hair, his head tilted to the side, soaking in every disgusting word, every mention of the pain I had for the last several months, and all the things it could end up being.

When I was done, he didn't ask questions. He moved even closer to me and wrapped me in his arms.

"Don't," I rasped, my face pressed to his chest before I knew what he was doing.

"Shut up and let someone hold you," he murmured in my ear, and I barked out a laugh.

"You're such an ass."

"I know." His lips were curled into a smile. I could feel them against my hair. "I think you like it."

For the first time since I'd met him, I lost the words to argue.

He was wrong to think I liked him. I one hundred percent did. That was what was always so terrifying about him to me. But he'd been right, too. I looked at everyone like they were one bad thing away from leaving.

He looked at people and assumed they'd bring something good to my life.

I had enough therapy in the first couple of years I had Jonah, encouraged to go talk to someone by Trina to help me work through the stress and fear and worry and changes I was dealing with, to know he was right.

Maybe it was time to let the remaining walls I had turn to ash.

Maybe it was time to start thinking of my future differently. Maybe I didn't have to be afraid of dying or abandoning Jonah and leaving him with Caroline.

Maybe, just maybe...

"Maybe I'll be okay," I whispered against Graham's chest. They were more for me, to voice hope in something instead of fearing the destruction.

Still, Graham's arm tightened around me, his lips against my temple as he declared, "Damn straight you will be."

For the first time, I didn't think about pulling away. I didn't mentally set up blocks, and I didn't try to tell myself all the reasons why I should be staying away from him, why this wouldn't or couldn't work.

Instead, I lifted my head, chin pressed to his chest, and met his rich, dark gaze. "So what now?"

There was a pause where he looked at me, brows knitted close together.

His hands went to the sides of my neck, back into my hair, and his arrogant smirk appeared right before he whispered, "This."

And then his lips brushed against mine, stealing all sense and defenses and refusals before I could conjure any.

"Oh," I whispered, right before he strengthened the kiss. His lips pressed against mine, nibbled at my bottom lip. My heart raced and my blood warmed, and I could do nothing but kiss him back, sinking into how *good* this felt.

There was no fear, no hesitation. The only thing I felt for the first time in a very long time was that this was *right*.

Being with Graham brought me peace and laughter and comfort. He allowed me to be. He was gentle while confident, he was patient while protective.

If I would have ever taken the time to dream of my perfect man, doodle him in diaries when I was a little girl, or consider what I wanted all those years ago when I made that vision board with Tracey, I would have drawn this man.

Maybe after all these years, it was time to stop trying to protect myself from all my fears and let Graham start battling them with me.

HE WILL STILL CUPPING both sides of my neck, fingers pressed into my scalp when he finally pulled back from my lips. "This might be the very first time I've ever gotten to see you, the real you, without you hiding anything from me."

My lips shook as I tried to smile.

"I like it, Holly. It makes you even more beautiful than I already thought you were."

My eyes fell closed, and I bit my bottom lip. "I feel like we still have a lot to work through. You live in..."

"Denver, I know," he teased. "And every couple has something to work through. We'll figure it out."

"But..."

He kissed me again, and this time, his tongue slipped into my mouth, tangled with mine, and I forgot the *but* altogether.

"There's Jonah," I whispered.

"There's the distance. There's a host of things we'll figure out. I want the chance to try, that's all."

He kissed me again, and I laughed against his mouth.

"You keep kissing me before I can say anything."

"That's because you're going to say something doubting us before we begin, and I don't want to hear it."

"Stop it." I laughed and smacked his chest, shoving him away from me.

He grinned back, lips dark and curled into his own smile. "Am I wrong?"

"Maybe." I crossed my arms over my chest and pressed my lips together. I tried for a frown and lost. My lips kept wanting to curl up.

"All right." He kissed my nose and then drifted his hands down my neck, my shoulders, and then my arms, until he was holding my hands. "Jonah. We'll start with him. I owe him time at the skating rink like I promised him, and I have new skates for him."

I blinked. "You what?"

"He asked me to take him skating. I'm going to do that so I can get to know him. Let me know when a good time for that is, and I bought him skates because I want *him* to like me, and he needs them. His are worn, and they weren't supporting his ankles properly."

"You bought him skates to bribe him."

"Absolutely."

I should probably be mad about that, but I couldn't muster up any anger. Instead, my eyes were filling with tears. Jonah needed something, and Graham bought it. No questions asked. Hockey skates were expensive, and while I tried to get the best gear for him, sometimes I had to make do with items from a used resale sporting goods store.

"Thank you," I rasped and sniffed, blinking my tears away. "He'll love them."

"I know you're scared and uncertain about this, but I think you know me well enough to know that no matter what happens, I won't make promises I can't keep, and I'll be gentle, both with your heart and Jonah's, as we figure this out."

My heart squeezed as I kept my gaze focused on Graham. His was so intent, so confident. That was always how he'd been. My objections took a hike, and one by one, they walked single file right out of my mind.

I made a decision, right then and there, to do the one thing in my life that was the hardest, to make a choice that made me feel the most vulnerable.

"I trust you," I whispered, and my chin shook as I said it. Trusting someone was terrifying. It gave them the means to hurt me. It gave them the upper hand, but Graham was right.

I knew exactly the kind of man he was.

He was worthy of it.

"Thank you, Holly. Thank you for that." His expression softened, like he knew exactly how much that cost me, and then he was kissing me again, his warm mouth against mine, his tongue teasing mine.

Heat swarmed in my lower belly, and all my nerves turned into something different, something so much better. We kissed until my lips were swollen, until my body was on fire, and then we kissed until Graham groaned and slowly pulled away.

"Come here." He drew me close to him on the couch, grabbed a blanket that had been on the floor, and draped it over both of us.

"What are we doing?"

"We're going to watch a movie, cuddle, and spend the rest of the time I get you tonight enjoying being together."

I had thoughts in my head of all the *other* things we could be doing, but we had time for that.

Suddenly, they didn't matter.

Graham was right.

We had plenty of time to figure out the rest.

THIRTY-ONE
GRAHAM

Man, I'd been nervous the other night before Holly came to the condo, but this was an entirely different set of nerves.

It was Wednesday. I spent the last two nights eating at the restaurant while she worked. Monday, Jonah was there for a bit, and I spent some time with him until Paul came and picked him up. We talked about hockey and school, and we colored in some of his coloring books while Holly stopped by and chatted when she could.

He wasn't there last night, and I'd barely had any time to see Holly, but she'd called when she got home from work.

We talked for hours. She told me all about Jonah and raising him, she told me about how when she graduated, she'd still wanted a job in finance, but outside of moving away, which she knew she couldn't do, the only financial firm in town was working with Cory Franklin, who happened to be married to a girl who hated Holly. It'd taken me a minute to remember she was one of the three girls who had been the reason me and my friends ate dinner in Caroline's office the first night I stopped into the restaurant.

I'd never forget the word *trash* being thrown around

then, loudly enough we could hear it. Of course we hadn't told Holly that at the time, but I was glad she didn't end up going to work for the guy.

At the end of the phone call last night, she did something I was hoping she would.

Something I thought would take her longer.

She invited me for dinner.

So now I was parking in one of the visitor spots in her cute neighborhood. It was a mixture of homes and town-homes, but they were all well-maintained, and the land-scaping was kept up well. Holly had a Fourth of July wreath decked out in red, white, and blue, and like most of the other homes I could see, there were two chairs out front, making it a cozy sitting area.

I climbed out of my truck and then grabbed Jonah's skates and flowers for Holly from my back seat.

Before I reached the door, it flung open, and Jonah stood in the doorway. "He's here, Mama!"

"Hey, Jonah. What's up, big man?"

I held out my hand for a low five, and he punched it with his fist. "Hi, Mr. Graham."

Holly appeared behind him, walking from around a corner at the back of their narrow townhome. "Hi there." She was wiping her hands on a towel, simply dressed in cutoff jean shorts and a pink V-neck shirt.

She looked relaxed, at home, and in total mom mode.

The tightness in her smile was the only thing that gave away her nerves.

I stepped across the threshold and handed the flowers to Jonah. "Can you give these to your mom for me?"

He shoved his face into the peach roses. "Wow. These smell great!"

I slipped out of my shoes and closed the door behind

me. Holly walked toward me, flowers in her hands, and the tight smile was now soft and easy. "Hi there. Thank you for these."

I glanced at Jonah, who was watching us closely, and to Holly. I'd kiss her every second of every day I saw her if I could, but I wasn't sure where we stood on this in front of Jonah.

"You're welcome." I set my hand at her lower back and went in for a hug.

She had different ideas, better ones, and pushed to her toes and kissed my cheek. "I'll give you a better one later," she whispered.

"Perfect."

"What's in the bag, Mr. Graham?"

"This is for you, but we have to wait until after dinner."

"What? A present?! Mama, Mr. Graham got me a present!"

"I heard," Holly said in a dry tone. "I think the whole neighborhood just heard."

The kid definitely had a set of lungs on him.

"Sweet!"

He ran off, leaving Holly and me alone, and me feeling like I was in seventh grade with my first crush on a girl all over again.

"Thanks for inviting me." I set down the gift bag with Jonah's skates in it by the stairs right off the door.

"This is weird."

"A little. But I like your home." It was mostly cream walls with pops of color from artwork. There were blankets tossed over the worn, dark brown sectional couch, and books spread out all over the coffee table. She might have tried to pick up before my arrival, but she hadn't gone overboard in making a home with a kid in it look perfect.

It looked lived in, aged some, sure.

Holly scanned her place like she was trying to see it from my eyes. "It's not a lot..."

"It's perfect," I assured her. My own home wasn't much larger, and the only reason I had that was because my dad handed me a substantial down payment. Holly had done this all on her own. There was no reason for her to be embarrassed.

"Come in," she finally said, giggling like she was as nervous as I was. "We're only making this weirder. Jonah wanted to help make dessert, so he's probably destroying the kitchen right now."

"Jonah bakes?"

"Brownies from a box mix. Don't get overly excited."

"I like brownies from a box mix." I liked it even more that he was baking and with her in the kitchen. "I used to love helping my dad in the kitchen. I'm glad you do that with him."

She smiled at me over her shoulder and then brought the flowers to her nose. "I remember."

My mouth split into a grin. *She remembered.*

"I've learned a few things the last few years working with Caroline, so I hope you like what we made. Nothing special, but Jonah loves spaghetti, and it was easy, so..."

"Holly." I reached out and tugged on her hand. She frowned down at my loose hold on her before lifting her confused and worried eyes to me.

"What?"

"I'm here because I like you. I already know I like you. You don't have to worry about impressing me. I'm already impressed." I tried to look around the corner for Jonah but couldn't see him, so I took a risk. A quick tug on her hand had her falling back into my chest. "And trust me, I was *very* impressed on Sunday."

I kissed her quickly but firmly, and as she turned away, her cheeks were peachier than the roses.

I took that as a win.

JONAH SHOVED the last bite of his brownie into his mouth and shouted, "Can I open my present yet?" Brownie dust flew out of his mouth.

"Jonah!" Holly cried. "Not with your mouth full. Please. Good gracious." She wiped crumbs off the table and brushed them back onto his plate.

I covered my own mouth so he didn't see me laughing.

There was no reason to be nervous at all. As soon as I saw Jonah dumping brownie mix into a large silver bowl when Holly guided me to the kitchen, the night became Jonah's show. He gave me a tour of their house and pointed out where his bedroom was. Took his time showing me all the things he liked in there the best. His Lego, a couple hockey posters, and some Nerf guns I promised him I'd play with him another night.

He kept up his one-man show all through dinner, talking about school and hockey and all the things he loved, barely giving Holly and me a chance to say anything to each other.

What we did share were a bunch of glances and smiles and even laughter.

I raised my brows to Holly, and she gave me a nod.

"Go get it, kid. But be careful. It's kind of heavy."

He clamored off his chair so quickly it tipped to two legs

before re-righting itself with a *thunk* of wood hitting the tile floor.

"He's so damn funny," I told Holly.

"He's excited." She glanced toward the front door. "I don't...well, he doesn't have a lot of men in his life, you know?"

"It might make me a jerk, but I'm kind of glad to hear that."

Her cheeks turned pink as she rolled her eyes. "Shut up," she mumbled.

"You always say that's not nice," Jonah scolded Holly as he carried back the large bag. It dragged on the floor, and he kicked it as he lifted it to the chair. "You should say you're sorry."

"Yeah, Holly," I teased and pouted. "You should say you're sorry."

She tossed her napkin at me and growled playfully. "Open it up, kiddo. What'd he get you?"

Attention diverted, and the subject changed, Jonah cried out, "I don't know, but I can't wait to see!"

He tore at the bag like he'd turned into a feral animal, and red paper went flying. Once freed from the bag, he dug into the wrapping paper with the same excitement, and soon, his eyes were rounding into large orbs, and his jaw was dropping. "Skates?" he asked, almost so quietly we had to lean in to hear him. He wiped his hand over the box of Bauer hockey skates and stared at me in awe. "You bought me new skates?"

"Thought you could use an extra pair." I didn't want to point out that the old ones were too worn and not sturdy enough. Holly was doing her best, and a great job at that.

He gaped at me and stared at his mom. I'd never seen

him so silent. And then he ran around the chair and threw his body into me. My arms wrapped around him on instinct.

"Thank you. Thank you so much, Mr. Graham! This is the best thing I've ever seen."

He shined his massive smile up at me and then to Holly, who sniffed and blinked harshly. "Isn't it amazing, Mama? I finally have my first pair of brand new skates! Mr. Graham is amazing!"

"It's really amazing, kiddo."

"Wow." He turned back and hugged me tight. I kept my gaze on Holly, watching her son hug me as her eyes filled with tears. My own started to feel the sting of dust in the air. "Thanks so much, Mr. Graham. It's really nice. They're my favorite."

I patted his back and wished I was comfortable enough with him, with both of them, to pull him into my lap and hold on to him even longer. "I'm glad, Jonah. I'm glad you like them."

"Like them! They're the best! When do we get to go skating again?"

"Friday," I told him. Holly and I had worked out the plans last night on the phone. "Your mom said I can take you Friday, so we'll break them in then, okay?"

"Awesome!" He pulled out of my arms and went back to his box, brushing his hand over the top again.

"Brand new skates that no one's ever worn before. This is so great." He bent over the box and hugged it. I gave up on blaming dust as my vision grew blurry.

He wasn't just a sweet and smart kid. He was thankful, too. And that said it all about how he'd been raised.

I looked to Holly to see her wiping away tears beneath her eyes, and I sucked back my own.

"Can I try them on, Mama?" he asked. "Just for a bit?"

"They should come with guards," I told her, in case she was worried about her flooring.

"In the living room," she said, nodding. "Give Graham and me some time to clean up, okay? And then we'll have to do bedtime soon."

"Bath, too?" His face scrunched up in displeasure.

Holly chuckled. "How about we give you a night off from the torture of clean skin?"

"New skates *and* no bath? It's like Christmas! You should be here *all the time,* Mr. Graham!"

He picked up his box and took it to the living room, having no idea that was what I would love most, too.

Something told me I only had to be brave enough to ask for it.

I stood and helped clear the plates and take them into the kitchen. It was around the corner from the living room, giving us a moment of privacy.

"You okay?" I asked Holly as I stood next to her near the sink. "That seemed like more than happy tears."

"It's...I knew he'd love the new skates. I didn't ever think he realized...you know? That he doesn't get new stuff like the other kids?"

"Come here." I pulled her in for a hug. "He's an incredible kid, Holly. His excitement and awe over that just shows how well you're doing with him. He doesn't *need* new things, but he appreciates them."

"But I want to be able to give him everything he wants." She sniffed against my T-shirt and slowly draped her arms around my lower back. "Sometimes it sucks knowing I can't do that, no matter how hard I try."

"Hey. That's because you're a good mom. He sees that. He loves you."

"I know." She pulled back. "I love him, too. So stinking

much. It's so weird sometimes when I look at him and think I've raised him, that he's my son...but also my brother. Sometimes I just want to be the fun big sister, but I have to be the mom, too. It's so weird."

"Does he know?"

She shook her head and flipped on the water to start rinsing plates. "No. I don't want him to. Not now when he's too young to understand. I don't want him to have to carry the burden of knowing our mom didn't want him, either. But when he's older, probably? He's asked me why I don't have a mom and why he doesn't have a dad, so we've talked about her some, but it's so heavy. I want to spare him all of that."

"That's what makes you a good mom *and* big sister, you know. You're looking out for him."

"He's an easy kid to love."

"So is his mom...his *real* one. The one who's been there for him."

I hadn't meant to say it. It slipped out. Based on the way her jaw unhinged, she hadn't expected to hear it. But the truth was out. Holly had a grip on me and my heart since the first night I met her. She lit up my life when I needed to shed my own pain. Losing her had brought it all back tenfold, for so much longer, and I wasn't sure I ever shook it away again fully.

At least not until I saw her again.

There was no point in hiding it.

"Mr. Graham!" Jonah shouted. "They fit! Come see!"

"Saved again," I muttered.

THIRTY-TWO
HOLLY

"Can Mr. Graham come listen to my bedtime story tonight?" Jonah was in his pajamas, teeth brushed, and ready for bed.

I'd spent every moment after dinner trying not to hold too tightly to the words Graham said. It wasn't an official declaration of love, but it was close enough, and we both knew it. I wouldn't dismiss it, but I had to figure out what to do with it.

Graham still loved me. I wasn't even sure how that was possible after all these years. It'd only been a week since he appeared in front of me, and everything was changing so quickly.

"I'd love that," Graham said, and of course he would. He loved everything these days.

"What story?"

"My favorite one," Jonah declared, and my cheeks immediately burned with embarrassment. They were doing that a lot these days. And all of them were because of Graham. "Oh, well...how about we tell a different one?"

"No! I want him to hear it." He turned to Graham.

"Mama's an excellent storyteller. She reads books super fun, too, makes all the people have different voices, but her own stories are the bestest."

"Well, I think I need to hear this bestest story then."

"You don't. You really don't."

"Please, Mama?" Jonah slapped his hands together like he was praying. "Pretty please. I like yours the best." He turned to Graham again. "It's awesome. It's a girl who lives all alone. She has no mom and no dad, and she's so sad because everyone left her..."

"Really?" Graham asked, and his brows rose on his head while he looked at me out of the corner of his eyes.

I wanted to hide my face and dig a hole and bury myself. When Jonah got started, he didn't stop.

"Yup. And then a prince shows up, and Mama says he's super handsome. And he was strong and had all these friends, and all of a sudden the sad girl isn't alone anymore."

"Really?" Graham's voice rose an octave.

"Ugh..." I muttered. "Maybe you should tell the story yourself."

"No! Come on." He tugged my hand and yanked me off the couch.

Graham stood behind me, whispering in my ear, "A prince, huh?"

Oh, that arrogant smirk was back. I was *never* going to hear the end of this one. It'd come to me one night out of the blue. The story had rattled off my tongue, not fully true because it was a prince in a castle with all the regular fairy tale trappings, but yeah, it was a rendition of sorts of Graham and me.

And I was sufficiently mortified he was hearing this, chuckling behind me.

"What else happens?" he asked Jonah.

"They got through all these battles, and they both get hurt, and in the end, the broken girl saves herself. She learns she has the powers she needed all along, and once she learns that, she gets a whole new life. She and the prince get married and live happily ever after, too, but I don't really like that girly part."

"I don't know," Graham said, and I could *see* his ego swelling even though he was behind me. "Sounds pretty great to me."

He had to be joking. I gaped back at him as we reached the landing. He shrugged, like it was nothing.

"What? I like happily ever afters, and I don't think they're girly."

"See," I said to Jonah. "Happy endings aren't boring."

Behind me, Graham laughed and then coughed into his closed fist.

Oh God. I couldn't believe I'd just said that. I glared at him as we entered Jonah's room. "Don't..." I warned.

"You said it," he whispered, with a glimmer in his eye.

"Where should I sit?" He scanned Jonah's room, which had a full-size bed and a beanbag chair. Jonah plopped down right in the center and patted his hands on both sides of him. "Here and here."

I paused, frozen, as I realized what Jonah was doing.

I'd never brought a man around him and had only had a couple dates in six years. And now...now he was welcoming Graham into his bedroom, no hesitation, like we were one big happy family, like he'd known Graham a lot longer than a week.

"Trust me?" Graham whispered, and it took me a second to realize it was more of a question.

I peered up at him, the way he was looking at me, like if

I wasn't ready for this, he'd deal with it and wait downstairs or sit on the floor.

But that was exactly why I trusted him. Why he'd always been the prince in my story. He always respected my pace, my decisions.

"Come on, guys! What are you waiting for?"

Graham looked at me, like he was asking the question with his eyes. *What are you waiting for?*

I nodded at him. I got it. What was I waiting for?

What could be more perfect than this?

I turned to Jonah and climbed into the bed, sitting between him and the wall so Graham could have more room on the other side.

"All right, Jonah." I adjusted so he was resting against my outstretched arm and ran my hand through his hair. It was so silky, and I took every opportunity I could, knowing someday he wouldn't allow it. Wouldn't want anything to do with this bedtime story.

"One day, a very long time ago, there was once a sad girl who was all alone. She only had one friend, and her mom and dad were both gone, leaving her to take care of herself. One night, she and her friend went out to a party and ran into a big scary monster who wanted to eat the sad little girl, but out of nowhere, a handsome and strong boy stepped in front of her..."

I tried not to watch Graham's reaction as Jonah settled into my story, but it was useless. He was tense as a board as he listened, oftentimes sucking a breath. I told the story of how he demanded this girl be her friend and how he showed her what true friendship was like. I told the story of how he made the lonely girl laugh and taught her to have dreams of her own, and then I ended it with the story of how another monster showed up, and both the boy and girl had to battle to survive. In the story, the boy teaches the girl how to fight, and in the end, the prince doesn't save her. They both end up saving themselves, and when they do that, they learn they should always be together, because they're stronger when they're together than when they're alone.

I cried the first year I started telling this story, but it'd been years since I did so. Tonight, with Graham's occasional sniffs, I found myself crying along with the story all over again. Most of it was fake, but there was enough truth weaved in to make it obvious whose story I was telling.

Not like he hadn't already figured it out.

"He's sleeping," Graham whispered with a raspy voice.

"He always falls asleep before I finish." I smiled at him in the small room, the hallway light illuminating his face.

"But you finish it anyway."

I could have brushed it off, made it seem like nothing. I trusted him. It was time I started proving it. "I like knowing they end up together in the end."

"Funny." Graham's smile went wide, and all I saw was a mouth full of teeth. "That's my favorite part, too."

"I FEEL like I should take back what I said earlier, but I won't."

We were on my front porch, my front door open. Behind me, Graham was looking down at me, cupping the side of my throat beneath my jaw. His thumb did a gentle sweep across my cheek.

"Especially not after hearing that story," he continued, like he wasn't turning my knees to jelly and my bones to mush.

After we left Jonah's room, he gave me a kiss that could only be described as scorching. He then brought me downstairs and didn't mention the story.

I'd been waiting for him to bring it up, and when he did, I dropped my forehead against his chest. "You were never supposed to know about that."

"Ah, but now I do." His thumb pressed to the soft flesh beneath my chin, and he tilted it up until I met his stormy, dark gaze. "I like knowing I was on your mind all these years."

I fought the urge to hide, even though he was staring so intently at me, and decided I couldn't.

I didn't need to hide from him or protect myself.

"You were never far from it," I admitted and licked my dry lips. My throat turned parched at the admission, and all my senses flared with that familiar flight-or-fight response being vulnerable brought me.

Instead of fleeing, I pressed my toes harder into the cement porch and rooted myself, waiting for his judgment.

"I know opening up is hard for you," he whispered, bringing his head down close to mine. "So thank you for that."

Graham closed the last whisper of space between us and kissed me. I sank in immediately and reached out, fisting his shirt in my hands. All too soon, and not nearly soon enough, he stepped closer, pressing his body against me and walking us backward until my back hit the door.

I chuckled against him and allowed myself to feel every part of this beautiful moment. The quickening of his breath, the deep, quiet groan that rose from his throat, the way his hands were gentle but firm and confident as the pads of his fingers pressed into my cheek and lower back.

I gasped when he pulled back, our lower halves pressed

together. His desire for me was evident, and my own arousal was rushing through me.

"What..." I tried pulling him back with my grip on his shirt.

"Soon," he promised and kissed my forehead. "We have all the time in the world to take."

We had all the time. A grin tugged at my lips. "Okay."

"Call me if your doctor calls, okay?" He asked it with another brush of his thumb over my cheek, like he couldn't not be touching me. Like he *needed* it, even if it was in the smallest ways.

But his words brought back the present. Reality. When Graham was around, I didn't think, and I didn't worry, but now it was front and center.

"Promise me, Holly. When your doctor calls, I want to be there with you."

"Why?"

Graham smirked at me like he found me adorable. "You know why." He kissed me again, quickly, and pried my fingers off his shirt, the sides now wrinkled from my hands. "Get inside and lock the door. We'll talk tomorrow."

Reaching around me, he opened the door. When I didn't move, his hands went to my hips, and he moved me back through the doorway.

"Good night, Holly."

I reached for the doorframe to steady myself. "Good night, Graham."

I closed the door and locked it, but I kept an eye through the narrow window next to the door and watched Graham jog out to his truck. Before he climbed in, he gave one last look back at my home. I didn't know if he saw me watching him through the sheer curtain, but I saw his smile before he got into his truck and shut the door.

He wanted to be with me when I went to the doctor. Caroline had volunteered, but that meant she needed other people down at the restaurant. Could I have taken her up on it? Sure.

But Graham wasn't giving me an option, and I knew it was solely because he wanted to be there for me. He wanted to support me and help me through whatever was about to come.

Which meant I wasn't alone.

And if I kept trusting him, I doubted I'd ever be alone again.

It was as terrifying as it was peaceful.

With a heavy sigh, I flipped off the lights downstairs and headed upstairs to bed. It was after eleven, and I had a long day, but sleep didn't come easy.

My bed suddenly felt too large, too cold, and too empty.

Soon. Graham had said.

My body warmed at the thought. Soon, maybe I wouldn't be spending every night alone either.

THIRTY-THREE
HOLLY

"I want to meet him."

My head jerked up at the intruder, who was now standing like a giant in the doorway to my office at the back of the restaurant. It used to be Caroline's, but once I took over all office management tasks, I kicked her and her messy organizational system out.

Cole had his arms crossed over his chest, decked out in his full police officer uniform, and if he thought he could intimidate me, well, he was right.

Even when I knew he was a good man and patient and an excellent father with a great sense of humor, when he put on his uniform, he became someone else entirely. Someone I definitely wouldn't want to mess with.

"Excuse me?" I leaned back in my office chair and spun it so I was facing him.

"This guy I heard about. I want to meet him."

"To threaten to beat him up if you don't like him?"

A twisted smirk curled his lips. "Or worse."

A laugh slipped from me, making Cole scowl. "You're joking. Trina would learn not to tell you things."

"The day my wife starts keeping secrets from me is the day we have problems, but Trina wouldn't do that, so we won't. I want to meet him, Holly. Make sure he's good enough for you and Jonah."

Something strange hit my senses, making my nose prickle and my eyes burn. Cole was always looking out for me, and as I looked at him, realization hit.

I hadn't been alone in a really long time. I had friends. Good ones who'd banded around me and supported me. I'd had Caroline and Paul my entire life, even when I fought against them. Cole was doing what any good friend would do.

"You'll like him," I said. "He plays and coaches hockey and teaches high school."

"I know. Already ran a background check."

Another laugh burst from me. I'd always wanted a sibling, and now I was sensing this was what happened when girls had older brothers from better families. Shameful that it took me so long to see what I had, but my eyes were opening.

"If you ran a check, then why do you still look so suspicious?"

"He took off when you needed help the most. Doesn't say much about him."

"Cole..." I stood from the chair and walked toward him. He had to know that wasn't the truth, not if Trina told him everything. "We were young, and I didn't let anyone tell him anything. That's not his fault."

I considered bringing up that he didn't exactly chase Trina down when she left town either but didn't think that would help his mood.

"Fine." I sighed when he kept glaring at me. "He's

taking Jonah ice skating on Friday. If you're off duty, we can do something after. Happy now?"

"I'll change my shift. You guys can come to our place."

"So you can torture him in the hidden room of your basement?"

A wicked gleam sparked in his eyes. "Only if he deserves it." Finally, a smile broke out. "Don't be mad that you have people around you who care. Maybe I want to meet him and check him out, but Trina seemed pretty certain he's special to you. Robbie and I just want to welcome him to town."

"He's not...it's..." My fears started to spiral. He was leaving. This was six weeks. Graham didn't need a welcome wagon when he was leaving.

But he loved me. He alluded to it anyway. And I was working on this whole new thing called trusting someone.

"Okay," I finally said. "I'll talk to him." I shoved a finger to his chest. "But no gun belts or taser guns or full SWAT gear allowed."

"You take all the fun out of everything."

I laughed. "That's exactly what Jonah says."

Cole grinned. "If he's as good as you say he is, then there shouldn't be any torture required. See you Friday."

"Wonderful," I grumbled, but I didn't say it to Cole. I said it to his back because he was already walking away.

Man...realizing I had a crew of friends around me who truly cared was great, but if they could be a bit less protective, that might be nice, too.

"Miss Jones?"

I braced myself for who I'd find in the doorway this time, only to smile at Annie. "I've asked you a hundred times to call me Holly."

She gave me a look that said her mother would smack

her across the back of her head if she tried. "You have a visitor. Want me to send him back here? Or do you want to take a break and eat with him?"

It had to be Graham...I grabbed my phone. "I'll come see him."

Before heading out to the front, I did a quick check on everything in the back. We were in the middle of prime prep time, and the kitchen was busy with prepping everything for dinner.

It didn't surprise me in the least that this would be when Graham would show up, but as I pushed through the metal doors and immediately found him at the hostess stand waiting, the men with him did surprise me.

Eli and Tanner were huddled close. A grin broke out on my face despite the fact that the last time I saw Eli I wasn't in a great state of mind, and he had at least had an inkling on my medical issues. Tanner, I hadn't seen since college, at least not in person, but I saw pictures every once in a while posted on Tracey's social media feed and from texts.

More friends. It was wild to me how I'd never truly realized how quickly my circle had grown and how it'd been filled with so many good and decent people. All people who knew my past, knew how I'd been raised and how I grew up and cared about me anyway.

It was the wonder of it all, the beauty of it and the shame at how I'd missed it for so long, that had me sliding up to Graham and slipping my arm to his lower back and snuggling in tight to his side.

His arm immediately draped around my back, and his hand rested at my hip. His hand squeezed, getting my attention. "You okay?"

"Perfect." I grinned up at him. "Hi, guys."

"Hi, guys," Tanner mumbled and then lunged for me.

"You can hi guys like you saw me yesterday when you *did* see me yesterday."

His arms wrapped around me, yanked me from Graham's hold, and then I shrieked as he lifted me high in the air. "How are things going, Spitfire?"

He used the nickname for me Graham had always used, but that was usually in private. I had no idea he'd even known it. Or remembered it.

"They're going well. Can you put me down?" He was so much taller than me that my feet were dangling in the air.

"And can you get your greasy hands off her?" Graham grumbled.

Tanner laughed because that was what he always did. Everything but hockey to him was one large joke and game. My feet hit the floor, and then Eli was there.

"You doing okay?" he asked, and this time I didn't hesitate or freeze to hug him back at his side when he opened his arms for me.

"Doing okay, I think."

"Sure seems like it. Heard you have a boy."

"Jonah. He's fantastic."

"Hopefully we'll get to meet him?"

I stepped back, right into Graham's side, and looked at the two guys I definitely hadn't expected to see. "How long are you here?"

"This guy"—Tanner pointed his thumb at Graham—"told me not to come, but I decided, screw that. Guys from my team are meeting up in Florida, so I'm heading there next week. Thought I'd stop here on the way."

"Tampa on the visit?"

"Nah." He shook his head. "Trace said she's busy with a project. Another time maybe."

I was hearing from her less and less over the last few

months, but she was a woman in a highly male-dominated engineering field. She was getting promoted and working hard, but her life had definitely shrunk to work, then home, and then more work. Granted, if I needed her, she'd be here as fast as possible, but the daily calls and interactions were much less.

"Bummer," I said and turned to Graham. "Did you guys come to eat?"

"Absolutely," Eli said.

I grabbed menus and set them at a table near the windows where I could sit and have a view of most of the tables and the front door in case other customers came in and needed help. After their waters and drinks were filled, I brought them back and took the open booth seat next to Graham.

"Let me know when you're ready to order, and I'll get that for you."

"I'll do it," Annie said, walking back with a stack of menus and a washrag in her hands. "You stay there, boss."

"Boss." Tanner snickered. "She calls you boss."

I glared at the fool. "I *am* her boss."

Annie returned and took our orders, and soon we were eating dinner and laughing. Once Graham was done eating, he draped his arm over the back of the booth like it was natural. Like he'd been doing it every day for years. It didn't take me long to melt into him, resting my shoulder against his.

"I might have something coming up soon," Tanner said, and his thumb started rapidly tapping on the table.

"What is it? A trade?" Eli asked.

"Maybe."

"Really?" Graham asked. "Where? I thought you had two more years left."

"I do, but the team is making changes, and Iowa's NHL team doesn't have room for me. It's kind of now or never, you know? I could stay for a couple more years, but I really want my shot."

"What's your agent saying?" Graham asked. "Is he looking? Or talking to coaches?"

"Yeah." Tanner's gaze shifted back and forth, his nerves catching up. Both thumbs started thumping on the table, and then he looked back. "Might be here."

He cleared his throat and quickly said, "But I'm not, you know...I'll be happy wherever, I just want my chance. So yeah...maybe the Carolina Ice Kings."

"No shit?!" Eli said. "That's incredible. That'd be, holy cow. That'd be awesome, Tan."

"Don't jinx it," he mumbled. "I didn't want to say anything, but I met with the coach yesterday. Kind of why I showed up here anyway after being told to stay away."

"Ice Kings." Graham sighed and shoved back his hair. "We won't jinx it, but damn...that'd be awesome. Does that mean you can't tell us who's leaving?"

"I don't even know if someone is. It's all speculation, and it could be anyone, but there are a few right-wingers who are getting older. Team's solid, though."

"They get close every year," Eli said.

I had no idea what that meant until Graham spoke up. "They'd be lucky to have you. You'd be sure to take them all the way to the finals next year." He turned to me. "The Ice Kings lost in the last series before making it to play for the Stanley Cup."

"So they're good."

"Yeah, they're good."

"It'd be a dream." Tanner groaned and fell back into the booth. Rubbing his hands up and down his face, he said,

"This sucks. The waiting. I need to get drunk off my ass and sleep for days, and I also need to run five miles. I don't think my heart can take it."

"Don't go into cardiac arrest around me," Eli said and popped a tater tot into his mouth. "I'm off duty."

Graham and I laughed. Tanner scowled at him.

It was just like old times, minus Tracey and the cheap beer Tanner used to drink.

"Where is Jonah?" Graham asked. "Isn't he usually here this time of day."

"Yeah, but our friend Ashley called. She's the one that has the foster kids." I'd told him about her the other day when I told him about Trina and Cole. "Her older daughters offered to take Jonah to the pool, so they're all swimming."

"Pool?" Tanner sat up straight. "I could swim some laps, get rid of all this nervous energy."

"It's in Ashley and Robbie's backyard, so no."

He pouted and chugged his sweet tea, making a lip-smacking sound. "What am I going to do?"

"I have an idea for tomorrow," I said. "If you're still around."

"I'll probably be in the morgue after this panic attack I'm about to have."

Eli chuckled and shoved a tater tot into Tanner's mouth. He chewed it and stole a handful off Eli's plate.

"What's tomorrow?" Graham played with my hair as he asked. "After skating, anyway."

"My friend Cole invited us over to their house. He's the cop."

"Got it. Can the hooligans come?" He gestured to Eli and Tanner.

"Count me out," Eli said. "I start another round of twelves tomorrow."

"I'll be there," Tanner said. "Not like I have anything else to do except wait."

"That sounded nice, Tan. Thanks." Graham must have kicked him because Tanner jumped in the table and cussed like a sailor.

"I just meant waiting sucks," he muttered, bending close to the table and probably rubbing his shin.

He had to sit for his news. I was waiting for mine. For once it didn't seem so scary and so nerve-racking.

"Maybe it'll all work out the way it's supposed to," I whispered, feeling uncertain of my burst of semi-positivity.

It sounded lame to my own ears. If everything happened the way it was supposed to, that meant I was supposed to have a mom who didn't love me, a dad who gave me a shitty upbringing. It meant I was supposed to struggle.

It also meant then that I was supposed to have the friends and family I currently had, and I was starting to think that was a really great thing.

"It will," Graham whispered and kissed my cheek. "It'll all work out."

Odd how it didn't sound so lame coming from him.

It sounded pretty damn close to perfect.

THIRTY-FOUR
GRAHAM

What a wild and surprising day. Tanner's visit was a total surprise, but a blast. It was like college all over again, with Eli camping out on my couch and Tanner sleeping in the guest room. Eli and he had played rock, paper, scissors for the extra bed. A best three out of five turned into a best five out of seven, into a best something out of whatever until Tanner finally lifted Eli up, threw him into the bed, and then ran and hid in the spare bedroom until Eli gave up shouting.

And that was only after I threatened to kick him out if he got the cops called on us.

Now, they were strapping on their skates. Eli's were rentals, but he'd gotten them sharpened, and it wasn't like he wouldn't survive on borrowed skates for an hour. Tanner had brought his gear with him because he never went anywhere without it. I was helping Jonah lace up his.

"You ready for this?" I tapped his helmet. "New skates and new friends and everything?"

He grinned at me through his cage. "I'm always ready for new stuff."

I didn't doubt he was for a minute.

We'd been able to get some private skate time at the local arena. I was surprised Deer Creek even had one, but it was near the high school and used for youth hockey and figure skating. It took a couple of calls, and maybe some begging, but I'd wanted time with Jonah to myself.

Him getting to skate with two of my best friends and with excellent skates was an excellent bonus.

Even better? Holly was in the stands, phone in her lap, and I knew she'd be taking pictures. It was eighty degrees outside, but she was dressed like it was twenty in her winter coat, hat, and gloves.

Meanwhile, the guys and I were in long pants and short sleeves. Jonah was decked out in his hockey gear, insisting he had to wear it so he could practice better.

Who was I to refuse a kid who wanted to be the best he could possibly be? He was the kind of kid coaches dreamed of.

"All right." I stepped out onto the ice, skated to the middle, and made an abrupt stop, sending ice shavings flying all over Tanner.

"What the he...h-e double hockey sticks?" he grumbled, and thank goodness he caught himself in time.

"You might be all pro soon and whatever, but I'm still better."

"Fat fu—reaking chance." He took off, chasing me across the ice. I was here for Jonah, but I couldn't resist trying to race Tanner. He'd gotten faster over the years, definitely more built and more in shape, but I'd always been leaner. Quicker.

We raced around the ice, and on the left turn, I caught Eli talking to Jonah in the center. They were both cheering for us, Jonah's little stick waving in the air. I'd thought I was still winning, but the scrape of Tanner's skates was louder. Closer.

I glanced back and shouldn't have. He reached out and grabbed my shirt. With a quick yank, he flung me to the wet ice. I slid until my back thumped into the boards. Neither of us had been going full speed apparently, and the fall wasn't enough to hurt anything but my ego. Tanner skated to the center with his hands in the air and came to a stop exactly like I'd done to him, sending a wave of ice to the top of Jonah's head.

"Hey!" he shouted, but there was laughter there too. I climbed to my feet and brushed ice off my pants.

I'd get Tanner back later. He could go pro, I thought as I skated to all of the guys in the middle. One of my best friends. This time next year, he could be at the end of a season with all his dreams and twenty-plus years of hard work behind him.

"Love you, man." I squeezed his shoulder and gave him a shake. Let him see how proud I was of him in my eyes.

He gave me a chin tilt and looked down at Jonah. "So, you've grown since I last got pictures of you. How old are you now? Thirteen?"

Jonah giggled. "I'm seven!"

"That's right. You ready to practice?"

"Always," Jonah shouted. "Can you make me as good as you, Mr. Graham?"

I squatted down low. "Me? Tanner plays for a professional team. Maybe we can make you as good as him."

"That's right. I'm pretty awesome."

Jonah shook his head. "I think you're the best."

I stood quickly and looked at Holly in the stands. She was smiling at us, perched on the edge of her seat like this was the most important game she'd ever seen.

Maybe it was.

With Jonah's words, it was certainly about to be the most memorable of mine.

I'd told the guys last night about Jonah's weakness and worries about shooting. Primary goal number one—give the kid some confidence while having fun.

"Remember what I said about the skates, right?"

Jonah nodded. "They need to be broken in, so I can't be on them long. I have to either take lots of breaks or put on my old ones."

"Right." I held out my fist. His gloved hand punched mine right back.

We spent the next half an hour skating with Jonah. Tanner and Eli chased him around the ice. I set up obstacles for him to fly around, and every time he made one of his perfect passes, we pretended he'd scored a goal.

By the time he needed to change out his skates to prevent blisters and pain, he'd made three goals, never once dropping his shoulder or lifting it like he'd done at camp.

"I'm getting better, aren't I?" he asked while I kneeled in front of him.

"Practice always does that, but do you want to know why I think you're doing better today?"

"No."

"Because you're thinking about having fun. You're not worried about missing. Or disappointing someone."

"Well, I wasn't really shooting at first. So it was fun. And it's not a *real* game. It's a fun one."

"Can I tell you something important? Something all people who play sports should know?"

"What?" He chewed on his lip like he wasn't quite certain.

"Kids should *always* be having fun when they're

playing a game. It's hard work, and you want to win, everyone does. But the minute it stops being fun, it means you've played a minute too long."

"Really?"

"I mean, that's what I tell the kids I coach."

I might have used more adult words, but the premise was true. I didn't want teenagers with attitudes on my team, taking everything too seriously. It always led to pride and egos and unnecessary fights. I wanted them out there dying to win because they were having so much fun they didn't want to skate off the ice. I figured the more you loved the game, the more fun you had playing it, the harder you'd play.

"Huh," Jonah mumbled. "I didn't think it should be only fun."

"There's hard work, sure." I finished tying his skates and got him to his feet. "And there's lots of practice. But what's the point of doing something you're not enjoying?"

"I dunno." He was silent for a beat. "So does that mean I can shoot more?"

We had ten more minutes on the ice, so I sent him out to where Tanner and Eli were taking slap shots at each other. Unpadded. Unmasked.

Idiots.

"Graham."

I immediately turned to Holly. She was at the boards, her face pale, phone in hand. "My doctor called."

"Now?"

"She rushed them so I didn't have to wait through another weekend. But..." Her gaze slid to Jonah.

"We can get him out of here, or they can take him to the restaurant or something." I'd throw him in the car and take him with us, but if it was bad news...

"I can just go..."

"Absolutely not. No way. You're not doing this alone."

"Okay." She shook her head, like she was trying to clear her mind, except even I could tell she wasn't thinking straight. She was gone, lost to worst-case scenarios and fears I'd seen her try too hard this last week to fight.

"Eli!" I shouted and waved him over. He was there in a blink.

"What's up?"

"Holly's doctor called. We gotta go. Can you get Jonah back to town? He can hang at the restaurant." I looked at Holly, who was staring at Jonah, but it was obvious she wasn't seeing him. She was seeing him live a life without her. I needed to get her to the doctor, get those results in. "Yeah. Yeah, of course. You need us to leave now?"

"No, in ten minutes or so, you'll have to get off when a figure skating lesson starts. You good?"

"What am I going to tell him?" she asked, still staring at him.

This was Holly, by now I understood. Her default was negativity and fears. Warranted given the life she had.

"Tell Jonah his mom had a stomachache, and I took her home for medicine," I told Eli and reached for Holly's hand. "Then later, you can tell him you feel all better."

"But..."

"You will be. You'll be just fine, remember?"

She stared at our hands and slowly lifted her face to meet mine. "I'll be okay."

It wasn't much, but it took all she had. I squeezed her hand. "That's the spirit."

"Go," Eli said. "We've got Jonah, and we'll be at The Grille unless we hear from you. And good luck. Chin up, Holly. Could be nothing, remember?"

"Right."

I dropped to the bench and tore off my skates and slipped into my sandals. I looked ridiculous, but who cared.

Holly needed me, and I needed her to be healthy, so I needed to get to the doctor as soon as we could.

"HOLLY JONES?"

The nurse might as well have shot a handgun for as loud as her voice was. In the silent waiting room, she could have whispered and still been heard. As it was, Holly jumped to her feet and squeezed my hand so hard the bones almost cracked.

She didn't apologize, and I didn't notice. It wasn't even the first or sixth time she'd done that since we checked in and took our seats.

The nurse guided us down a hall, one left and then a right, and then we were being led into an office.

Not an exam room like I'd expected. Holly dropped into one of the faux-leather seats, and I took the other. She still hadn't let go of my hand, but she hadn't said much either. The only way I knew she knew I was there was the death grip on my hand.

I wasn't complaining. If she needed to break all the bones in both of my hands, I'd happily hand them over so she could get through this.

"Dr. Myers will be just a minute," the nurse said. She set a file on a flat-looking screen that was definitely not a computer and then left and closed the door.

"The results are in that file," Holly mumbled. "I don't even think I want to know anymore."

I adjusted in my seat so I was facing her as best I could,

gripped the armrest of her chair with my free hand, and gave it a quick tug. It angled, and Holly was faced to look at me.

"It could be dozens of things. Fibroids. Something else. Endometriosis. Constipation."

That last one broke the icy facade she'd worn before we left the rink. "I'm not constipated."

"It says it's a symptom." I went on teasing, and it helped. At least a little because she smiled, and my fingers weren't in immediate peril.

"You'll be okay either way. I checked, Holly. Even if it is the worst, the survival rates are high, and you're young. You're flying to the worst-case scenario because that's the way you've always lived, but life isn't always one step away from death and ruin."

"I'm trying to believe that. I'm trying, but it's so hard."

Two quick thumps hit the door, and then it opened.

Holly's face paled, and this time I think she broke my pinkie.

I faced the doctor and tried to read her expression as she closed the door, kept her face blank, and gave me nothing.

"Thanks for coming in today," she said. "Sorry for the late notice, but like I said on the phone, I didn't want you to wait longer." She gave me a passing glance and went back to Holly.

"I have good news and bad. Which would you like first?"

"Bad." Always the bad. There was no way to prepare myself for this. I'd tried not thinking about it. I'd tried living with the pain. I'd tried *hoping*, but my life didn't work like that. Despite the blocks I'd torn down and broken through, I was still expecting the other shoe to drop.

Things had gotten too good. I was with Graham. He was more fantastic than he used to be.

Hell, I was having a blast with Eli and Tanner and watching my little family of friends grow.

Something had to fall. Something had to turn it all sour.

"The bad news is we didn't need that biopsy after all, so I'm sorry for putting you through that unnecessary pain."

I blinked. Blood rushed from my face, straight to my toes. Might have left my body altogether. "What?"

A soft but still wary smile broke out on Dr. Myer's face. "The biopsy was an extra precaution, as you remember, so you don't have to keep waiting for tests and pushing everything back."

"I remember."

Next to me, Graham was listening intently. I knew I

was hurting his hand. I kept seeing him flinch in pain out of the corner of my eye, but every time I tried to loosen my grip, I kept coming back to him.

I needed him. I needed him for more than this.

The last week with him had shown me how much I was missing out on, how much Jonah was, and how much I wanted to give him everything with Graham. There wasn't anyone else who'd be good enough.

But if I were broken...

"I don't understand," Graham said, frowning at me and then the doctor.

She slipped something out of the file the nurse left, set it on that flat lamp-looking thing, and flipped a light on.

"This isn't going to sound like good news, but I promise you it is." She kept her gaze on Holly. "It's not cancer, and it wasn't tumors on your cervix, Holly."

"What is it?"

"Fibroids." The doctor smiled then, it was serene and hopeful and full of genuine peace. "I know that sounds bad, but they're not cancerous. They're basically benign cells that grow, but they don't turn to cancer."

"I can get rid of them?" Holly asked, and this time when she went to squeeze my hand, I pulled my fingers out and took ahold of her hand in both of mine. This time, I held on to her. Let her know she had someone there, holding her, taking care of her.

"We'll have to discuss treatment. We should be able to get rid of these three here quite easily." She pointed to some blobs I couldn't detect, but I wasn't the doctor. "These might cause some concern, but don't get worried. It just might mean a different kind of surgery. The thing to know is really, out of everything we considered, this is the *best outcome*, Holly."

I was reading the relaxed features on the doctor's face, but Holly must have read something else. "But it's not a great outcome. It's not...it can still be bad."

"There is a chance, given the placement of this." She pointed out all the fibroids. Six of them. On her cervix, her uterus, and her left ovary. "We might have to remove the ovary, and in the future, *years* down the road if they return, you might need a hysterectomy. But at least through the next few years, you should be okay. This type of fibroid tends to be slow-growing, which means they've been there awhile before you started having any issues, maybe even years."

"With one less ovary." She didn't glance at me, but she swallowed thickly. "Kids?" she asked. "Will it...I hadn't even considered it, not really, but would I be able to have kids someday?"

I saw it then. Holly laughing with our kids. Both of us teaching them to cook, maybe dancing in the kitchen along with baking. We'd take them to parks, she'd bring them to watch me coach hockey. I'd teach my kids *and* her how to skate. All the things I started to see with her all those years ago...and now they could be gone.

"Have all the kids you want. Lots of women only have one functioning ovary. It might take longer to try, but it shouldn't be a problem. We'll keep an eye on you every six months and then yearly check-ups to see if the fibroids return. But the hysterectomy is the worst-case option, years away. I truly believe that."

Holly was quiet for so long I thought she'd turned to stone. And then she turned and smiled at me. "I'm going to be okay."

Tears slipped down her cheeks, and I didn't care if a doctor was in the room. I leaned forward and kissed one away and then wiped the others. "I told you. You should really start listening to me."

Holly chuckled.

The doctor smiled.

"Call my office next week so we can talk to you about scheduling the surgeries to start getting them removed. It'll be a few visits, but the procedures are very low-risk and outpatient for the most part."

"Okay. Thank you."

The doctor grabbed a tissue and handed it to Holly. "Any questions for me?"

Holly shook her head. "Outpatient, that's just a morning or something, right? Because Jonah..."

"We'll make sure he's taken care of," I assured her.

"Outpatient, usually just a couple hours in and out and then resting for the rest of the day, maybe two. But you won't be in the hospital, not any more than overnight if there are issues."

"Okay. Thank you again. I just...I really thought it'd be worse than this."

"It's normal to let your fears get away from you when this stuff comes up. No one blames you for that, but now you get to go celebrate."

"Celebrate," Holly muttered, like the concept was foreign to her. "I get to celebrate."

"And I get to be tortured by your cop friend."

I got a strange look from the doctor I ignored.

Because Holly was smiling, and when she smiled, it was all I ever saw.

I KISSED her against the truck until it became almost indecent for the public. I kissed her in the cab of my truck until she laughed and pushed me away. I kept reaching over and kissing our interlocked hands on the way back to Deer Creek, and as we made the drive to the restaurant to pick up Jonah and tell Caroline the good news, I couldn't stop touching her.

"It still doesn't sound great."

She was staring at her phone.

"Swear to God, Holly, you don't take a night to enjoy the good news you just got, I'm chucking your phone out the window."

"You wouldn't." She hugged it to her chest.

"I absolutely would."

"I've been so worried for so long, and there are always risks with surgeries."

I reached out and plucked the phone from her fingers and dropped it into my door.

"Graham!" she shrieked.

I pulled into the parking lot and shoved my truck into park in the first parking spot I could find.

"I can't believe you did that!"

I grabbed her cheeks and kissed her. I slipped my tongue into her mouth until the fight went out of her, and she responded, leaning in. Only when she whimpered did I pull back. "You got good news today. Tomorrow is going to be even better. I'll be here to help with your surgery stuff, and then you'll be *fine*. Jonah is happy. Someday, I'm going to move here and find a job, and then after that, you'll still be fine. You'll be better than that. You'll be happy."

"You...what...you?"

At least she wasn't worried even if her voice and words didn't work right. "Spitfire," I drawled and brushed my lips over hers. "Did you really think you'd ever be able to get rid of me again?"

"But...it's been a week."

"No." I opened my door and hopped out. "It's been six years, and I'm tired of waiting. Get used to it, because you're not ever going to be alone again."

I shut my door, waited for a second, and then hurried around the truck to get her door. "You coming in to tell Caroline the good news or not?"

"I suppose you're not giving me a chance, are you?"

"Not a chance." I lifted her out of the truck and carried her into the restaurant. Folks gave us strange looks, and Jonah ran right up to us.

"You don't look like you have a stomachache," he declared, before I could set her on her feet.

"That's because she's all better, little man." I looked down at Holly. Her hair was a frazzled mess, her lips full and pink, but there was a glimmer in her eyes that was new.

One I wanted to start seeing much more frequently.

"That's right, Jonah. Graham's made me all better."

"I LIKE HIM," Trina said. "He's sassy but sweet, and I love the way he looks at you."

"I think he's sexy," Ashley cooed. "His butt looks fantastic in those jeans."

I laughed around the rim of my water bottle. "Keep your eyes on your own man's butt."

"But..."

"Not buts or butts," Trina declared. "You look good. Happy. It's kind of weird."

"Thanks. You look like you're going to puke," I told her.

She laughed. "You're not wrong. I've been throwing up every morning. Thank God the girls are at their mom's this week now. It'd be impossible not to tell them yet."

"I'm happy for both of you," Ashley said. "Both of you, and Trina's right, Holly. You're happy with Jonah, but this is a new look on your face. It suits you. And the guys like him, too."

"How can you tell?"

"They haven't shot him yet."

I blinked at Ashley. Trina shrugged.

Animals. My friends were all animals.

"Woo-freaking-hoo!" Tanner ran out of the hallway, stopped, and froze when he saw us. "Where are the guys?"

"Outsid—"

Before Trina could finish, Tanner ran at me and tossed me into the air. "I'm a freaking Carolina Ice King, Spitfire! I got it! I've made it!"

Tears poured out of my eyes before I could stop them, and I threw my arms around Tanner's neck. "That's amazing!"

"What's going on?" Cole asked, standing in his doorway. He frowned at Tanner, probably because he was holding me.

"He did it!" I shouted to Graham, who was standing right next to him.

"No kidding!?"

"No shit! My agent just called!" Tanner shouted. He practically dropped me to the floor and I stumbled before righting myself. "I made it!" He threw his arms out in the air. "Who's the man, now!"

Graham and Eli both rushed him, and soon the three were in a dog pile in a strange man's living room, who was watching the mayhem with a smile on his face. Robbie was beside him, then in front of him.

"NOW it's time to celebrate!"

He went to the kitchen. Beers were opened. Wine was poured. Even I had one. We celebrated Tanner's great news. I cheered to my new friends, and soon, I found myself tucked off to the side with Cole.

"I like him," he declared, so much like Trina but with more potential malice. "He's good for you."

I looked at Graham, shoving his hands through Tanner's hair, and grinned up at Cole. "I'm going to marry him someday."

His eyes widened with surprise and then crinkled at the edges as he smiled. "Good, because I'd kick your ass if you ever thought of letting him walk away."

An arm looped around my lower back, and I was pulled to Graham's side.

"What are you two talking about?"

"Nothing," I quickly said, because no way was I telling him what I just told Cole.

Cole's smirk appeared slowly, taunting me. He looked at Graham. "Your future wedding."

He sauntered away and went to shake Tanner's hand again. Crazy how everyone had gotten along immediately. Guess I had good taste in friends.

"Our wedding?" Graham asked, a teasing tilt to his voice. "Has the broken but healed princess finally found her prince?"

Well, when he put it that way...

I smiled up at him, lifted to my toes and kissed him. "I'm pretty sure they'll even live happily ever after."

"You're damn right they will."

EPILOGUE

Five years later

MY BODY BEING close to freezing and my hands almost always encased in gloves had become my favorite feeling. My favorite place above all other places was now the Crystal High School hockey arena.

Jonah handed a player a green water bottle and quickly scurried out of the way. At twelve, he was in the stage of acting too cool to do the things he did when he was younger, and still so much a child. It was hard to balance the expectations with his need to grow up while having the memory skills of a mouse. Hockey, in whatever form he could get it, playing, watching, or helping Graham, was still his favorite thing. The one constant thing about him I could count on.

Another player jumped off the ice and Jonah handed him another water, grinning broadly at something Graham said to him. These were the moments I treasured the most. The moments when Graham never failed to treat Jonah as if he was his, even if he now legally was. The moments when

I got to watch the most incredible, loving, and patient husband treat our children with more kindness and grace than I'd ever remembered experiencing in my entire life.

Cold tears swamped my vision, and I sniffed them back. I probably only had one or two more years left of being able to sit in the stands and watch Jonah on the bench, handing players skates and grabbing water bottles and towels from the bench floor wherever they were flung when players jumped to the ice for their shift. At least, until he was hopefully sitting on the bench or on the ice as a player. If that happened, it wouldn't be with his dad as his coach, which was a bummer.

Graham was decked out in his Crystal High School coaching colors. He still hadn't been able to find a job in Deer Creek, but Crystal was only the next town over, so he was close. He landed his job teaching chemistry the summer he decided to stay for six weeks.

I truly had no idea when he did all that that he'd be here all these years or that we would have been married three years ago. That on that same day, Jonah would ask if he could be adopted so we could all share the Marchese name.

Or that a year and a half later, we would get the best surprise of our lives.

Somehow, the surprises kept coming, and life kept getting better.

"How's she doing?"

Trina sat down next to me and flicked the tiny green ball on top of Anna Grace's hat. She and Cole came to as many games as they could, which was a lot considering they now had their hands full with their own four kids. Two from Cole's first marriage, and two with each other.

"Sleepy, cranky, and teething." I grinned as I said it though. I didn't take a moment of my life for granted, nor the fact I was able to have kids naturally in the first place. After years of surgeries, fibroids, and eventually losing an ovary, I had started doubting it'd ever happen for us, but at some point, in time, Lady Luck had decided to glance in my direction again, and there I was.

Spending a Friday night with my daughter, named after Graham's mom, my best friend on one side of me, and my father-in-law on the other.

Who would have thought.

"Let me at her." Trina wiggled her fingers and reached for the buckle on my baby carrier.

Next to me, Jordan scoffed. "Grandpa privileges come before friend privileges, Miss Paxton. We've discussed this."

"Unfair."

"Fair," he stated, like he was getting ready to state in case in front of a judge. "You see her more. If anyone's getting their *well-washed* hands on that baby, it's me."

I chuckled. It was possible I'd become *slightly* neurotic after Anna Grace's birth about germs and touching and hand washing.

"Not nice, Jordan."

"Come on, come on. My turn." He slapped his gloved hands together.

Graham wasn't an exact replica of his dad, but man, it was close. Jordan was older, nearing sixty and had bought a condo on the mountain so he could visit on the weekends but still give us privacy. It was the best of both worlds, especially since he was nearing retirement.

I might not have had a good dad in my life, and there were moments the reality of what I missed out was a painful pierce to the heart, but being around Jordan had been healing. It took three visits with him to get over the awkwardness of who I was, how our paths would have initially crossed had I been at my father's trial, but after the third visit, he pulled me aside and told me he was proud of the life I'd built. Enjoyed the person I was. He assured me he didn't see me and think of missing Sophie, or become angry at my father, and somehow, slowly after that, I began trusting him too.

Hard not to trust a man who reminded me so much of Graham in the first place.

"All right, all right."

I unbuckled my daughter from her carrier, and before I could tug her feet out of the holes, Jordan pulled her into his arms. She was eight months old, happy as a clam most days, and was born with Graham's curly dark hair. Doctors had told me she'd probably lose it in the first few months, but it was still there, a fluffy little mop on her head when I didn't make her wear a hair tie.

Jordan gently bounced her in his arms, and I glanced back to the game, to the man at the bench, and found his focus on me instead of the game.

A soft smile curled his lips, and I blew him a kiss.

He turned back to the game, and I sat back and enjoyed watching every moment. It didn't matter that he hadn't blown me a kiss.

I'd get one later.

A better one.

GRAHAM

GAME NIGHTS WERE EXHAUSTING. After a week of morning practices and then school, having to be out until nearly ten o'clock at night had my bones hurting like I was closer to my dad's age than thirty-five. It also meant little time with the family, and I hated missing out on bedtimes and baths and all the chattering that happened during the end of the night. Considering Anna Grace wasn't sleeping, Holly was equally exhausted, and missing tonight made it all worse.

I clicked the front door shut of the new house we'd bought shortly after learning Holly was pregnant. The townhome had been great for us while Jonah was still young and we were getting our feet beneath us, but with a baby coming, and hopefully more on the way, I finally sold the home in Denver I'd been using as a rental property to grow more passive income and bought a house close to town.

If Holly wanted to, she could now walk to work. Jonah biked to middle school, and it was only a fifteen-minute drive for me to get to school.

The house was quiet as I entered, but that wasn't surprising. If Jonah was awake, he was playing video games with friends, and if Holly was still awake, I knew exactly where to find her.

Slipping out of my shoes, I dumped my wallet and keys on a tray by the door and headed upstairs. Anna Grace was an easy baby, full of smiles and few tears, but Holly was always slow to put her down to sleep in her crib, snuggling with our daughter every last second that she could.

The pale light in the hallway coming from Anna Grace's room proved my theory correct, and I headed in that direction, stopping as Holly's soft voice whispered into the hall.

My lips curled up as I listened, and then I carefully peeked into the room. She was in the glider chair, feet kicked up on the ottoman. I couldn't see Anna Grace beneath the bundled blankets in her arms, so I figured our daughter was eating.

And while she was, her mom was talking.

"There was once a prince, young and bold and brave, who loved a young, broken girl very much..."

I slunk to the floor in the hallway with my back to the wall and closed my eyes and listened.

Like Jonah, and someday hopefully Anna Grace, this was also my favorite story. I didn't need to listen to Holly to fall in love with it, but man, I loved listening as she told it.

After all, it was my story, too.

Our story.

"YOU SCARED ME." Holly jumped as she reached the hall, one hand pressed to her chest. "How long have you been out here?"

I climbed to my feet and instantly went to my wife, wrapping her in my arms. "Since the story started."

"Why don't you ever come in?"

"I like listening. Like knowing you give our kids that."

Her arms wrapped tightly around me, and she inhaled, snuggling into my embrace even deeper. "Good game tonight."

"Thanks." I kissed the top of her head. "She sleeping?"

"Soundly, for now."

"Ready for bed?"

She burrowed into my chest and squeezed me tighter. "Always, husband. My prince."

"Come on then." I spun her around and gently guided her toward our bedroom down the hall. "Let's go create a whole new *not-safe-for-kids* scene in that story of ours."

I followed Holly's amused chuckle into our bedroom, ensuring the door was locked behind us, happier than I ever could have imagined being. I had a boy, who might not have been mine by birth but was my son all the same, a healthy daughter, and a wife who never stopped showing how deeply she loved all of us.

Loving Holly had been as frustrating and daunting as it'd been easy. Fortunately, she'd given me the chance to scale all her walls years ago, and now there was nothing but all that light and goodness I'd seen in her from that very first night. Years later, I never would have guessed we would have been settled in Deer Creek, raising a family, but there we were, living out our very own real-life, happy ever after.

And as I stripped my wife and showed her without words how much she meant to me, like everything else Holly did, she gave it back in a multiplied measure, making me feel like I could always be the man she needed, the man she loved and trusted. A man who could truly scale castle walls and make all her dreams come true.

THANK you for reading Love Me Boldly! If you enjoyed this story, please remember to leave a review!

Want to read more of my books similar to Love Me Boldly? Check out Sneak Attack! A second chance romance, tempers collide when Eden returns to a town she swore she'd never see again, only to run into her ex-boyfriend, and finds out he's a single father. Download it here! https://amzn.to/3IBlFvm

THANK YOU

2025 marks my twelve-year anniversary in the writing and publishing world from when I published my first book, Just One Song. I truly had no idea that publishing one book as a "bucket list" challenge to myself, would lead to this amazing, decade-plus career. From the friends I've made along the way, to meeting other authors and book signings and meeting readers, my world is so drastically more amazing than anything I could have ever imagined. I'm so unbelievably thankful to every person who takes a chance on one of books. Thank you for being a part of this wild journey with me!

HUGE thank you to Nina and all the incredible women at Valentine PR for throwing your full enthusiasm and support behind me and these books. I love with working with you.

Thank you so much to my editing team for all your amazing hard work and refining the hot mess drafts I send you.

Shannon, you're the best. Always. Forever. Your talent is astounding and I'm thankful I can call you a friend.

Ratula, I couldn't do this without you. Thank you so much for being so incredible!

To my Sweeties: I love you ladies and your excitement for my books!

To all the bloggers who devote their time and passion into reading books, book tours, release events, leaving reviews, promoting and pimping – you are all rockstars! Thank you for all the love over the years.

My family— I love you all to the moon and back. I don't know what I would do without you in my corner, cheering me on every step of the way. Your support is everything to me and I love you all with all of my heart.

To my friends who have encouraged me for the last several years and always been there to support me. Tamara, Cassy, Niccole, Bree, and Lauren. Thank you so much for loving me!

And last but definitely not least – to you, the reader. I'm blown away with every release how much you adore my books. You have made my dream a reality and I hope I can cheer you on with yours. Please don't forget to leave reviews on Goodreads or whichever retailer you've purchased this copy from. It helps us so much!

ABOUT THE AUTHOR

A long-time dreamer, Stacey Lynn has always loved the emotional journey of two different and complex individuals finding their way to a happily-ever-after.

The author of over fifty romance novels, many of which have been best-selling titles on Amazon, AppleBooks, and Barnes & Noble, she loves being able to turn her vivid imagination into a career that brings entertainment and joy to her readers. Focused on emotional, small-town romance, she happily admits her books might require keeping tissues nearby.

Born in Texas and raised in the Midwest, she now makes her home in North Carolina and loves all things Southern. Blessed with her ultimate tall, dark, and handsome hero, and four children, she loves every minute of her wild and wonderful life.

Subscribe to her newsletter so you can stay up to date on all her new releases. www.staceylynnbooks.com

OTHER BOOKS BY STACEY LYNN

A Deer Creek Novel ~ small town romance

Love Me Gently

Love Me Boldly – May 2025

The Kelley Family ~ small town romance

Undeniable Love Novella (free on all retailers)

Unending Love

Unstoppable Love

Unbreakable Love

Nashville Steel ~ football romance

Sneak Attack

Time Out

Tight Spot

Risky Game – releasing October 2023

Las Vegas Vipers ~hockey romance

Final Shot (free on all retailers)

Game Changer

Dream Maker

Rule Breaker

Shot Taker

Goal Chaser

Secret Keeper

Ice Kings Series ~hockey romance

Playing With Fire (free on all retailers)

Playing To Win

Scoring Off The Ice

Hooked One Her

Hard Checked

Fighting Dirty

The Rough Riders Series ~football romance

Dirty Player

Filthy Player

Wicked Player

Cocky Player

Love and Lies Duet ~angsty slow burn, romance

All the Ugly Things

All the Beautiful Things

Love and Honor Duet ~angsty, romantic suspense

Twisted Hearts

Unraveled Love

Love In The Heartland ~small town romance

Captivated By You

This Time Around

Long Road Home

Before We Fell

Crazy Love Series ~small town romance

Fake Wife

Knocked Up

28 Dates

Weekend Fling

The Fireside Series ~small town romance

His to Love

His to Protect

His to Cherish

His to Seduce

Just One Series ~rockstar romance

Just One Song

Just One Week

Just One Regret

Just One Moment

Standalones

Remembering Us